Autobiography
of Us

Autobiography
of Us

A NOVEL

Aria Beth Sloss

HENRY HOLT AND COMPANY   NEW YORK

Henry Holt and Company, LLC
Publishers since 1866
175 Fifth Avenue
New York, New York 10010
www.henryholt.com

Henry Holt® and ▥® are registered trademarks of Henry Holt and Company, LLC.

Excerpt from *Macbeth*, by William Shakespeare. Copyright Penguin Books, 1967, 1995, 2005.

Library of Congress Cataloging-in-Publication Data

Sloss, Aria Beth.
   Autobiography of us : a novel / Aria Beth Sloss.—1st ed.
      p. cm.
   ISBN 978-0-8050-9455-8
   1. Female friendship—Fiction.   2. Life change events—Fiction.   3. Pasadena
(Calif.)—Fiction.   I. Title.
   PS3619.L74A97 2013
   813'.6—dc23   2012020616

Henry Holt books are available for special promotions and premiums.
For details contact: Director, Special Markets.

First Edition 2013

Designed by Meryl Sussman Levavi

Printed in the United States of America

10 9 8 7 6 5 4 3 2 1

For Dan, who told me so

Autobiography
of Us

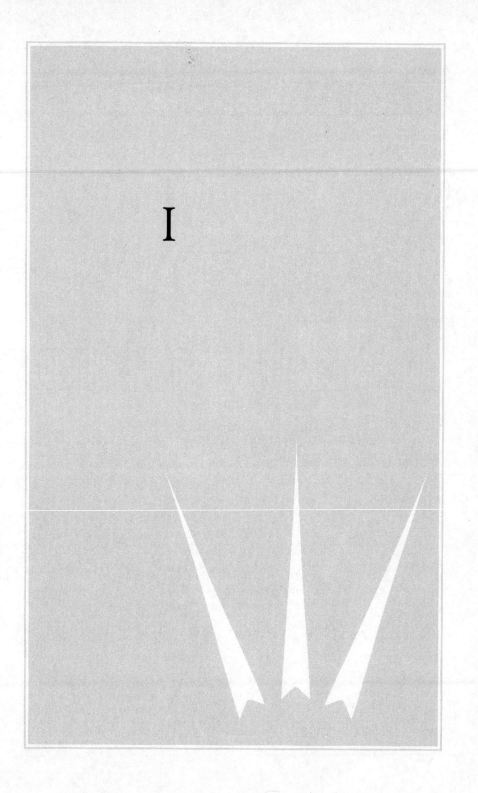

I

Chapter 1

SHE died before her time. Isn't that what people say? Her name was Alex—Alexandra, though only our mothers and teachers ever called her that. Alexandra was the wrong name entirely for a girl like her, a name for the kind of girl who crossed her *t*'s and dotted her *i*'s, who said *God bless* when you sneezed. From the day she arrived at Windridge, we were the best of friends. You know how girls are at that age. We found each other like two animals recognizing a similar species: noses raised, sniffing, alert.

Funny, isn't it? To think I was once young enough to have a friend like that. There were years she meant more to me than anyone, years our lives braided into each other's so neatly I'm not sure, to be honest, they ever came undone. Though how does one even track such things? Like the movements of the moon across the sky, she exerted a strange and mysterious pull. Even now, I could no more chart her influence than I could the gravitational powers that rule the tides. I suppose that could be said of anyone we love, that their effects on our lives run so deeply, with such grave force, we hardly know what they mean until they are gone.

I was fourteen the day she appeared in my homeroom. A transplant from Texas, our teacher announced, her hand on Alex's shoulder as though she needed protecting, though it was clear from the start Alex didn't need anything of the sort. She must have come straight to our classroom from home that day, because she wasn't in uniform yet. Instead of the pleated navy skirts and regulation white blouses we had all worn since the third grade, she had on a red flowered dress with smocking across the front, ruffled at the neck in a way my mother never would have allowed. I remember being struck right away by how pretty she was—*unfairly* pretty, I thought. In those days I was a great believer in the injustice of beauty, and I saw immediately that Alex had been given everything I had not. She was thin through the arms and slender rather than skinny, with a pale, inquisitive face that might have seemed severe if it hadn't been for the frank snubness of her nose and the freckles that stood out against her cheeks. Her dark hair she wore loose around her shoulders, her eyes startling even at a distance, the color a deep, sea-colored green, the right slightly larger than the left. Released to her desk, she chose the route that took her directly past mine—accident, I thought, until she turned her head a quarter inch and winked.

I was as blind as anyone as to why she picked me. I had by that age already established myself as a shy girl, bookish, and in the habit of taking everything too seriously. Of the fifteen girls in our homeroom that year, Ruthie Filbright was the prettiest, Betsy Bromwell the nicest, and Lindsey Patterson the biggest flirt. But it was me Alex winked at that September morning, me she approached at tennis that same afternoon. Me she rolled those eyes at when Lindsey flounced past, twirling her racket; me she flung herself down next to on the bench, kicking her legs out in front of her, her shins scabbed in a way I was aware I should have found ugly but did not. What I saw was that her shoes were covered with some sort of embroidered silk, that her fingernails were painted a shocking pink—the shade, I would later learn, *Cyclamen*. That she was, depressingly, even prettier than I had thought.

"Boo," she said, frowning at a splotch of ink on her wrist. She rubbed it with her thumb, then brought her wrist to her mouth and licked it.

"Boo yourself." I felt my cheeks heat right away.

But she was busy looking around, her expression caught somewhere between amusement and boredom. "Don't tell me," she said. It was a thrilling voice, surprisingly deep for a girl her size. "They're every bit as bad as they look."

"They're nice enough."

She crossed her arms over her thin chest. "And you? Are *you* nice?"

"That depends," I said slowly. "There are different kinds of nice."

She smiled. Her mouth was the one real oddity in her face: It was too large, too wide, the upper lip full in a way that erased the usual dip in the middle. Still, it was a surprisingly sweet smile. "So you *are* different."

I didn't need to look up to know everyone was watching—Ruthie and Lindsey and neat-faced Robin Pringle. I could feel their eyes, those girls standing clustered close to the fence, pretending to bounce tennis balls or check the strings on their rackets while they watched the new girl drag the toes of her ivory shoes carelessly back and forth in the dust. And they were watching me, Rebecca Madden, who until this very moment had been just another quiet girl in the corner, easily passed over and as easily forgotten. "I don't know," I said finally. "I guess I'm more or less like everyone else."

She brought her head down close to mine then, so close I could smell the sharp floral scent of what she would later inform me was her mother's perfume—*filched*, she would say, from her dressing table and applied liberally to her own wrists. "Now, if that were true," she said softly, "what in the world would I be doing over here?"

She lived, we discovered after school that day, just three blocks down on El Molino, in a beautiful old Tudor surrounded by bougainvillea and a high wall that ran around the perimeter of the property.

"Hideous, all of it," she announced as we walked. "You'll see. Eleanor's had the place done Oriental—oh, I don't care for honorifics. It's Eleanor and Beau around here, and they'll expect you to call them the same. Anyway, the whole thing's silk and tasseled pillows and these awful little Chinaman figurines, which she insists positively ooze the West Coast *esthétique*. Meanwhile, I only know everything about California there is to know. It might have behooved her to ask my opinion." She gave me a sidelong glance. "Aren't you going to ask how I know everything about California?"

I straightened up. "How do you know—"

"I'm going to be an actress. Isn't it obvious? I know what you're thinking," she added quickly. "But I'm not talking about the pictures. I mean the serious stuff, the Clytemnestras, the Heddas. Shaw, Brecht, et cetera. None of this fluff. It used to be about talent, you know. Look at Marlene Dietrich, for Christ's sake. No—wait." She shut her eyes. "Don't tell me. You don't have a clue." She blinked at me. "Poor thing. Never mind—I'll have you out of the Dark Ages in a jiffy. As for *la* Marlene," she went on, "there's no doing her justice with words. You've got to see her to understand. She came through Houston on a tour last fall—this awful cabaret thingy, really juvenile stuff, but, I swear, I would have sat in the audience and watched her slice bread. I mean, I could have sat there in my goddamn seat forever." She put her hand on my arm. "Have you ever had one of those moments?"

6

"Which kind?"

She looked at me intently. "The kind where you feel like everyone could go to hell. Like you wouldn't care if the whole world blew to pieces."

I pretended to think. "I'm not sure."

"Then you haven't found it."

"Found what?"

"Your something," she said, impatient. "Your heart's desire."

"You're saying yours is acting."

"Listen, I'm not exactly thrilled about it either. I would have preferred something with a little more"—she clicked her tongue—"*gravitas*. That's the thing about callings—*they* choose *you*."

"But how do you know?"

"That's like asking how anyone knows to breathe." She'd stopped walking now, her hand still on my arm. We were standing under the shade of one of the big palm trees that lined that stretch of El Molino, and in the late-afternoon stillness I heard the drone of a honeybee circling overhead. "Look, I wasn't given this voice for no reason. I'm not saying it to brag. I'd a thousand times rather have been given just about anything—a photographic memory or the ability to speak a dozen languages. Something *useful*. But I'm stuck with what I've got. Not to mention what I haven't. Schoolwork, for starters," she went on. "Oh, some of it I do alright with. Reading, for one. I happen to be a voracious reader. You?"

"I like to read," I began. "I—"

"I'm perfectly tragic when it comes to arithmetic," she went on. "And teachers are always telling me I've got to improve my penmanship. Frankly, I have neither the time nor the inclination." She looked at me. "I bet you're the type whose papers get held up in front of the class. I bet your goddamn penmanship gets top marks."

I shrugged. "I do alright."

"Because you're a realist. Don't look like that—it's a compliment. Anybody with the slightest smidge of intelligence is a realist. The point is that you get the appalling fact of the matter—that we're alone. Doomed to lives of quiet desperation or whatever. Thoreau." She squinted at me. "You *do* know Thoreau."

"Of course I do." I pleated the material of my skirt between my thumb and index finger, feigning concentration to cover the flush I felt moving up my neck. I am, as you know, a terrible liar.

"Listen to me." She gave me a dazzling smile. "If we're going to be friends, you'll have to learn to ignore me when I get like this. I go on tears, that's all. There are things better kept to myself, Eleanor says. Problem is, I'm an only—child, I mean. Afraid I don't always remember to think before I speak. Sometimes things come out without"—she chewed on her bottom lip—"arbitration."

"I'm an only, too."

"Were there others?"

"Other what?"

She gave me a penetrating look. "Eleanor had three before me. Or two before and one after, I can never keep it straight. You know—dead ones. Was it the same with yours?"

"I don't think so." I felt myself frowning and tried to relax my forehead—Mother telling me I looked pretty when I smiled, that frowning never did anyone's face any good. "My mother traveled before she had me. Turning pages for a famous pianist."

"You're kidding." She stared. "And now what?"

"And now what, what?"

We started walking again. "What happened to her and the pianist?"

"She got married, silly," I said, laughing. I'd always found the story romantic, though I had a feeling if I admitted that, Alex would only shake her head or roll those startling eyes. "She and my father met in a restaurant. She was out with Henry Girard—the pianist—after a concert one night. Daddy had just come back from the war." I tried to make it sound as though I could hardly remember, though of course I'd memorized every detail: my mother at a table with the famous pianist, her blonde head gleaming under the chandelier; my father in the corner with his wounded leg stretched out in front of him; across from him, his date, a woman whose face—no matter how many times I tried to picture it—remained blank. My mother young and beautiful in a green dress; Henry Girard aging, brilliant, bending his gray head over his soup. My father waiting until his date excused herself to the ladies' room to stand and walk over to where my mother sat—a face like that, he said, impossible to ignore. "They got married not long after."

"Sounds exciting."

"It was," I said, glancing at her, but she only looked thoughtful. "She always says he swept her off her feet. She says he—"

"I meant the working with the famous pianist bit."

I shrugged. "She doesn't talk about it much."

"Like the dead babies."

"Not exactly like that."

"I think I would have liked one," she went on, ignoring me. "A sister, anyway. I'm fine without the brother. I never would have known, obviously, except my parents get in these god-awful fights. Beau was saying something about family once, taking responsibility, and Eleanor just shrieked at him, *If you blame the dead ones on me one more time, I swear—*" She stopped. "*The dead ones.* Ghoulish, isn't it?"

"Maybe a little."

"I'm headed toward something sanguine, in case you were wondering." She looked at me pointedly. "From the Latin *sanguineus*, meaning *bloody*. Hopeful. Optimistic. Point being, I believe we're capable of righting certain wrongs. We might be all alone in the world, *en effet*, but that doesn't mean we have to be lonely." She stopped me again, and now we were at the edge of the small park across from her house, the canal that cut across the middle sluggish and choked with cattails, the far bank studded with juniper. "So? What do you say?"

"To what?"

She put out her hand, palm flat. "Blood sisters." She wiggled her fingers. "I saw you fiddling with a pin in your hem earlier. Hand it over."

"I don't know," I began, startled. It must be clear by now: I had never met anyone like her.

"Sure you do." She gave me another one of her smiles. "Come on, Becky. In or out."

I hated being called that, but I didn't dare tell her. She was looking at me closely, her eyes darkened to something like charcoal; after a moment's hesitation I reached down and undid the latch on the pin, dropping it in her hand.

"Good girl! Now." She closed her eyes. "Do you solemnly swear?"

She pricked her own finger, then mine. At first I was too busy watching the drops of blood form on our fingertips and worrying about staining my blouse to hear much of what she said: I remember that she kept her eyes closed as we pressed our index fingers together, her voice solemn as she recited our vows. At a certain point I shut my eyes too, more to shut out the glare of the sun than anything. But as I stood there in the afternoon heat with the sharp scent of juniper filling my nose, I realized with a start that I was happy. That the world might fall to pieces and I wouldn't care, not the littlest bit.

I should have told you all of this a long time ago. The truth is that we weren't like everyone else in Pasadena, your grandparents and I: house-poor, they'd call us now. My father was the first in his family to graduate anything beyond high school, putting himself through college before the war working odd jobs as a soda jerk and a shoe-shine boy, the government paying for law school when he came home early from the war with a bullet in his leg. It couldn't have been easy, building his way up from nothing, though if you asked he'd say it suited him just fine, thanks. He was a great fan of Lincoln and Adams, your grandfather, fond of quoting them and others on the subject of freedom and the dignity of man. *Lay first the foundation of humility*, he often said—Saint Augustine, I later discovered, though at the time I'm sure I attributed it to him.

My mother held a far more complicated position toward her past. The Pooles were old Virginia stock, a family I knew mostly through the Christmas cards they sent every December like clockwork, their signatures scrawled across the bottom revealing little despite my scrutiny. "Daddy was a wonderful man," Mother liked

to say, pausing for effect, "but he didn't have a head for business."
Her father had killed himself after losing everything in the Crash,
leaving my grandmother to raise Mother and her two younger
sisters on little more than sheer determination and the sales—
piecemeal—of what had once been an impressively comfortable life:
A hundred acres parceled off bit by bit; the rambling old Georgian
my grandmother hung on to till the bitter end; a grandfather clock
with a cuckoo that sang on the hour; a pair of horses, Duke and
Ranger, whom my mother had spoiled with sugar cubes and apples;
a baby grand piano my grandfather had played from time to time
and whose departure my mother had mourned bitterly, the sight
of it being rolled through the front door too awful, she said, for
words; box after box of heirloom jewelry; sets of family silver—all
of it sold off by the time Mother was in her late teens. When she
left for California at the age of eighteen, there was nothing to take
with her save the twenty dollars my grandmother slipped into her
pocket on her way out the door. "I escaped," Mother declared. Or:
"I got out." She always did have a flair for the dramatic. A flourish
she put on everyday life, like the silk flowers she copied from the
ones at Neiman's, sewing them herself and tucking one into her
chignon before she swooped out to a meeting of the Pasadena His-
torical Society or an afternoon tea at the club.

She was quite beautiful, your grandmother. I must have shown
you pictures.

But I don't mean to suggest we were poor. We were anything
but. We simply lived as thousands of others before us have lived,
tucked up against the limits of our means. The life we led demanded
certain expenses, Mother's pen scratching busily as she tallied up
our bills on the first of each month, doling out the amounts allotted
to each category for the upcoming weeks: *House: upkeep*, one column
might read. *Car: maintenance; Gas; Groceries; Walter: personal.* And
so on. Her father's loss had imprinted in her the necessity for if not

economy then at least delegation. Funds went where they were needed, Mother directing the flow of monthly income as though mobilizing troops: there, not there, *there*. And so our house was large if not overly so—more important, it was in the right sort of neighborhood; there was my schooling—private, Mother insisted; there were the cars, kept long after they had begun to rattle and hiss; a small garden at the back of the house, where she grew prize-winning roses; a yearly membership to the club we could easily have gone without, Mother declaring when my father suggested as much that we might as well go around barefoot and begging for alms. That without the club, we were, to put it plainly, *sunk*.

I must have been an unusually unobservant child, or perhaps I simply kept myself occupied, my nose always buried in a book; I don't know. I don't remember minding the differences between my classmates and me until Alex, that's all. But then I never had what you might call close friends. What free time I had I spent reading, out on the patio or at the kitchen table. I planted myself there with my book and a glass of lemonade until my mother came in to start dinner, announcing that there were peas to be shelled if I was offering, and even if I wasn't she bet she could find something more useful for me to do.

Still. I would have had to be blind not to see the differences between Alex's family and mine. That first afternoon I met Mrs. Carrington—I could no more have called her Eleanor than I could have broken into song—I found it hard to look at her directly. She dazzled, the jewels at her throat and in her ears winking in the lamplight, her hair blonder even than my mother's and set in soft waves. She was languid where Mother never sat still, fond of using long cigarette holders she referred to as *quellazaires*. Mr. Carrington proved equally intimidating, dark like Alex and handsome as a movie star in his crisp white shirts and linen sports coats. Oil money, Mother told me later, Alex's grandfather one of the first to strike it rich in what was then known as the Gusher Age, which made me laugh.

Their house was filled with similarly beautiful things: fine porcelain vases and heavy damask curtains, thick silk rugs Alex treated so casually I could hardly bear to watch—scuffing her shoes across them after coming in from a hard rain, spilling crumbs, waving a full glass of milk around carelessly as she read to me from one play or another, her voice rising and falling with that wonderful air of drama that seemed to infuse everything she said or did with a sense of the utmost significance. There was a pool in the backyard, set like a sapphire in the lush grass, the bottom tiled with faded paintings of sea creatures I dove down again and again to examine: an orange lobster, a monstrous fish, a tiny, iridescent crab.

I'm embarrassed to admit how quickly I succumbed to shame. How, that first afternoon I came home from Alex's, I registered the differences between our houses with a dismay that struck me to the core. Suddenly everything wore the look of fatigue: the chandelier above the dining room table scratched so badly on one side that the glass appeared cloudy, the velvet couch my mother had reupholstered herself beginning to pale in irregular circles where people had sat over the years. Even the antique French end table in our hallway my mother prized had gotten nicked along the legs over the years, giving it the look of a castoff—which, in fact, it was. The table had been a gift from Mrs. Peachtree, a neighbor who left it for my mother when she moved away. It was only right, Mrs. Peachtree said, my mother had always loved it more.

\I/

It was an easy walk from where we lived on El Molino over to the Capitol Theater, its floors tiled in an old pink and green pattern I would later learn to identify as Art Deco, the marble refreshments counter tacky with a permanent residue of spilled sodas and ice cream. The man who owned the theater worked for Alex's father or had worked for him once, I never quite understood—point being, we never had to pay a dime.

We must have seen a dozen movies that first fall, Alex and I. This was 1958, remember. We saw *Gigi*, which Alex hated, and *Cat on a Hot Tin Roof*, which she adored. It was at the Capitol that we saw *Vertigo*: Kim Novak, blonde and doe-eyed, her face always angled upward as though searching out the source of the light that shone down on her like some alien sun. After, Alex announced she'd drawn up a list of all the roles she meant to play before the age of twenty-five. It was important to keep abreast of these things, she said. To have goals. She'd do Cleopatra, she said. Good old Hedda. Lady Macbeth. Hell, just about everyone Shakespeare had to offer but Juliet, she said.

"What's so bad about Juliet?" I said. This was out on the bench down by the canal, where we liked to sit after school, throwing pebbles into the water.

"Backbone," she declared. "Lack thereof. At least Madeleine has her own fish to fry. Not that I care for the whole damsel-in-distress thingy. Fluff is fluff. Never mind if it's Shakespeare or the pictures." She took a handful of clover from the grass and stood, dropping them one by one to the ground. "Do you think I'd look like her if I colored my hair?"

"Like who?"

"*Madeleine*, dummy. Right before she jumps."

"Exactly like her." I threw a stone into the water and watched the ripples spread outward across the surface: I was nearly fifteen and I had my own ideas about love, each more foolish than the last. "You don't think Romeo and Juliet are romantic?" I asked after a minute or two. "More than, I don't know, what's-his-face and Kim Novak."

"Madeleine," she corrected me absently. "Romantic, not romantic—not like it ended well for either of them. Anyway, I've decided I'm against it." When she turned to face me, her expression was serious. "Love."

"But if you don't fall in love and get married, what do you do?" It was an honest question. In all my favorite novels—*Pride and Prejudice, Little Women, Anne of Green Gables*—marriage was the inevitable conclusion, the heroine's fate tied up neatly with a bow.

"Do?" She stepped up on the bench so she stood over me, twitching her skirt out from underneath her. "TO BE, OR NOT TO BE: THAT IS THE QUESTION—"

"Hush," I tugged at her hand.

"—WHETHER 'TIS NOBLER IN THE MIND TO SUFFER THE SLINGS AND ARROWS OF OUTRAGEOUS FORTUNE—"

"Someone will see," I begged, tugging again. The park was empty, but I could think of any number of people who might pass by at any moment—my mother, hers, one of the other girls from school. "Please."

She turned to give the canal an elaborate bow before dropping down beside me. "*I choose my destiny.*" Her voice was particularly wonderful to listen to when she got excited, so round and full it seemed less to speak the words than to toss them around like the wind. "My heart's desire, remember? If you don't have that, you drown."

I shrugged: I'd recently gotten in the habit of doing that whenever I didn't know what to say. "I guess."

"Don't," she said fiercely, sitting up straight. "You *guess* you feel like a Coke. You *guess* you'd like to go for a swim or not. You don't guess about your life, you *choose*. Or else—"

"Or else what?"

"You get swallowed up like the rest of them." She turned her gaze on me. "Your mother, for starters."

"I told you. She fell in love. My father swept her off her—"

"Exactly."

"I don't see what's so terrible about that."

"Nothing. If you want to be like everyone else, I mean, it's just peachy." She looked at me. "Is that what you want?"

"Of course not." I tried to sound indignant, though the truth was that I wouldn't have minded in the least. It shouldn't surprise you to hear that in those days I did everything I could to go unnoticed. Being called on in class was enough to send the blood rushing to my cheeks, my voice shaking in that way it still does on those rare occasions I am forced to speak in front of a crowd.

"God knows it's easy enough." She turned back to the canal and watched the slow-moving water. In the afternoon stillness, the low croaking of the bullfrogs formed a hoarse chorus; behind us, hummingbirds darted between the lemon trees that lined the park's edge. "Eleanor's already on the warpath," she said finally. "Next year's *the* year, she says. Time to spread our wings. Flap, flap," she laughed a little bitterly. "Baby birds, the both of us. Fledglings. You should see the calendar she tacked up in my room: ballroom lessons, etiquette lessons, fox-trot. Elocution, for crying out loud. God forbid I should study anything worth knowing. God forbid I should actually improve my *mind*. Did you know Shakespeare wrote thirty-seven plays and one hundred and fifty-four sonnets? Do you have any idea how long it takes to *read* thirty-seven plays and one hundred and fifty-four sonnets? Meanwhile, there's Eleanor saying it's time to start thinking about a dress for cotillion. Don't I worry about that, she asks." She shook her head. "As if I don't think about it all the goddamn time."

"She's only trying to be helpful," I murmured.

"We're not little girls anymore, Rebecca." She looked at me almost sorrowfully. "I'll be fifteen this March. Tick-tock."

"I know that." I thought about my own mother, the frown she got as she stood behind me in front of the mirror mornings before school, her hands patting at the stray pieces of hair that refused to lie flat. Of course she wanted everything Alex had been complaining about for me: The week before, we'd passed a flyer tacked up on the community board at the club, announcing ballroom-dancing lessons for the fall, Mother telling me briskly not to worry, that we'd figure something out. "It's just—"

"Just what?" Alex said, her voice dangerously quiet. "You thought everything would stay like this forever?" She gestured in the direction of the canal, and I followed dumbly, searching around us as though the answer might be written in the spiny leaves of the junipers or across the smooth bark of one of the lemon trees.

"Of course not," I said.

The truth is that I understood very little of what she was saying. Before Alex, what thrills I'd experienced I'd found in my imagination, the result of burying myself in book after book. I depended, I mean, on escape for my various joys. It had never occurred to me that real life might offer the smallest portion of the happiness I found in reading, the ordinary scaffolding of my day-to-day a thing I'd made a habit of burying under a thousand imagined lives, each more inviting than the last. And then she came along and it was as though life were a Christmas tree and I'd discovered the hidden switch, the whole thing lighting up in a blaze of color.

Chapter 3

WOULD it surprise you to learn there wasn't much for girls like us to do in those days? We were bright girls, after all, and not without certain resources. But Pasadena at that time was a different world. At Windridge we studied sewing alongside the humanities; we jotted down Latin declensions in our notebooks beside recipes for chocolate cake or a diagram for a foolproof cross-stitch. *Amo, amas,* we wrote. *Whip egg whites until soft peaks form.* We were expected to do well but not overly so. My own parents gave my report cards no more than a passing glance, Mother saying once that so long as I was minding my manners I could likely keep her up to date on everything myself. "If there's a problem," she said, "we'll get a phone call from Miss So-and-So, isn't that right?" She smiled at me, showing her dimples. "I don't expect there will be any problems."

There *was* a girl two classes ahead of us at Windridge, a Martha Clarkson, whose parents were rumored to have sympathized with Communists after the war; it was believed that because of that she was allowed to do as she pleased, that in the aftermath of that disgrace her mother and father had, for all intents and purposes, defected from parenthood. She certainly looked as though no one was paying her any attention. She wore a large, ill-fitting sweater the color of mustard over her blouse no matter the weather, and her hair always had the wild look of something left to its own devices. The few times I stood close to her in line at the cafeteria or found myself partnered with her in dance class, I saw that her nails were bitten down to the quick, the skin on either side of them bloodied. *Ruined*, my mother called it, shaking her head whenever the Clarksons came up in conversation. "That poor girl," she sighed.

She would go on to study physics and Latin at Cal State, Martha Clarkson: In the spring of her senior year, the news went around that she'd been accepted to law school at Pomona. Ruined, in other words. I remember squinting in the bright sun to find her onstage at Windridge graduation, her hair cut by then in a blunt bob that did her squarish face no favors, her thick, black-framed glasses disguising what I had once observed during dancing were surprisingly blue eyes. She was a tall girl, taller even than I was. I shot up during the summer before tenth grade, a betrayal I counted among my body's greatest. It must have been in part because of that that I registered Martha Clarkson so acutely that morning, the way her head stuck out above all the rest of the girls in her row. *Queenie*, my father called me in moments of affection, and I might have thought of that as I watched Martha Clarkson cross the stage to accept her certificate, the fact that she did indeed look regal in her own way. But what I thought instead as I sat there drawing circles in the grass with my toe, already bored, was that she must have felt burdened by her height the way I did, that she must have found it excruciating. It must, I told myself as everyone stood to applaud, have been part of what had spurred her on to Cal, to physics and Latin, that sense that she didn't belong. That she was only ever playing the part of a girl like all the rest.

I would not be a Martha Clarkson: My mother would never have allowed it. But the day Mr. Percy brought the frogs into the classroom that first spring after Alex arrived, I stood my ground next to her, more than half the other girls in the room crying out for infirmary passes, complaining of headaches, dizziness, nausea.

"Shoot me." Alex pulled on her gloves, snapping them over her wrists. "I mean it. If I ever turn into a fainting violet or whatever, go ahead and pull the trigger." She sniffed. "I, for one, happen to find the smell of formaldehyde bracing."

I glanced around the room. Besides us, just four girls remained. "They say biology's the key to everything."

She rolled her eyes. "Oh, they do, do they?"

We found the station assigned to us and sat down in front of the metal tray containing our frog, the sides of the tray shallow, cold to the touch.

Alex slid the cover off. "For Pete's sake!" She sat back heavily on her stool. "No one said it would look so pathetic."

"I think he looks peaceful."

"Never knew what hit him, poor bastard."

"They're raised for this," I said doubtfully. "I think."

We stared down at the damp grayish body, the small flipperlike feet spread wide, the skin dull against the metal. "Bred for death," she said drily. "Much better, thanks."

At the head of the room, Mr. Percy cleared his throat. "You'll see that the diagram provided at each station outlines each step in detail," he said. "I'll be here if there are any questions. And to all you brave souls strong enough to endure, my undying gratitude." He was kind, Mr. Percy, younger than most of our teachers, and one of just two men at Windridge. The other, Mr. Watkins, was ancient and hard of hearing, and everyone made fun of him behind his back.

Alex gave herself a shake and picked up the knife. "Alas, poor Froggy," she said loudly. "I knew ye not." I watched as she reached down into the tray, her fingers enormous in those gloves. There was a clatter as the knife dropped —"Christ!"— Alex's face when her head came up this time ashen. "It's rubbery. Slick too. And in case you were thinking the knife would just go in, it doesn't. It *resists*."

Out of the corner of my eye, I saw Mr. Percy rise halfway out of his chair.

I picked the knife up from the tray and nudged the lab notebook her way. "You take notes."

"What do you think you're doing?"

"I'll be fine."

"Fine?" I could see her struggling. "I give you five minutes, and then let's see who's fine," she grumbled, but she flipped the notebook open and turned to a clean page.

I lowered my head and began to cut.

How do I explain? I'd planned on blustering my way through; I considered myself not unaccustomed to the ugliness of death. The lizards that hid in the cracks of our garden wall sometimes died in among my mother's roses, and it was my job to collect and carry them to the bin, their bodies hitting the bottom with a sickening thud. I'd thought this would be only a little worse. But no sooner had I pulled the gray flaps of the frog's stomach apart than everything disappeared. The room went quiet. Silent, really, the silence turning everything around me unfocused, the edges of the room softened as though painted over in watercolor. The frog's skin proved thin as onionskin, easily removed; I pulled the yellow ropes of fat along the belly through the incision and laid them flat against the tray; I took out the liver, dark and flat as a dried plum between my tweezers; I probed the gallbladder and picked out the kidneys, which lifted away from the flesh like a pair of dry seeds; I sliced out the ugly little heart, the tissue gleaming a deep, gelatinous scarlet. Somewhere to my left, Alex groaned, and I lowered my face over the tray until everything disappeared again but the heart.

"Look," I breathed, but she buried her face in her hands.

"You look."

I pulled my chair in closer and bent down over the tray. I had that exquisite sense of focus that came from being lost in one of my books, my universe narrowing itself to a single point. I unwrapped the wet skein of the intestines and pulled them taut against my palm; I turned the kidneys onto a separate tray with the forceps. I flipped the blackish liver over onto the glass slide and felt the give of it under my gloved finger, dense and resistant as meat. I drew the head of the microscope down and examined the oily honeycomb of cells under the lens, the pattern a delicate feathering, I thought, not unlike the one waves leave along the sand.

"Fine work." Mr. Percy stood over me. "Fine work indeed." He pushed his glasses up his nose. "Wonderful to see you girls get involved. There are any number of— *hrrmph*—opportunities here at Windridge, you know. Excellent resources." He stood, arms crossed across his chest now, as though waiting. "Seems a shame no one ever takes much of an interest."

"Yes, sir," I said. "I'm enjoying it very much, sir—"

"I was just saying, Mr. Percy," Alex interrupted, holding the notebook aloft as though it were a fan and she might, at any moment, snap it open and begin to dance, "that biology is more or less the essence of life. Don't you agree?"

"The what?" He stood there, blinking.

"The key to everything." She beamed at him. "Isn't that right?"

"Perhaps." His glasses had already begun their slow journey back down his nose and he pushed at them again, using his knuckle to edge them into place. "That is, I like to think it's the most directly applicable of the sciences. A *living* science." He coughed. "It being all around us and all."

"It is, isn't it?" Alex gazed at him.

He reddened. "Yes. Well, then—carry on." He nodded as though we'd asked his approval and turned back toward his desk.

"We'll do our best, Mr. Percy," Alex called after him. He ducked his head—embarrassed, I thought, or flattered. "*I'm interested,*" Alex said, turning to me and putting one hand to her chest. "Oh, absolutely, Mr. Percy, I'm so interested I could lie down and kiss your darling biological feet—"

"Hush." I glanced around the room to make sure no one had overheard.

She smiled broadly, tucking a pencil behind her ear. "I think it's adorable."

"It's got nothing to do with adorable."

"Then why are you blushing?"

"I'm not—" but then I stopped. I saw—like one of my heroines, only decidedly less heroic in her misfortune—Martha Clarkson walking down the hallway with a frown of concentration creasing her pale forehead, her skirt sagging, her blouse covered up by that sweater. *Ruined.* "Well," I said slowly. "Maybe just the tiniest crush."

"And why not?" She flashed a smile and I feigned absorption in the contents of the tray, feeling a shiver of something equal parts guilt and pleasure. "Not much to look at, is he, but at least he's got a head on his shoulders. More than anyone can say for those Browning boys." She picked up the notebook again, looking bored. "Now give me something to write down so we can get out of here already. I'm famished, and as it turns out I don't care for the smell of death."

It can't have been long after that day in Mr. Percy's classroom—a week, maybe two—that Alex had the first of her many classes after school. "Elocution," she said, sticking out her tongue. "Told you." I'm sure I pretended it was mere coincidence when I found myself walking along East Walnut toward the public library. It was a stately old building, large and full of light. The librarian, a kindly old lady named Mrs. Farmington, was more than happy to point me in the direction of natural sciences.

"It's for a school project," I told her, as though I needed to explain. I'd never set foot on the second floor, but it was even quieter up there, the sound muffled by thick carpeting and endless shelves of books. I located the section that housed the biology texts easily enough. I must have spent a good three hours there that first day, poring over diagrams and tables, the print often so small I had to bring my face down close to the musty-smelling pages. I went back the very next week. Dance class this time, Alex declared grimly when we said goodbye in front of school. "Tick-tock," she said. Eventually I worked up the courage to check out a book, then a second, the due date stamped in the back with a satisfying *thwack!*

I remember those as some of my happiest hours. To sit at the end of those narrow aisles with the afternoon sun filtering through the windows, the smell of old books heavy in the air, the whine of the overhead light like the honeybees that gathered in my mother's garden, come June, by the dozens—it was as close as I have ever come to understanding worship. My father was the only regular churchgoer in our family, but on the rare occasions my mother and I joined him, I was always surprised to find how much I liked it. I couldn't tell you much of anything about Father Timothy's sermons; I don't believe I registered more than a handful of words over the years. All I heard as I sat between my parents in the hard-backed pew was the cavernous silence that continued even as he spoke, and the hundreds of small sounds under that sound, the echoes produced by the shuffle of feet moving against the wooden floors or the noise of someone swallowing. The library had that same persistent quiet, a stillness that I'm afraid made it all too easy for me to lose track of time. I often climbed the stairs with every intention of leaving within the hour, only to find myself startled by the click of the lights as Mrs. Farmington turned them off, one by one, signaling it was time to go.

It was in the anatomy books that I found the most astonishing things: diagrams that unfolded like accordions to show tendons and muscles, pages of illustrations mapping out vast territories of veins. A single drawing that outlined all twenty-six bones of the foot. I lost myself in them the way I'd always lost myself in books, only instead of Catherine from *Wuthering Heights* weeping over Heathcliff or Emma Woodhouse getting into trouble over one thing or another, there was the fascinating architecture of the human skull, or the fat gray bellows of the lungs. There were the twin arches of the clavicle, the tiny, saclike alveoli clustered together like buds on the verge of blooming. I traced the bones of the leg up through the hip girdle and let my fingers wander over the pattern of veins. Later, I would stand in front of my bedroom mirror wearing nothing but my slip and start all over again: *lingual artery, carotid, coronary, hepatic.*

I was careful to visit the library only on those days when Alex had something else—her *goddamn elocution* or whatever it was. I told my mother I was going to Alex's straight from school; to Alex, I said I was going home, that my mother needed me for one thing or another. Each time I lied it bothered me less, as though lying were a sweater I stretched with each use until the shape of it molded to my body. Then there were moments I wished I could take it all back, afternoons as I hurried down the sunny stretch of East Walnut when I longed to do it all over again, to go back to that afternoon in Mr. Percy's classroom and erase that first lie as easily as chalk from a board. No, I might have said. It's not Mr. Percy. *This* is what I love—holding the tray aloft, the microscope. The tiny, waxen heart.

But the truth is that I was afraid I would lose her. Not because

I'd finally found my heart's desire, and it was something so crude, so entirely lacking in glamour that I understood immediately Alex would never approve. And not because I had grown up a lonely child, unaccustomed to explaining my many peculiarities, or even because I was already used to maintaining a certain border between private and public, to turning a particular face to the world. *Keeping up appearances*, Mother called it: the silk flower pinned behind her ear; the tear in my uniform stitched up by her neat hand; the complicated recipes she clipped from magazines and followed to the letter, the heat in that small kitchen making her pretty face gleam. *We have to try harder*, she told me as she stood behind me before bed, setting my hair in curlers. *A challenge*, she called it. No, I was afraid I would lose Alex because I knew I'd in some sense already let her go. Because, I mean, I'd found something I loved as much as I loved her.

And so when she asked, I lied. I'd learned how to roast a chicken, I told her, holding up my hands as though to show my scars. I'd spent the day helping my mother polish the goddamn silver.

How little we know the ones we love. How little we know of anyone, in the end.

Chapter 4

OF course I lost her anyway. His name was Bertrand Lowell.

He was a year ahead of us in school, a Browning boy like the rest of them. All anyone said about him growing up was that he was a genius, rumored to have received a near-perfect score on the Wechsler-Bellevue. We were juniors at Windridge the day he punched his history teacher in the eye for reasons that remained unclear; even the other Browning boys in the room that day couldn't put words to the particulars. All anyone knew was that the teacher had been rushed to the emergency room and that Bertrand reappeared in the hallways the following Monday without further explanation. The Lowells were rumored to have made a sizable donation to the school, a story supported by the fact that the teacher—just as quietly as Bertrand had been let back in—was let go at the end of the year.

He hardly looked the part. He was tall and thin, the kind of skinny mothers clicked their tongues over at the pool as they watched their sons cannonball into the deep end, spines gleaming in the California sun. By the time we were in our first year at the university and Bertrand Lowell was in his second, what adolescent fat that had rounded out the corners of his body was gone. Even at nineteen, he dressed like a much older man: dark fitted jackets, dark chinos, and dark shoes. He brushed his black hair down so it lay flat against his head; his cheeks were sunk in like the flesh there had been scooped out with a spoon. He had a wide mouth, thin, mobile lips, and light-blue eyes so pale the pupils seemed to float there in the whites, untethered.

Not that any of that really mattered—the shiny black shoes or the sleek black hair, the slender, almost feminine frame. All anyone cared about was the story of that punch, the way it trailed behind him through the years like a red balloon. It was because of that that all at once every girl in school would have done anything to get his attention. To have known, even for a moment, that he had noticed us.

But even that's not right, exactly. I lost Alex twice: The first was long before Bertrand Lowell. She went to a theater camp somewhere north of the city the summer we graduated Windridge—one last hurrah, as she put it, before her mother put her foot down.

"She says I might as well get it out of my system," she told me. "It's like someone telling you to go take one last walk with your dying dog. Morbid, really. Macabre." She frowned. "Either or. Point being, I won't have any spare time come fall. Too busy chairing the Junior League, according to Eleanor. Pledging Theta Alpha whosie-whatsit."

"I'm going to miss you."

She grinned. "I know."

"I'm going to be so goddamn lonely." I tried to make my voice light; I'm sure I didn't fool her for a second.

"You'll have a fabulous time. Lounging around at the pool and sleeping late every day—I'm jealous." She got that far-off look she sometimes did when she was reading me a scene from one of her plays, her lips parted slightly to expose the front tooth that bent inward—the result, she insisted, of being dropped as a child, though I could never make up my mind as to whether I believed her or not. "I must be mad, running off to the middle of nowhere with a bunch of God-knows-who when I could spend a perfectly gorgeous few months right here with you. I mean, I must be off my rocker."

"I'll write every chance I get."

"Dear Penelope." She threw her arms around my shoulders.

"That was weaving," I mumbled into her hair, but it seemed no sooner had she embraced me than she was already letting go, fluttering her hand over her shoulder like a handkerchief as she disappeared through the front door.

I spent those long, hot days helping my mother with her gardening or in the kitchen, the heat with the oven on close to unbearable. I'm sorry to say I never bothered feigning much of an interest in either activity; of the two, the garden interested me more, though even that I could have done without and mostly did, carrying out my chores with an enthusiasm halfhearted at best. Still, I had to admit it was something to witness my mother at work in the kitchen. She could coax a meal out of anything—a few carrots, half a cabbage, a package of Minute Rice. The results were inspired, products of a happy marriage between her resourcefulness and her artist's eye for color and symmetry: Lettuce leaves fanned out around the edges of each plate for salad Niçoise; a few Birds Eye peas lined up along the border of the boiled new potatoes; a sprig of parsley arrived stuck into the mouth of a broiled fish for an effect she called *festive*—the taste, she said, nothing without the art of presentation.

I passed far more hours in the kitchen with her than I would have liked those summer weeks. With school over and Alex away, it was harder to think up excuses. Morning, I cracked eggs and chopped onions before slinking off to the library whenever I could, telling my mother I'd found a partner for tennis at the club. I knew what she would think about all that reading if she found out: *Bad for the complexion. Ruins the eyes.* A little back-and-forth before the sun went down, I announced instead. Working on my backhand, I said, Mother looking at me with that crease in her forehead she sometimes got.

"Isn't there anything else you'd like to do?" she asked at breakfast one morning. "Something a bit more social?"

I shrugged. "Tennis is social."

"Shrugging is for Italians, sweetheart," she said absently, frowning down at the little pillow she was mending. She sewed during meals more often than not—*settles my nerves*, she said, though I believe the truth is that she couldn't bear to waste the time. "And I'm afraid I don't see how hitting a ball back and forth over a net all day qualifies as social."

"Internal dialogue," my father said, lowering the paper to peer at me. "Far less taxing on the spirit than the other sort. Isn't that right, Queenie?" He winked and I ducked my head gratefully. How I wish you could have known your grandfather then! Already an older man, seven years my mother's senior and fine-looking without being what you'd call handsome. An honest face, people said in those days. He was what by that point already qualified as a dying breed, a good, kind man who loved his work and family, who went uncomplainingly to the office each morning, worked long hours, and came home weary and smelling of tobacco and ink. Of course he worshiped my mother; we both did.

She licked the end of her thread. "I'm glad you two find this amusing."

"Now, Eloise—"

"It just so happens invitations are going out next week for this

31

fall's charity balls," she went on, "but apparently I'm the only one at this table who cares about Rebecca being included in this season's most important events."

"I care," I offered.

"As do I," said my father, raising his coffee cup in salute.

My mother eyed us to see if we were mocking her and decided we were in earnest. "I have it on good authority that the boards are particularly selective this year. Eleanor," she said, with a nod in my direction. "I ran into her at Swenson's last week. Positively brutal, she said."

My father closed the paper and tilted back in his chair; he wore the expression of deliberate concern he always assumed when my mother sounded unhappy. "I'd like to know what would recommend a girl better than tennis," he said finally. "Seems healthy enough."

"Rebecca?" My mother appealed to me.

"I think a few girls from school might be going to the beach later on this afternoon," I said slowly. "I could make a call or two."

My mother gave me the smile she reserved for those rare occasions I surprised her. "The thing about tennis, Walter," she explained with exaggerated patience, "is that it's exclusive. The girls have no opportunity for *mingling*. It's all fine and good to spend time at the club, and under ordinary circumstances . . ." She let her voice trail off. "But these are extraordinary times, don't you agree? What with Rebecca headed off to college so soon and all. Extraordinary measures. Isn't that right, sweetheart?" She turned to me again and I sat up very straight, doing my best to look ready, my entire being bent toward mingling.

"Alex said they'll have dance class for all us first-years this fall."

"You see, Walter?" She beamed at me.

"What I don't understand is how it won't be chaos," I said. "There are twelve girls in our house alone."

"And you're all going to have the most fabulous time." A few pieces of hair had come loose from my mother's chignon; they floated by her ears like strands of corn silk, moved gently back and forth by currents of air. "Just think of all the new friends you'll make!"

"I don't need new friends."

She looked at me reproachfully. "Sweetheart."

"I don't."

"*Really*, darling, it isn't healthy—"

"It must be difficult," my father interrupted.

"Sir?"

"Your Alexandra," he said gently. "You must miss her."

I swallowed against the sudden lump in my throat. "I do."

"And she's been a wonderful friend to you over the years," my mother said briskly, her needle darting in and out. "But you'll want to be careful."

"I don't know what you mean."

She tied a deft knot, snapping the thread with her teeth. "*There.*" She held up the pillow in triumph, the new cover stretched taut across the front. "Isn't that better? I never cared for that old blue ticking. Too Frenchy, and I don't mean that in a good way." She gave me a conciliatory smile. "I'm not saying anything we all don't already know, darling. All your father and I have ever wanted is for you to *enjoy* yourself. Spread your wings."

"Flap, flap."

"Hmm?" She frowned. "Besides, Alexandra can afford to be careless. Theater camp, for goodness' sake! I can only imagine the kind of young men who attend that sort of thing. Hardly husband material." She clicked her tongue. "Eleanor must be furious."

"They're eighteen," my father protested mildly.

"And I've put two and two together, and last time I checked they'll be nineteen soon enough, then twenty." My mother's face could look quite stern, those light eyebrows knit together in consternation. "Am I to be persecuted for thinking of the future? Why, when I think of how Daddy—" Her eyes filled with tears.

"Eloise." My father looked at me desperately. "Please."

"But I have you," I said, too loud. "I have both of you."

"That's right," my father said, soothingly. "You're both right. It's just, Eloise, don't you think she's a little young to be thinking about marriage?"

My mother stood then, tucking the pillow under her arm and wrapping her spool of thread and needle into the sewing pouch she carried around the house in the pocket of her housecoat. "If everyone's already made up their mind," she said, wounded.

My father and I stood together as though her reproof had been a command, the remains of our breakfast scattered across the tablecloth. The toast crumbs Mother would clear away later with the special scraper she'd recently ordered from a catalog, saying she'd seen one at a luncheon and apparently they were all the rage.

"It does look like a nice day for the beach," my father offered, stooping to peer out the window opposite his chair.

"The weather's glorious," Mother sniffed.

"We could go together?" I already knew her answer.

"Me? Goodness, no. I've got scads of things to attend to around the house," she said briskly. "Not to mention there's pie to be made for a luncheon Mary-Lou is having tomorrow. There's only to be *one* pie, mind you, and mine is it, which means it has to be perfect. You know how those girls get about their pies." She put on her brave face. "You go on ahead, Rebecca. Only if you feel like it, of course."

I nodded slowly, as though I was thinking something through. "I thought maybe I'd write a letter or two first."

She sighed again, gathering up the rest of the pillows from where she'd stacked them on the floor; sometimes it seemed my mother

34

had an entire vocabulary of sighs, each subtly different in speed and volume, the pressures behind the release of air varying one to the next. "Has so much really changed since you wrote her yesterday?"

"The world, I should think," my father said, leaning over to drop a kiss on my head.

I must have written Alex at least two or three letters a week that summer, spending early mornings out on the patio with a glass of lemonade and the stationery my parents had given me for Christmas years ago, my initials stamped at the top in indigo ink.

It's hot as blazes, I wrote. *The club's packed to the gills. You should see the bathing suit poor old Mrs. Ostrong had on the other afternoon—it must have been from the turn of the century. Prewar at the very least. Are they keeping you busy up here? Have you played Cleopatra yet? Are the other girls nice? Are any of them half as talented as you? Do you miss me?*

Her letters came fairly regularly at first: *Dear Pen, First few days here miserable, as to be expected. Bugs thick as thieves. Bed made out of goddamn iron, not to mention lumpy mattress. Company lacking. Present curriculum skewed toward saccharine. If I have to sing "I'M GONNA WASH THAT MAN,"* etc., *one more time, I swear, though at least the voice coach has a decent head on his shoulders. N.B.: Girls from Santa Barbara slippery little eels & not to be trusted! You should see what some of the idiots here try to pass off as intelligence,* she wrote. *One of my bunkmates actually asked if Marlowe was still alive—I told her, yes, alive and well and living in London with the queen. Prefers scones to crumpets. Cruel, I know, but* honestly! *I have zero tolerance for the prodigiously uninformed.* Another: *Darling Penny. I woke up this morning in a panic over the early tragedians. Dreamt I was being quizzed by a panel of directors (bearded, white-haired) & they all started shaking their heads when they asked for Aeschylus and I said WHO? I've only read the littlest bit of Sophocles. Euripides another story completely, thank God, but what about Aeschylus? Have you read him extensively? Bunkmate Laurie has loads & the plays are nothing short of marvelous. Situation to be remedied immediately upon my return. We're to read this fall like absolute* mad, *do you hear?* Little by little, however, the frequency of her letters dwindled and then stalled; soon enough, her correspondence had been reduced to the occasional postcard. *P: My Othello's a complete drip,* one said. *Have you ever seen a red-haired Iago?* Another read simply: *"In bocca al lupo"* means GOOD LUCK—the bottom signed with a sketch of a wolf's head, a row of *x*'s followed by a single A. By August, even those had stopped coming. Meanwhile, I kept writing religiously, spending every afternoon in a state of mild agitation until the mailman came. But one by one my letters disappeared into a silence so vast it seemed to follow me wherever I went, a heaviness like the humidity that weighed on me as I hurried up El Molino toward the library or made idle chitchat with my classmates at the club before diving into the pool, testing how long I could hold my breath while my mother sat in a deck chair drawn close to the other mothers, their laughter so loud I could hear it underwater.

Chapter 5

OF course there were all kinds of expenses that went along with going to college, expenses that in retrospect I understand must have weighed heavily on my parents. At the time I saw them as little more than nuisances, I'm afraid. In those days, tuition was still free at California's state schools, but there were books to buy and formal dresses Mother claimed she didn't dare try her hand at herself, new shoes she deemed *obligatory*. We spent three consecutive afternoons at Bullock's that last week of summer, during which she took such obvious pleasure in the selection of each item—the agonizing over this dress or that one, the buttons on this one declared *cunning*, the collar on another *divine*—I finally told her she was better off choosing them herself, that if she didn't mind I would wait in the dressing room and she could bring me what she pleased. I needed no less than three pairs of gloves for the charity balls, the invitations for which Mother set out on Mrs. Peachtree's table as they arrived; there was a new quilt for my bed at the dorm, the old one I had used since childhood worn and yellowed by the sun beyond repair; new stockings, packed between layers of tissue; a jacket Mother had sewn herself, a smart linen thing she presented to me with a flourish as we sat together on my bed my last afternoon at home, fanning ourselves in the heat.

"Better than Neiman's, if I do say so myself," she declared. "It should go beautifully with that blue muslin. Of course, you'll want to bring that new taffeta for the formal dances. The yellow one with the flowers will have to do for the rest." She looked at me critically, the tip of her tongue caught between her lips. "I'll have to take in the waist. You've lost weight."

I glanced at my reflection in the mirror that hung on the opposite wall. My face was sober, unsmiling. "Maybe a little. The jacket is perfect." And I meant it. For all her modesty, she was a wonderful seamstress. Her mother had taught her when she was young—out of necessity, I suppose—and now she could stitch together an entire blouse in the time it took me to cut a single sleeve from a pattern.

"I can't say I like your color," she said now, squinting at me. "How about an orange juice? A nice glass of milk?"

"I'm alright, I guess."

She busied herself folding the jacket, smoothing it down beneath the tissue. "People can be cruel. Girls especially. Don't think I don't remember."

I did my best to smile. "I'll be fine."

"Of course you will. You're a Poole girl, and we Poole girls always land on our feet. You know, I was already working at your age," she went on. "School was never really in the cards. Daddy never would have allowed it, even if he'd lived long enough to see us all out of diapers. Still, I distinctly remember feeling relieved to have something to do. Something that took my mind off things." She pressed her lips together: I could see her choosing her words carefully. "It isn't healthy to have too much time to sit around and brood."

"I haven't been brooding."

"You remember what I said about Alexandra." She looked at me intently; I would have done anything to smooth the crease from her brow. "She can afford to dabble, that's all I meant. I'm afraid we don't have that luxury." She pleated her skirt, a nervous gesture I recognized as one of my own. "I don't have anything against her, darling. It's just that I'd hate to see you make choices that lead to nothing but disappointment."

With a great show of deliberation, I turned my gaze toward the rug, the faded patch where the light through the windows had struck it repeatedly over the years, bleaching the crimson threads to pink. "I have no intention of disappointing anyone."

She fussed with the tissue wrapping the stockings. "Sometimes I forget how young I was when I met your father. Heaven knows what would have happened to me if he hadn't come along. He rescued me, you know." She paused. "I don't think I've ever said it quite like that."

"I thought you loved working for Henry," I said, surprised.

"It was fun for a while. But I had to think of my future, didn't I?" She left the stockings and brushed something off the collar of my blouse, her hands going automatically to straighten the shoulders. "Don't look so down in the mouth about it, sweetheart. I never considered it a permanent solution. Much too much traveling, for one, and I'd like to remind you that Henry didn't exactly make it easy for me. What would I have done if I hadn't met your father? Taken a job as someone's secretary in some ugly old office? Come home every night to a grimy little room, dinner on a Sterno?" She stood then, snapping the lid of my suitcase shut and giving it a pat. "Be sensible, darling."

"Then you don't regret giving it up—the traveling. The music."

She tilted her head. "You're full of questions today."

I turned my attention to the skirt I'd laid aside to wear the next day, patting it down with exaggerated care. "Everything's going to be so different."

"It's only natural to feel a little apprehensive. All this change! But really, you'll find it does you good. Invigorating, I should think." She put her hand on my shoulder, fingers tapping. "He used to practice like this—Henry, I mean. On his own arm. It just came to me now—isn't that funny? Of course, he was getting on in his years, but it didn't have a thing to do with age. Said it helped him understand the keyboard, to *see* it. A pure kind of vision, he called it." She ran her hand down my arm, her fingers flying now. "He'd play anything in sight—the table at a restaurant, the dashboard of a car, his own leg. Sooner or later, though, he always had to sit down and play the real thing. I always thought it must have come as the most tremendous relief." Her hand came to rest on mine. "You're going to have the most marvelous time." She tipped my head up so I had to look at her, her hair gleaming in the late-afternoon light. "You know that, don't you?" I nodded. "Marvelous," she repeated.

We had an early dinner that night, after which I escaped to my room, telling my parents I was tired and needed to tend to a few things before bed, the two of them exchanging looks as I kissed them good night. They would have liked me to stay awhile longer, I'm sure—Mother especially must have wanted me to linger, to sit and discuss the details of the next day over dessert and coffee. But I felt distracted at the thought of the next twenty-four hours and vaguely ill, and so I pretended not to see their disappointment, leaving them with their coffee as I turned and fled. I stood for a minute in front of my packed bags, suddenly exhausted, and then I turned the sheets back and crept into bed, too tired to so much as unbutton my blouse.

\|/

The knock on my door woke me from a deep, dreamless sleep. It was after ten, late for a call, but my mother only shook her head when I sat up.

"Sounds as though she had a fabulous time," she said from the doorway. "You may as well say hello." I swung my feet out from under the covers and crossed the room. "Don't forget you'll need your rest for tomorrow," she added. "Both of you."

"I won't be long."

"You might ask if she still plans on driving you to campus." She turned to the side to let me pass and brushed at her housecoat the way she did when she had something to say but wouldn't. "Goodness knows you won't need your old mother hanging around."

"I'll ask," I said. "Can I have a minute?"

"*May* I," she said automatically.

"*May* I have a minute? Please?" She must have heard the desperation in my voice, because she only reached out to smooth my hair back from my face before turning away and disappearing down the hall. I picked up the phone immediately and clamped the receiver between my ear and shoulder. "When did you get home?"

"Hello to you too." Her voice on the other end of the line was oddly worn—breathless and crackling with fatigue. She was *exhausted*, she said. She and her father had driven all day to get home by dark and she was *famished*, she said. She was absolutely beat.

"We're due at the dorm by one tomorrow," I reminded her, winding the telephone cord around and around my finger until the tip turned purple. "My father was going to take the bus so we could have the car, Mother and I. I didn't know if you'd be back in time. But if you think you'll still be able to drive, of course I'd rather—"

"I said I would, didn't I?" she said, a little impatiently. "I'll be there by noon. Noonish. I got held up, that's all. Unavoidable delays."

She hadn't packed, she said. She hadn't even *unpacked*, for Christ's sake. "And for the love of God, please stop worrying," she said. "I can hear you worrying all the way down the block, so just don't. It's driving me absolutely berserk."

Morning found me dressed and at the breakfast table long before anyone was up; I made a pot of coffee and drank cup after cup while I waited for my parents to come down, Mother reaching out to tip my chin up as she came into the dining room, the lilac scent of her perfume strong.

"A little rouge?" she said, sinking into her chair. "Brighten you up? What about a touch of lipstick?" She drew one of her gold tubes from the pocket of her housecoat and slid it across the table. "The saleslady said it's their most popular shade." She watched as I dabbed it on my lips and pressed. "Keep it. It's better with your complexion. Brings out your eyes." She frowned. "You look a little tired."

"Too excited to sleep?"

I tried to return my father's smile. "Something like that."

"You'd tell me if you thought we needed to run out to Bullock's for another pair of stockings, wouldn't you?" Mother checked her watch. "We have the time if we leave this minute. Do you have enough sweaters?"

My father stopped with his toast halfway to his mouth. "It's ninety-five degrees today. They're saying over a hundred by the afternoon."

"If it were up to you, Walter, I swear," she sighed. "She'd go off for the year without so much as a toothbrush."

He looked at me fondly. "She's going to be just fine. Aren't you, Queenie?"

"I certainly hope so."

My mother pushed her napkin across the table at my father.

"Crumbs," she said, gesturing at her chin. "Honestly, Walter. You wouldn't send a soldier off into battle without the proper ammunition, would you?"

My father wiped his chin slowly and folded his napkin back under his plate; he was such a careful man, your grandfather, his every movement methodical. "We could certainly manage another sweater."

I said I thought I'd be alright without the sweater. My mother poured out the orange juice for everyone and reminded me to call the moment I arrived. "The *minute*," she said. "Or else we'll start to worry, do you hear? It's not every day your only daughter goes off to college all on her own. Never mind me—" She produced a handkerchief from the pocket of her housecoat and dabbed at her eyes. I nodded and said I was looking forward to it, though the truth was that my hands had begun to shake in that way they had at the dentist's or one of the schoolwide spelling bees Windridge held every fall. I pressed the tumbler of juice to my forehead: The cool glass felt marvelous. To my father's offer of a piece of toast, I said, no, thank you. Too jittery to eat, I said.

"Look," I said, holding up my hands, and the three of us watched my fingers tremble.

\|/

I must have blamed my fatigue for how newly strange Alex appeared to me when she pulled up outside my house a little before noon. She wore her hair curled at the ends so it flipped up around her shoulders, her cheeks pink across the tops as though she'd been sitting in the sun.

"Look at you," she said. She was grinning as she reached over the gearshift to throw her arms around me, and I thought for a moment in a great rush of relief that everything would be fine. "Look at us, the dashing coeds."

"You look terrific."

"This?" She touched her hair. "I figured it was time for a change." She watched me lift my suitcase into the backseat. "Don't tell me that's all you're bringing. For Pete's sake, Beau had to go by the dorm earlier and drop off my trunk and about a million books—he was livid, I tell you. Absolutely livid."

I slid into the passenger seat. "I'm leaving my sweaters and things at home until it cools off a bit," I lied.

She shrugged. "Suit yourself."

Together, we turned and waved to my mother where she stood in the doorway, watching. "Goodbye!" we called. "Goodbye!"

She stood up on her toes to wave. "Goodbye," she called. "*Bon voyage!*"

I caught a glimpse of her in the rearview mirror as we pulled away from the curb, her arm still raised, the blue of her housecoat cheerful. We'd made plans to have my father pick me up that Sunday and bring me home for dinner. The university campus was just a few miles from our house, and of course I could spend the night in my own room whenever I liked. Still, it was one of those moments that gives weight to the smallest particulars. I have never, as you know, been a great fan of change, and everything seemed fraught with my leaving: the scent of our neighbor's clematis through the open windows, the sun heating the car door under my arm to near unbearable, a dragonfly that veered drunkenly through my window and out the other side as we turned the far corner onto Rio Grande, the sound of my mother's *bon voyage!* ringing in my ears long after she'd disappeared from sight. It came as a shock to realize I had never spent more than a night away from my parents before. Strange to think they would not be just down the hall that night when I went to bed, that my father would not be at the table when I came down in the morning, reading the paper and cutting his toast into neat triangles, that my mother would not be there when I came home every day, sitting in the living room with her sewing or stand-ing bent over the banister, oiling it until it gleamed, her hands cool as she brushed the hair back from my face, offering lemonade, a glass of iced tea, a bowl of fruit.

I don't believe Alex noticed a thing. She was in high spirits as we drove: The program had been a scream, she announced. Really, if I could have seen the theater they got to perform in, I would have flipped, she said. Absolutely flat-out flipped. Some of the other actors hadn't been half bad, but the real excitement had been that they'd had an entire cast and crew for the stage machinery and a separate crew for lighting, not to mention a few girls for costumes and another few for makeup. *Very* official, she said. And did I want to know the best part? An agent had approached her after one of the last performances and given her his card.

"It was my Desdemona that did it. *Alas the heavy day!* Et cetera. The director had me do the whole thing a touch treacly for my taste, but he called it brilliant. The agent, I mean." She flicked her sunglasses to the top of her head and eyed me. "*Brilliant*. Imagine!"

"Imagine," I echoed.

"Not to mention," she went on, "Eleanor laid down her arms when I told her, if you can believe it. I think it was the agent thing that did the trick. She said if I was that dead set on acting, I might as well go ahead and give it my all. Everything worth anything deserves a little dedication, she said. So now I've got her blessing, more or less. As long as it doesn't interfere with my so-called duties." She held up her left hand and waggled her ring finger. "Ding-dong, in other words. *Try not to embarrass us, Alexandra*, she says. As if her droning on about Beau's handicap or the latest goddamn polo pony she's thinking of snapping up isn't embarrassing. I swear, if I have to sit there through one more lecture about the importance of proper seating etiquette or whatever, I think I'll—"

"Sounds like you were busy."

"I just said."

"It must have been hard to find time for much of anything else."

She glanced at me, then back at the road. "You're angry I didn't write more."

"No—"

"Look, it wasn't my fault. Something went funny with the mail there toward the end, and by the time I had all your letters, it was time to go. You have to believe me." She frowned at the road. "You're not actually mad, are you?"

"Not especially."

"Promise?"

"Scout's honor." I held up my hand, fingers crossed.

"God, don't even start with that. I was a Brownie back in Houston and I'm still recovering." Her face had relaxed but her forehead held the suggestion of a frown, a faint tracing of parallel lines. "I couldn't stand you being mad at me, you know," she said intently. "I don't think I could stand it one second."

"I'm not mad."

"So you're happy for me."

"Sure I am."

She was quiet a moment or two. "I'm finally going to make something of myself, Pen."

"Forget I said anything."

"Can't. I'm not the forgetting type. I do, however, forgive." She grabbed my arm and squeezed. "But I won't forgive you even an inch until you tell me you're happy for me. And you have to sound like you mean it."

"I am," I said, laughing a little. We'd stopped at a light and she was turned sideways in her seat to face me, her expression pleading; she was my best friend. We were driving to our first day at the U and there was no one I could talk to about it except her. "I couldn't be happier."

"Things are going to be different from now on." She was still clutching me; her fingers dug in around my wrist. "Freddy says——"

"Who?"

"The *agent*," she said impatiently. "He's got connections at MGM. Fluff, I know, but he says I have to start somewhere. I can't just go straight to the stage, he says. Not in this day and age." She clicked her tongue. "It all starts with the pictures now."

"Sounds thrilling," I began. "Sounds like——"

"Problem is, I need practice. Stage time. Freddy said I've got to start gunning for New York, effective immediately. Of course, I'll have to work like a horse. It'll be tough as hell while I'm still going to school and trying to keep Eleanor happy. But *Broadway*, for God's sake."

"It really does sound——"

"Let me guess," she said, shooting me a look. "Thrilling."

"Well, it does," I said. And then, because I didn't know what else to say, "it really does." We turned off the main road into a narrow drive lined with hydrangeas, the lawns on either side lush and green, impeccably trimmed. The university campus was much larger than Windridge, but our dormitory was tucked into one of the far corners in a quadrangle with the other girls' dorms; when the college went coed, they must have grouped the girls' dorms away from the main campus intentionally, though at the time I worried only that we were farther from the library than I would have liked. I caught a glimpse through the hydrangeas of a few girls walking here and there along the path: They looked glamorous in their neat blouses and narrow skirts, many of them wearing their hair cropped short in an angled cut I hadn't seen before. Sophisticated, I thought, as Alex pulled the car into the lot. My mind went immediately to the clothes Mother and I had packed the day before—the cotton blouses she'd sewn from patterns we'd picked out together months earlier, the skirts that had at the time seemed the height of fashion, the dresses from Bullock's—all of it, I knew, wrong. "So this is college," I said, trying to make my voice light.

Alex tipped her head back against the seat and slid her sunglasses down, her timing—as always—impeccable. "Rah-rah," she said.

It didn't take long—a week? Maybe two?—before she disappeared. She joined the student theater company and started staying out till God knows when, somehow coaxing Mrs. Perkins, our house mother, into giving her an extended curfew. In those days, girls—*coeds*—were still required to be inside by nine. The boys, of course, were free to come and go as they pleased. "Extraordinary circumstances," Alex called it, in any case. She was rarely home, often returning to her room only to sleep. Mornings she arrived at breakfast—if she came at all—with just enough time to grab something and *run*. She seemed to operate in a state of perpetual distraction, her bottom lip caught between her teeth, her gaze in those brief moments I caught her in the hallway focused on some distant, unseen point.

There were other changes, subtle but perceptible. I noticed first that her beautiful eyes were often reddened around the rims, tearing slightly as though from cold; she let her hair grow long again and took to wearing it knotted carelessly on top of her head, secured with a pencil; she wore a new shade of lipstick I privately thought much too bright; she grew thinner, her face taking on the translucent quality of bone china; at some point during that winter, she took to wearing a pair of oversize tortoise-rimmed glasses, which she had a habit of pushing up the bridge of her nose in a gesture of wearied tolerance. She seemed never to be without a cigarette. She was always in a rush: She had rehearsal, or a meeting, something she called a *read-through*. "Another goddamn read-through with the director," she'd complain in mock exasperation. "I'm late," she'd declare, a plume of smoke rising from her hand. "Not now, darling. Later? Would you mind terribly?"

Cullers Hall. That was the name of our dormitory—the house, we called it, and it had in fact been the university president's home for a number of years, converted not long before we lived there, when the college accepted its first class of girls. 1956, I believe that was. We each had our own room across a hallway we shared with ten other girls, three from our class at Windridge—Robin Pringle, engaged to Benji Spaulding by the end of our sophomore year, red-haired Lindsey Patterson, and Betsy Bromwell. I believe it was Betsy who first knocked on my door to ask if I might like to come to dinner with her and the others; she had a kind face, kind eyes. We called her Dove because of that, and she smiled and said she liked it just fine.

In the wake of Alex's new absence, we became friends, those girls and I. Ordinary friends, the kind I'd managed to make it through my years at Windridge more or less without. I sat with them at meals and visited them in their rooms; we all took to sitting out on our stoop before curfew, Lindsey smoking one of the skinny cigarettes she claimed were all the rage, Betsy and Robin and I keeping busy with our needlework or just sitting. From time to time Alex joined us on her way in or out; she might lean up against the brick wall beside the stoop as we chatted and close her eyes, as though she were one of those lizards from my mother's garden absorbing the warmth of the stone through her skin. More often than not, however, on those rare occasions she wasn't at the theater building or in rehearsal, she shut herself up in her room, stretched out on her bed with her cigarette and a collection of coffee cups balanced precariously on her quilt, a script spread in front of her in apparent disarray.

"I'm working," she'd say with a trace of irritation if I knocked

on the door. "No, hang on: So long as you're here, you don't happen to know the Latin root for *canker*, do you? *Cancerous? Cance-
rum?* No clue? Gosh, no, no dinner, thanks. I couldn't eat a thing."
One hand reaching for her cigarette. "Freddy says it's best at my
height that I go for a Hepburn thing. *Roman Holiday. You* know."

"I really am sorry," she might say sincerely whenever a boy
called for her on the hallway phone—and, believe me, they called—
those glasses balanced all the way down at the tip of her nose or
used, as they were from time to time, to scratch delicately at something above her ear. "I'm afraid I'm terribly tied up at the moment."
Or: "I'd love to, honest, but it's the most atrocious timing," or sometimes, when she was tired or something had tipped her mood to
dangerous, a curt "can't." *Cruel*, Lindsey called it, Alex reminding
her that she could do as she pleased. "Last time I checked," Alex
snapped before vanishing back into her room, "it was still a free
country."

I admired her enormously for that, for her ability to simply,
unapologetically, disappear. But it must be clear by now that I
admired everything about her, that she was everything I was not.

Chapter 6

I did try to tell her once. Alex, I mean. It was our junior year at Windridge—spring, it must have been, March or early April. We were on our way home from school when it began to rain, one of those sudden torrential downpours Pasadena is famous for at that time of year. You could see the rain sweep down the broad streets as it approached, a heavy gray curtain dropping over one house after the next. The street we were walking down that afternoon was lined with trees, which might have provided refuge, and—better yet—houses whose owners would gladly have let us in. No one locked their doors in those days. We would have been taken in in an instant and given cookies and lemonade, a dry towel. But no sooner had I begun to slow my pace than Alex grabbed my hand and pulled. I was already drenched—my fingers slick, my arms— and her hand kept slipping against my skin. Rain streamed down the street's slight incline, the bark on the palm trees gone glossly black and reflective, as though lacquered.

We ran for what I would later swear was miles, though of course it was only a few blocks, Alex in front with her hair streaming out behind her like something out of Ovid, some changeling creature. We turned in to her driveway and collapsed on the front stoop of her house just as the rain stopped, as abruptly as it had begun, both of us gasping, sopping wet.

"I'd like to run to the ends of the world and back." She shook her hair back off her shoulders, though pieces of it clung to her neck like strands of seaweed. "I think I could run forever—I mean it." She said it with that fierceness she had even at that age, and I pretended to be busy with my socks, pleating the material between my fingers and watching the colored water drip onto the stone. "I bet I could run far if I wanted. Fast, too. I bet I could outrun all of them, even those Browning boys."

"Sure you could." My uniform skirt had begun to bleed. Streaks of blue ran down my legs through the mud in a way that worried me, my socks not only filthy but stained as well, the cost of replacing everything, I knew, prohibitive.

"I will, too. And soon." She shrugged. "Soonish. People here lack depth," she said seriously. "Zero gravitas."

"But where would you go?" I asked, careful to keep the rising panic from my voice.

"Anywhere. Everywhere. Travel expands the mind." This she said carefully—quoting, it seemed clear, something she had recently read. "I've been thinking maybe the Amazon. It's supposed to be marvelous down there. The natives believe the earth is carried around on the back of an animal. Isn't that the most marvelous thing you've ever heard? A lion, I think it is, or a turtle. Actual living flesh, is the point, creeping around with the weight of the world on its shoulders."

"I think that's blasphemy," I said uneasily.

"But the best thing I read about the Amazon is what happens when you get into the jungle," she went on, ignoring me. "Deep, I mean, at the absolute center. There's a tribe of women who rule the place. They hunt and kill all their own food. Do everything men do. Men aren't even allowed. Or maybe," she frowned, "once a year or something. They must let in a few to mate every now and then. Point being, they otherwise do without. And you want to know the best part?" She raised her hand to the right side of her chest and slowly, seriously, made the shape of an X. "They cut it off."

"It?"

"The right one. It gets in the way of the bow." She leaned in close. "They slice right through. No medicine or anything. Imagine— they've probably never done it on a white woman. All that blood would be shocking as hell against skin like ours."

I felt a pang in the right side of my chest, where I was still flat as a board. "But it's only these natives who do it," I said worriedly. "Isn't it?"

She sighed. "That's really not the point, Rebecca."

Perhaps I felt she'd just shared something with me and I wanted to do the same. Or maybe I felt a shiver of excitement at the danger in what she'd said, or I heard her disappointment at my question and wanted to prove myself to her once and for all. I don't know. All I know is that I took her hand as she started to turn away— grabbed it, with an urgency I believe surprised us both.

"Look." I pointed to the pale blue V of veins along the under- side of her wrist. "Do you have any idea what these do?"

"I'm cold," she said, frowning.

"This'll just take a minute." I traced the veins up to where they disappeared, an inch or two below the rolled cuff of her blouse. "I was reading about it the other day. There are three big veins that run through your arm—the brachial, the basilic, and the cephalic."

She peered down. "I don't see anything."

"You can't see them, exactly. You have to know how to look."

"So what—now you're God?"

"I think it's interesting, that's all," I said, faltering. "It's like Mr.

Percy said, remember? The best parts are all around us. Everywhere you look. For instance, our hearts." I held up my fists. "Did you know? They're only that big."

"Good for them," she said, turning away again, bored. But instead of going inside, she stood there a moment, her hand resting on the doorknob. "I wouldn't be scared," she said finally, her back still to me. "In case you were wondering." She half-turned then and made that slicing gesture across the front of her chest again. "I wouldn't mind a bit."

I fiddled with the hem of my skirt, the material sopping. "I would."

"I know, Rebecca," she said, her voice heavy with something I didn't recognize, and then she pulled the door open and went inside.

Chapter 7

BUT I said I lost her twice: The second time was Bertrand Lowell. It was May of our junior year at the U when he called for Alex, her voice as she told us she'd said yes unusually husky. I remember thinking it sounded as though she'd been crying. We all circled around her where she sat by the hallway phone, tilting her head back to exhale a thin stream of smoke. "Why the hell not," she said. "I've been living like a goddamn nun." She stubbed her cigarette out in the ceramic dish we kept beside the phone. "I deserve a little fun, don't you think? It's been ages since I had a little fun."

Their date was on a Friday. I remember because it was the weekend before exams and it was unseasonably chilly, the breeze strong enough that I took a scarf when I left for the library that afternoon. I kept a study carrel there in a corner of the fourth floor so the other girls couldn't accuse me of being a grind. So long as I didn't try to work in the dorm, no one could accuse me of anything besides being out, though in retrospect I don't suppose I was fooling anyone. Still, I liked working there enough not to care. It was smaller than the old Pasadena library, but the windows were big, the carpet kept meticulously clean. French literature—that was the section directly behind where I worked, and, when I tired of reading, I often let my gaze drift to the names written in gilt lettering down the spines: *Sartre, Gide, Baudelaire.*

It was late by the time I left my carrel the night of their date, dinner long over. I remember I was half delirious from studying and glad to be out in the fresh air, the breeze carrying the smell of the jacarandas that lined the far quad. An unnatural quiet had descended across that part of campus, the only sound the low vibrato of the creek frogs. I gazed up at the sky as I walked, in no particular hurry to get home. I liked picking out the constellations, each angle fixed to a star precise as a pinprick. Andromeda, Cassiopiea, Ursa Major and Minor.

But I won't pretend I was so engrossed in the skies that I forgot about Alex and Bertrand Lowell. I'd been thinking idly about their date all day while I worked: I pictured them walking down Sunset to the theater, the way he might, smiling, remove a fallen leaf from her hair. As I crossed the footpath over to the women's quad, where yellow lamplight spilled through the windows of Cullers Hall down across the grass, I felt that sudden desire to be home that still strikes me from time to time, a loneliness that makes me want to shut myself up somewhere familiar. The moon slid out from behind Bellweather Hall and I quickened my pace, half-running as I crossed the last pathway to Cullers and pushed the heavy door open, taking the stairs to my bedroom two at a time.

I'd just pulled my nightgown over my head when Alex burst through the door.

"What in the world—"

She pushed past me and threw herself on the bed. "Disgusting," she said. Her face was very pale. "I'd like to know who gave them the right to be so disgusting."

"Who?"

She glared at me as though I was being purposefully obtuse. "Men," she snapped. "Bertrand Lowell." She'd had to hit him to get him to stop, she said. She'd asked first, nicely, and he'd stopped for a minute. His kitchen hot, she said. *Hellish*, both of them sweating like pigs. They'd started out just kissing, and because it felt good, she'd let it keep going. His fingers went to the buttons of her blouse next: She let that go too. It wasn't until they moved up from her knees and up the back of her legs under her skirt that she tried to push him away. He laughed and told her she was gorgeous. Somehow her skirt ended up around her waist. He was strong, she said. Stronger than he looked. They were down on the floor and he was pinning her, she said; he had her by the wrists. It wasn't until it started to hurt—and it *hurt*, she said fiercely; no one ever said it would hurt like that—that she'd managed to work her hand free and bring the flat of her palm against his jaw, her ring cutting a half-moon just in front of his ear.

You little bitch. He'd actually called her that. And then he'd sat there on the floor, cradling the side of his face with one hand as she grabbed her purse and ran.

This was 1965, remember. The words we had for what he'd done fell short of adequate. We might have said he'd been *filthy*. We might have called him an *animal*, said he had acted *abominably*. When she'd finished telling me everything, I went right out into the hallway and poured a glass of milk from the refrigerator in the little kitchenette we all shared. I was surprised to see as I put the bottle back that my hands were shaking; they looked like someone else's hands, my fingers holding the glass so tightly the knuckles shone through the skin.

When I opened the door, Alex was sitting up on my bed and rummaging busily in her purse. "There!" She held up a lipstick, frowning at the tube. "*Scarlet Sunset.* Christ. A little imagination wouldn't have killed them." She drew on her red mouth and blotted with a tissue. "Of course, we'll have to keep the whole thing quiet," she went on. The last thing she wanted was a fuss, she said. Besides which, there wasn't much to tell. She was tired—*God*, she was positively *dead*. She'd had much too much to drink. It was a wonder she hadn't gotten sick. She brought out a compact and checked her reflection, touching up her eyes while I stood there like an idiot with my glass of milk. I had thought she might need to have a good cry. That she might rest there on my bed awhile, gathering her strength, until we came up with a plan. "Everyone makes such a thing about sex," she said now, examining herself in her little mirror. "I've got my career to think about, for crying out loud."

I sat down next to her on the bed and watched as she twisted her hair back into place, driving the pencil through that elaborate knot with what seemed to me to be unnecessary force. "But it's awful what he did," I said finally.

She gave me a bland look. "Honestly, I can hardly remember."

"You just told me—"

She snapped her purse shut and stood. "And now I'm saying I don't remember."

She stood there, tapping her foot against the rug. When it was clear I wasn't about to say anything else, she went to the door, giving me a look; after a moment's pause, I agreed to silence—nodding, unhappy. I stayed sitting on my bed a long time after she left, drinking the glass of milk down myself, every drop, before turning off the light. I don't know what the hardest part of the whole thing was—trying to pick out the truth from everything she'd said or trying to explain to myself how and why exactly I felt betrayed.

Chapter 8

THAT next week was, as I said, exams. I would have shut myself up in the library till all hours even if Alex hadn't come into my room that night and said what she did. As it was, I stayed deliberately late and left the dorm before breakfast was set out, my pencils sharpened and tucked into the side pocket of my purse. Still, it was strange to see her standing there in Betsy's driveway when we all met that next Saturday morning before Robin's wedding—her hair falling loose around her shoulders, her yellow dress cut low and tight. Looking, I mean, as though nothing had changed. She gave a languid wave when she saw me, her cigarette leaving a *Z* of smoke hanging in the air.

"Hail the conquering," she called. "How'd you do?"

"Fine, I guess."

She rolled her eyes. "Don't be modest, Becky. It doesn't suit you."

"Oh, leave her alone," Betsy broke in. "You're just jealous." She gave me a reassuring smile. "We're all jealous, aren't we, girls? Wouldn't we all like to be as smart as Rebecca?"

Lindsey patted her curls—copper-colored and tucked under in the style my mother had encouraged me to try. "Some of us will have to settle for being dummies."

"Dummies," Alex said slowly, "with a little foresight." She reached into her handbag and pulled out a flask; Lindsey broke into applause.

Both ceremony and reception were being held at Robin's family's country house in Indio, a town some hundred-odd miles southeast of Pasadena in an area known as the dusty territory of date farmers and ranchers. I stayed mostly silent in the passenger seat beside Betsy, listening to Lindsey chatter on as she and Alex passed the flask back and forth in the backseat, both of them rolling down the windows to smoke. The landscape dulled as we drove, the trees giving way to great dry swaths of land that stretched out toward the horizon, pale as bone, dotted here and there with scraggly bushes whose branches scraped low to the ground as though bent to the task of finding water. Dust blew up around our wheels in clouds the sickly yellow of pollen—the car coated with it, we discovered when we stopped, thick enough you could write your name with a finger.

We must have driven at least two hours before pulling into a long, winding driveway guarded on either side by date palms, their trunks dusted over so thickly with that yellow dirt the bark looked shaggy, like the coat of a wild dog. I'd been out to the property once before, years earlier when Robin and I were very young and our mothers had briefly become friendly. I'd forgotten how big the house was, though my mother had leapt to remind me of it the moment I told her about the wedding. *Stunning,* she'd called it. I never did find out when it had been built, but everything about it spoke to a kind of history missing from our house, its structure massive but oddly haphazard—rambling, maybe, is the better word.

"What's that funny thing?" Lindsey held a hand to her forehead, shielding her eyes as we walked up the path toward the house. She pointed to where a balcony jutted out on the third floor, the railing looped around and around with roses.

"Widow's walk," I said automatically.

"Gosh, how cheery," Alex snorted.

"You know the strangest things, Rebecca." Betsy tugged at the hem of her dress. "I swear."

"They're more common on the East Coast, I think. Robin told me her grandmother had it built after Mr. Pringle—Senior, obviously—died last year. She came from Boston, remember?" I looked up at the flowers strung along the white rail, the deep-pink blossoms falling open like mouths. "They were meant for sailors, in any case. Or, rather, the wives they left at home. They stood on the walk and watched the horizon, waiting."

"Not too morbid or anything," Lindsey said.

"They lived in this house together for twenty-five years." I squinted into the sun. "Maybe she likes to stand out there and think of him coming back."

"Or maybe she gets up there with a shotgun in case he does," Alex said, shading her eyes with her hand. "I bet she kicked up her heels once the old man was gone. I mean, I bet she runs around this place happy as a pig in—"

"Look who beat us here," Betsy interrupted, pointing across the lawn to where the boys were crowded around a table set with ice buckets and tumblers, a row of tall bottles standing guard over an enormous bowl of limes. Off to the side of that little circle stood Bertrand Lowell, wearing a pale-pink shirt and a woven hat, holding a glass of something iced.

"Hello, hello." Charlie Thornton was the first to call out. Most of the boys standing in that group waved. The shyer ones nodded in our direction or stared down at their shoes—freshly shined, the leather gleaming. They wore suits, navy and light gray and dark gray and black; a few had on jackets pin-striped with blue. They looked different than they did at school in their everyday clothes, and they stood as though they knew—their shoulders thrown back, spines ramrod straight. These were nice boys, all of them, the kind with whom any of our mothers would have been glad to see us paired off. There was Doc Rhiner, dark and bushy-browed, and tall Larry Templeton with his cowlick of blond hair; there was Charlie Thornton, the star of the track team; Oliver Hinden, who'd grown up next door to me and whose widowed father and little brother had on occasion spent Easter Sunday at our house, Mother saying it was the neighborly thing to do. There was Buzz Fletcher, reed-thin and elegant as a professor in his small wire glasses.

When Alex got close enough, Charlie Thornton took her by the elbow and kissed her on the cheek. He'd been in love with her forever and had given up trying to hide it years ago.

"Charles, you prince," she said, accepting the yellow rose he presented with a flourish. "Let it never be said that you lacked persistence."

"I call it dedication." He beamed at her. "And you're worth every bit."

She twirled the rose between her fingers. "Looks like you boys have kept yourselves busy guarding the bar."

"Well, maybe." The rest of the boys nodded. In front of me and to the right, Bertrand Lowell raised his glass to his lips and a few drops of condensation rolled down the side, dripping onto his pale pink shirt.

"You made it." Oliver Hinden handed me a drink. "And in one piece, even."

"Barely." I was glad to see him, his round, familiar face, and I smiled to let him know.

"When's the big solo?" Charlie picked up a pitcher and started pouring.

Alex shrugged. "After the cake, I guess."

"Is there even a piano?" Betsy peered around.

Alex took a glass from Charlie. "Last time I checked, Marlene didn't need any help when she sang 'Falling in Love Again.'" She threw the drink back in one long swallow, wiped her mouth with the back of her hand, and held out her empty glass. "Besides, I don't plan on feeling much of anything by the time I get up in front of the crowd. *In vino veritas*, correct?"

"Correcto!" cried Buzz.

"Marlene?" Betsy whispered in my ear.

"Dietrich," I said. "Never mind."

"We were about to head on over into the shade. It's hot as anything in this sun." Charlie gestured at the edge of the lawn, where a cluster of avocado trees bent over a few chairs. "Shall we?" We moved together then, Charlie leading and the boys jostling one another, us girls trying to navigate that grass in our heels.

"Careful." From somewhere behind me, Bertrand Lowell appeared and caught Lindsey's arm just in time.

"Gosh, thanks," she said, steadying herself against him.

I saw what was happening right away: the smile that slid across her face as she looked up at him from behind her curls, a smile Bertrand Lowell returned, holding her elbow with his other hand as they walked across to the circle of chairs and sat down. I followed Alex through the grass and sat down in the chair Larry Templeton was holding. I took a long sip from my glass. I didn't have much of a taste for alcohol in those days, but for all my mother's efforts—the cocktail parties she pressed me to attend around the holidays, reminding me to speak to everyone, anyone, the dancing lessons I understand in retrospect we could ill afford—I never did learn to feel at ease around groups. Besides Oliver, there wasn't a boy there I felt close to comfortable with.

"It's over." Buzz looked around the circle. "Our boy's gone and done it now."

"There but for the grace of God . . ." Doc grinned, shaking his head. Someone whistled; Larry gave an exaggerated shudder. They were boys, when you got right down to it—twenty, twenty-one, round in the face but still too skinny through the arms and legs, happy to sit with a cold drink in one hand, pretending to loosen their collars at the thought of marriage.

And I—I stayed where I was, my drink sweating lightly against my palms. I stayed and watched Alex shred the petals of her yellow rose to pieces as she leaned in toward poor Charlie, deliberately letting the front of her dress dip down, letting the straps slide to the edges of her slender shoulders. Lindsey laughing a little too loudly, her head thrown back.

And then there was Bertrand Lowell. Sitting across the circle with his strange pale eyes staring straight at me.

At a certain point I excused myself, telling Betsy I'd catch up with them by the tent. The car ride had given me a headache, I said. I needed to walk. I headed back through the trees toward the main house, where I made my way to one of the bathrooms on the first floor. I'd spent the night before at the house on El Molino, Mother insisting on helping me do my hair up that morning in an elaborate arrangement.

"There!" she'd declared as she slid the final pin into place. "Look at you." Her voice had held an almost negligible vibrato. "You've gotten so pretty."

And we'd looked together—both of us, I believe, surprised to find that in that moment it was true.

The day had turned uncomfortably hot, however, the air heavy,

The heat was causing the whole thing to slide down my neck, working little tendrils loose here and there around my ears. I was standing at the sink, doing my best to pin everything back in place, when Alex walked in, pushing the door open without so much as a knock.

"Oh," she said. "It's you." She looked as though she was doing her best not to burst out laughing. "Well, all hail the queen, I guess." She lit a cigarette and dropped the match on the floor, grinding it under her heel; I saw that what I'd taken for laughter was anger. "I'll say this for Linds, she doesn't waste any time."

I busied myself with my purse right away, fiddling with the clasp. "She doesn't mean anything by it."

"Snap out of it, please. She knows exactly what she's doing." She waved me off. "Look, I can hardly blame her—the man's brilliant. Filthy rich. He's got Kennedy's nose, don't you think? The dead one. Bobby's a touch beaky for my taste. Not to mention, he's already got his own place—down on Melrose, did you hear? Gosh, there's no need to look so morbid." She peered at me through the smoke. "You didn't think he was my first, did you?"

I could feel myself blushing furiously. "Of course not."

"It was that agent at that summer program, if you must know." She frowned. "Fred. Freddy. Bled all over his hotel sheets like a stuck pig. *Call me Lady Macbeth*, I told him, but he didn't think that was funny. I thought it was pretty goddamn witty, considering."

"You never told me."

"I didn't tell a soul, silly. The whole thing was mortifying." She used her pinky to remove a bit of tobacco clinging to her bottom lip. "I fell for the oldest trick in the book. The auditions that *happened* to be switched at the last minute? The director who was dying to meet me but *happened* to have been called out of town? The emergency strategizing lunches—which, incidentally, I ended up paying for more often than not." She shook her head. "Makes me sick just thinking about it."

"But that's awful."

"What's awful is the man stank of onions. Positively reeked," she declared. "And don't get me started on his hands. Christ, his *hands*. Ham-fisted or whatever, and he moved them like a goddamn—but, look, now I'm embarrassing you again." I started to protest and she wagged her finger, shushing me. "So you're last. So what? Most men find the whole vestal virgin thing quite charming."

"Since when am I last?"

"As of *tonight*, fine, if you insist on getting technical. You and Robin were the only contenders, and one assumes conjugal rights. Lindsey confessed to me ages ago. Some stiff in the philosophy department, poor thing. Sounded like a complete snore."

"And Betsy?"

"Betsy *est verboten*." She frowned. "I've got that wrong, haven't I. Doesn't count, that's my point."

"I don't know why not."

"Book of Ruth? Sappho? Freud's theory of childhood trauma? Christ, Rebecca—Isle of Lesbos?"

"Betsy? I don't see that."

"No, I don't expect you would." Her voice was amused.

I took my time fishing out an extra pin from my bag, guiding it into my hair. "I'm not completely ignorant about sex," I said finally. "I just haven't found the right person."

"Poor Oliver."

"It's certainly not *Oliver*."

"He's not so bad. Not exactly the brightest bulb in the room, but he'd do in a pinch. Not to mention the dead mother was some sort of heiress—isn't that right? Coal, I think. Unless it was diamonds. Filthy rich, in any case." She eyed me. "You could do worse."

I shook my head. "It'd be like kissing my brother."

"Zero sparkle." She nodded. "You're like me—you'd take a rat over a jellyfish any day. They're all rats or jellyfish. The trick is finding one who's just rat enough."

"Someone like Bertrand Lowell," I said carefully.

"Someone who thinks for himself, yes. Someone who hasn't memorized the goddamn handbook."

"So you've forgiven him. Him *and* this Freddy person."

"Grow up, darling." Her face looked drawn, her eyes big and round as a child's. "This is only the beginning. Robin won't even graduate—did you hear? Benji's getting shipped off to France next week for naval duty. Daddy dearest finagled him out of any real slogging through the Orient, but still: Off he goes to save the motherland. Meanwhile, poor old Robin'll be knocked up before the summer's over." She shook her head, disgusted. "Twenty bucks says we never hear from the girl again. Good riddance, I say. We need another wet blanket around here like we need a goddamn hole in the head."

"She seems so happy."

"There but for the grace of God . . ." she sniffed. "Those idiots actually got it right for once."

It was quiet for a moment or two. "Look, about Lindsey—" I began.

"Last time I checked, Lindsey was perfectly capable of taking care of herself."

"She doesn't know what she's getting herself into." It was hot in the bathroom, and I'd begun to feel faint. "I happen to think it's unforgivable, what he did. Both of them, Bertrand and your Freddy."

"I don't remember asking—"

"I'm entitled to my opinions," I interrupted, the loudness of my voice in that small space startling.

She leaned into the wall; she looked so small standing there with her head tipped back against the painted wood, her shoulders rounded to balance the arm holding the cigarette against the opposite elbow, her legs crossed. "How bold of you," she said, smiling a little. "How *un*-Rebecca."

"We should go," I said wearily. "We'll miss the beginning."

"Hang on. So long as we're baring our souls and all." A small bluish vein on the side of her forehead had begun to throb. "I'd like to ask a question. Am I allowed one goddamn question?"

"You're drunk."

"Good deduction." She peered at me through the smoke. "Why haven't you ever come to one of my plays? Three years, and you haven't so much as showed up for the first act. And, please." She held up her hand. "Don't make up some ridiculous excuse. I can't bear being patronized." She lit a fresh cigarette and flicked the old one to the ground, where it burned a moment longer before turning to ash. "You might as well come out and say it."

"I don't know what you're talking about."

She held her chin up then, angling her face as though she wore her big glasses and was peering out at me through their enormous lenses. "You think I'll never make it. That I'm lacking a certain something: *Panache.* Freddy's word. *Not a whole lotta panache, kiddo, but you're going to make some man very happy.*" She was trembling now, the hand that held her cigarette shaking visibly. "He actually said that the other night."

"You've been seeing him all this time?"

"A little credit, please." She looked disgusted. "He called me up out of the blue to say he had a sure thing. *Streetcar,* for Christ's sake. I hung up on him, of course, but two minutes later the director calls and says he'll be expecting me. Says he's heard wonderful things and that he's looking forward to it. I cut rehearsal to get my hair done, for crying out loud. And then Freddy shows up at the theater the morning of with that hangdog look of his to say it was all a mistake. That they booked someone ages ago and he must have missed the goddamn memo. Did I want to have goddamn *breakfast*." She shook her head. "I don't have *it*, is the point. The thing."

"You're going to be famous. Everybody says so."

"Oh, screw everyone," she said heatedly. "What do *you* say?"

"I think you'll do whatever you please—just the way you always have. I've always thought that's extraordinary." I tried to smile. "I guess I think it's always been the most extraordinary thing about you."

She stared at me a moment longer and then her face changed, the color rushing back into her cheeks. "You do, don't you." She crossed the small bathroom in two steps and put her arms around me. Her hair covered my face, my eyes. "Bless you."

She was holding me too tightly and I tried to laugh, just to see if I could breathe. "Since when do you care what I think?"

"Don't be ridiculous. You're the brains of this operation," she went on. Smoke was everywhere and my eyes burned, but she kept her grip on my shoulders. "The rest of them can go to hell."

"No one can hold a candle to you. Lindsey's not even one little bit as pretty as you—"

"*Pretty*." She pulled back to look me in the face. "What does that have to do with anything?"

"It's everything," I said, confused. "Isn't it? Look at Elizabeth Taylor. Look at Jean Harlow. Kim Novak—"

But she was staring at me with a curious expression. "You're right," she said. "Maybe it's time I face facts." Her face was very pale in the overhead light, her skin with a shine to it as though she'd begun to sweat. "Maybe it's all we've got."

"Looks?"

"Sex."

I glanced down at my shoes, the tips damp from the grass. Her fingers had been cool on my shoulders, surprisingly so; I could feel the ghosts of their imprints on my skin. "We've got a little more than that, don't you think?"

"Speak for yourself." I started to protest but she cut me off.

"Time to toast our fallen flower," she said lightly, already turning away as she spoke. I stood there a moment, trying to figure out who she meant, before I followed her through the door.

Of course I'd been to one of her plays. It was something terribly modern, or modern for those times, anyway. I'm sorry to say I don't remember the title or who wrote it. The important thing is that it was awful—the costumes garish, the stage set with clusters of potted palms, a girl with a flute ruining what gravitas the opening moments might otherwise have held. There seemed to be some conflict between the flute girl and the boy who came onstage soon after her, but because I'd slipped in just before the curtain went up and decided to stand at the back rather than bear the embarrassment of walking down the aisle to search for a seat, I had a hard time hearing either of them properly. They had yet to learn, it seemed, the art of elocution.

The play couldn't have been more than ten minutes in when there was a clang—a bell, maybe, or else some sort of gong—and Alex appeared from behind one of the palms as though summoned. She was barefoot for reasons I was never able to discern and dressed in what can only be called a robe. Grecian, the intention must have been, though it was jeweled or sequined, sewn along the hem with something that sparkled, and draped over one shoulder in a way that left the other bare. It was a few inches too long and dyed a deep vermilion: On anyone else, it would have looked ridiculous. Of course Alex carried it off to a T.

She had what I believe you would call presence—a thing I have come to think you are either born with or go without. There was a languor to her movements, an ease I imagine any fine actor must have in order to inhabit that world of fictions so thoroughly you believe that even the smallest motion is genuine—the smile, the frown, the outstretched hand. She must have known how quickly she held us in her thrall. Still, what I realized as I watched from the back of the dark theater that night was that she was wonderful for one very simple reason: She loved it. Loved being up there in front of everyone, loved it with a determination that shone through her every inch. Even when she was meant to be distraught or furious, even when she was pounding the false wall at the back of the stage or mourning, so far as I could tell, the loss of that poor girl with the flute—even then she burned with a joy I can say, quite truthfully, I had never witnessed in her before.

But it will be clear to you that I never said a word to her about having been there. I never told her how marvelous she'd been, how I'd wished—suddenly, foolishly—for flowers to throw to her at the end, something remarkable. Lilies, I remember thinking wildly. Orchids. I left the theater as swiftly as I'd come in, walking through the crowd before breaking into a run as I cut across the main quad, the night air cool against my bare arms. I ran—ran as I had never run before, hard and fast, down past Cullers and out along the far edge of campus, weaving my way through the fragrant jacarandas until at last I hit open road. I had never been down that particular street, I don't think, though it is difficult to know if I would have recognized anything that night, the trees a blur of shadows flashing past long after my legs had begun to burn.

For a while there I let myself believe I would never stop. I would go on, I told myself, in those brief, staccato thoughts the mind produces under duress—on and on. The ends of the earth, just as Alex had said. Darkest Brazil. The Amazon, where my body would grow hard and thin and I would feel no pain when the knife sliced through. Farther, I thought as my arms went loose and rubbery, a stitch taking hold in my side. I would run on and on to a place where the things of the world I lived in could no longer touch me.

But at a certain point my legs turned heavy; eventually I slowed to a walk. My breaths made ugly sounds in the stillness, and I stopped at last to lean up against a banana palm, the trunk rough through the thin material of my blouse. I stayed there for what felt like hours before starting back toward campus, the road in the darkness giving off a pale glow like the moon.

Chapter 9

IT was night by the time the wedding party dispersed. The atten-
dants snapped up the chairs behind us as we filed down the aisle,
the sound of them clattering shut loud through the buzz of voices;
two parallel lines of torches lit the path from the ceremonial arch
to the tent, where the tables waited under the high white dome.
Betsy and Lindsey took their seats two tables down with Buzz and
Doc. My name card put me between Oliver and Charlie and across
from Alex, who smoothed her skirt against the back of her legs as
Bertrand Lowell pushed her chair in and sat down to her left.

"Nice evening." Oliver leaned forward, resting his forearms on
the table. He gave me a wink. "How was the drive?"

"Fine." He looked a little hurt and I tried again. "We saw a
deer."

"Did you hit it?"

"We came close." We'd been rounding a corner somewhere
north of Palm Springs when it stepped into the road, its slender
head jerking up like a puppet's.

"Pity." Charlie shook the ice cubes in his glass. "Could have made a trophy out of it." He glanced at Alex, her head tipped forward toward Bertrand Lowell. "Guess I'll go round up some more drinks!"

Across the table, Alex laughed at Bertrand Lowell, who raised his light eyes in my direction.

I looked away quickly. "I'll take something with tonic, please."

I drank the glass of whatever it was Charlie brought back to the table, and then I had another. Waiters came by to make sure my wineglass stayed full; they popped champagne corks one after the next. Every now and then I heard the tiny *sssst* of moths crumpling into the candle flames. The flowers formed a screen at the center of the table, and as everything went on around me I pretended to listen to whomever was talking, nodding or laughing at the appropriate intervals. I didn't hear a word. I was too busy watching them through the latticework of petals: Alex and Bertrand Lowell. I watched Alex dip her head toward him so the length of her hair swept across the remains of her dinner; Bertrand Lowell said something in a low voice and reached across her, casually brushing a few green curls from the ends of her mane as though it didn't mean a thing. Believe me, it meant everything in those days to touch a girl like that.

I sat there pretending not to watch from across the table, my body angled toward the front where everyone lined up to toast the bride and groom. To my right, just beyond Buzz's flushed face, Lindsey sat staring straight ahead. When at last the cake was cut—Benji fumbling it, of course, crumbs scattering down the front of Robin's dress—and the band started up, it was a relief to stand. I took the hand Oliver offered me and walked with him out onto the dance floor.

Oliver wasn't particularly light on his feet, but he tried. There wasn't much more you could ask of a boy like him. It was hot out there in the crush of people, but I felt better immediately; the air had movement to it, at least, and when Oliver spun me my skirt twirled out, blowing up a little breeze. The band was surprisingly good. After a few songs, we were both breathing hard. Beads of sweat stood out across Oliver's forehead.

"You alright?" He was gazing down at me with a frown.

"I'm having a ball."

"It's the funniest thing—" He stopped.

"Tell me."

"It's just," he looked sheepish, "I could have sworn I saw you coming out of McCarren the other morning."

"*Moi?*" I forced a laugh.

"Is there another Rebecca?" He smiled, but his eyes stayed serious. "I thought I was wrong, except the same thing happened a few weeks before. I thought maybe there was someone . . ."

"Someone what?"

"I don't know. Some premed guy." He turned me clumsily. "My father's got me thinking they're everywhere. Dime a dozen. Everyone but his son fighting to get out there and save lives."

"Premed!" My voice was too loud; the sound of it made me cringe. "Thanks, but no thanks."

"You're funny tonight."

"Funny how?"

"Just . . . not quite yourself." His face turned serious again. "If there *was* someone, you'd tell me. Wouldn't you?"

"And if I tell you there's no one?"

"Guess I'd have to believe you."

"There's no one."

He gave me a look. "How do I know you're not—"

"Hush." I put my fingers to his lips, and his eyes went wide and startled.

After a few more songs, he brought me to the edge of the floor and went into the crowd and came back with fresh drinks. I didn't especially like standing there: I kept hearing Alex's laugh, or thinking I saw Bertrand Lowell's dark head dipping under the overhang of the tent. When Charlie came over and mock-bowed, I looked at Oliver, motioning with my empty glass. He glanced down at his, still half full.

"Don't let me stop you," he said.

"I'd like to see you try." I tried to say it lightly, but he only frowned as Charlie pulled me away.

He was a wonderful dancer, Charlie, much better than Oliver. He knew to keep his hand on the small of my back and the tips of his fingers on the other hand barely touching mine. He spun me out and reeled me back in; all at once I was having a terrific time. When he dipped me, I laughed with genuine pleasure. The song finished and we paused a minute, catching our breath.

"She's enjoying herself tonight," he said, jerking his head back toward our table.

"I suppose she is."

"And you?" He looked closely at me. "You're not drunk enough."

"No," I said. "I don't think I am."

He went off through the crowd and came back with another round of drinks. I'd already drunk far more than I should have, but the more I drank, the less I cared that Alex and Bertrand Lowell were still out there somewhere in the throng or sitting at the table, feeding each other forkfuls of cake. The more I drank, the easier it became to focus on how nice it felt to dance, to feel the swing of my body and the heat of Charlie's hand against my back. I'd barely caught my breath when a boy with light-brown hair and brown eyes took my hand and pulled me back onto the dance floor. I think he told me he was Robin's cousin. I heard myself say something inane: *She never told me she had a cousin!* or *Isn't she a riot?* The words floated back at me from somewhere very far away. Women drifted past in their big dresses like large, pale fish, someone laughed and the sound flashed like a color, a burst of yellow that hung in the air, shimmering. I was having a harder and harder time hearing. Betsy sailed by in her green dress with Doc, his thin face bright with happiness. Robin appeared out of nowhere, leaning forward through a tangle of chiffon and lace to kiss me on the cheek. *Darling! Congratulations!* It wasn't until the band stopped to take a break, the singer stepping to one side to cup her hands around a cigarette, that I realized I'd lost track of Alex completely.

I took the hand of whomever I had been dancing with off my arm and murmured an apology.

"Hey," whomever it was said.

Oliver's face appeared to my right, flushed and gleaming.

"Have you seen Alex? It's important," I insisted.

He shook his head. "Listen," he started, "Charlie can be a real animal with those drinks," but I pushed right past him.

What a sight I must have been as I made my way through the crowd! The front of my dress sagging from the heat, the gauze I'd pressed down so carefully at the beginning of the night drooping now, my hair falling out from all its pins. I kept catching my heel in the soft ground as I followed the path of torches and then the little trail leading to the cabins where we would spend the night. There was a heaviness to my arms and legs and I remember thinking, despite everything, how nice it would be to sit down right there in the grass and stretch out under the light of all those flames.

"Rebecca," someone called. "Rebecca."

I kept walking, holding my arms out to either side for balance. It wasn't really that dark. The stars were shredding the sky to pieces, and a thin veil of light fell down across the grass. Still, I felt dizzy, unsure of where my feet were landing. I'd never understood the saying until then, but it was true: My head was swimming. I got lost somewhere among the torches, and when I found myself at the main house, I kept going. I needed to use the bathroom. The front door was wide open.

"Hello?" I called into the darkness. The hall was pitch-black and I had to feel my way along the wall. "Hello?" I tapped a table, the corner of a mirror. Partway down the hall I found the door to the bathroom and pushed it open. When I flipped the light on, little suns exploded inside my skull. I turned the light off, used the toilet and washed my hands in the dark, and then I went back out into the hallway. My dress was making the strangest noise, a rustling as it moved in and out with my breath. It was loud—too loud, I realized. I followed the sound down to the end of the hall, to a door whose knob I found easily; when I put my ear to the wood, the sound was right there, a skittering combination of wood against wood and wind and something else. I turned the knob and the door swung open. Light leaked into the room from a single window, and in the confusion of the dark and that lone thread of light, I saw a flash of yellow—there one second and gone the next, disappeared around the corner through a second door. A patch of pale pink gleamed in the dark.

"Tag," said the pink shirt. "You're it."

I cleared my throat. "I was looking for the ladies', actually."

The music from the tent buzzed in the background. Or something buzzed: It might have been a fly or a trumpet for all I knew.

"The indomitable Miss Madden." There was a faint snapping sound and a small orange flame sprang to life, then a second. Bertrand Lowell drew on his cigarette. "You happen to be just in time for a drink."

I stayed where I was. Bertrand Lowell let out a long breath into the dark, and the pink shirt collapsed in on itself a little.

"Don't make me come over there and get you." His voice was low. "I'm drained, you know. Positively worn out." He had a seamless way of speaking that I found unnerving. Every word he said was like another car in a train he sent gliding through the air; it occurred to me that in all my years of knowing him I'd never heard him say more than a sentence or two. It was cool in that room, and the heat back under the tent would only have gotten worse—the women would be fanning themselves with their place cards, the men pressing their handkerchiefs to their foreheads. Mrs. Pringle clutching her fourth glass of champagne as if someone might take it away.

"I shouldn't," I said.

"One drink."

I hesitated a moment longer. "Just one," I said finally. "But then I really do have to get back to the party."

Bertrand Lowell and his pink shirt lay directly diagonal to the door I'd come in. To the left of him, the window threw its broken thread of light across the floor; next to that was the door where the flash of yellow had gone. I raised my arms for balance again as I walked.

"Quite a show." I could see his nose by now, the glow of the cigarette catching the tip. "Do you do trampoline work as well?" I laughed. I couldn't help it. He was right: I felt ridiculous walking so carefully, but I was just aware enough to be afraid of my own sense of gravity. Little by little, my eyes got used to the dark, and there he was—Bertrand Lowell, sitting on a table pushed up against the wall.

"Here we are." The light from the window fell away as though a cloud had drifted over the moon. I looked down toward my feet for balance, and when I glanced up, I was nearly on top of him. The toe of my shoe brushed the table leg. "Easy," he said.

"I'm fine."

"Pull up some table."

"I'm fine," I said loudly.

"You mentioned that." The ice rattled again. "That was a yes to a drink?"

"Do you always do things in the dark?"

"Only on special occasions."

"It is, isn't it." I was glad the dark hid my blush. "I think they'll be very happy together."

"Slim to none."

"Sorry?"

"Chances of that happening."

"That's an awful thing to say on someone's wedding day."

"Good thing I said it, then, not you. Awful Bertrand Lowell." He sounded very drunk.

"You've tried the lights?" I pictured him sitting in the dark with Alex, the yellow dress leaning in, and I felt a little sick.

"Goddamn desert." I heard liquid pouring. "Here. Sounds like you need it."

My hand bumped his as I took the glass, and I tried not to pull away too quickly. The glowing tip of the cigarette floated down toward the table; he tapped his fingers against the wood. "I'm afraid you've caught me in a funny kind of mood," he said. "Weddings bring out the honest man in me. What would you say if I told you I've been trying to figure you out for a while now?"

I tried to sound casual, as though people said this kind of thing to me every day. "That depends."

"On what, exactly?"

"Whether or not you've come to any conclusions."

"So you *do* want to know."

"Do you happen to have another cigarette?" I was twenty-one, remember. It meant something different in those days. I could have counted on one hand the number of times I'd been kissed; I don't know that I'd ever sat in a dark room alone with a boy before.

"*Natürlich.*" My fingers glanced off his knuckles again, and I tried to hold the cigarette steady between my fingers as the lighter clicked. "Wouldn't have figured you for a smoker."

"Sometimes," I managed, coughing.

"Special occasions, I presume." He lit another cigarette.

"The smell makes me ill." I managed to breathe the smoke out smoothly this time, and it clouded the little circle of light around his face. "I've never understood the draw, though of course some people can't get enough of it. My mother, for instance."

"It's the addiction that does it." Something clicked against his glass like a spoon. "The way it is with most things, isn't it. Makes you sick as a dog if you try to stop."

"Which is why I never wanted to start."

"Smart girl." In the dark, everything registered so precisely. I knew he'd shifted closer: I felt the warmth of his body raise the temperature of my skin, the length of his arm close enough to raise the hairs on my arms. "But that's the thing about you, isn't it?"

"I don't know," I said. "There are smart girls and then there are pretty girls."

"So you've picked your side and you're sticking to it." Bertrand Lowell shifted his weight again. The table creaked. "Though people say you look like her, don't they?"

"Some people, sure."

"Can't say I see it. No offense."

"None taken." It didn't matter that I agreed with him: It stung to hear the words. I pictured her sitting exactly where I sat, her shoulders straight where mine slouched, the fine silk of her dress gleaming in the dark. I imagined the picture in his head of us side by side, the shadow I drew next to her. "I don't see it either."

He clapped his hands. "Bravo. Most people have the damnedest time recognizing their—shall we say—limitations. Your friend there, for instance, seems dead set on having her name in lights. Broke my heart, the way she went on—"

"Do we have to keep talking about her?" I was speaking too loudly.

"I was merely going to point out that some people harbor delusions of grandeur." Now he was close enough that I could smell the sweat and soap beneath the liquor on him. "Call me old-fashioned, but I prefer the truth."

I put my drink in the hand with the cigarette and dropped my other hand down so I could wipe my palm against my skirt. "It just so happens I know all about the truth. Especially with regards to you."

"That doesn't sound nice."

"You're the one who's not nice."

"Pity," he said. "A good girl, after all."

It had been quiet for a bit, but now in the distance there was the sound of someone singing. "By which I suppose you mean having morals is something you look down on. Because you're different from all of us." I cleared my throat. "Nearly all."

"Tut-tut." He clicked his tongue. "I've always found jealousy terribly unattractive. *The green-eyed monster which doth mock the meat it feeds on*, and so forth."

"I'm familiar with Othello," I said coldly. "And I'm not jealous. I'm merely pointing out a fact. You think being different means being better."

"And how exactly am I different?"

"That's just it," I rushed on, triumphant. "You aren't. You're exactly like the rest of them. Wealthy and entitled, accustomed to sailing through life as though the world owes you your happiness. But you happen to be smart, too—"

"I'm smart now, am I?"

"—and you think being smart gives you license to be cruel. You've hurt people deliberately, and you think being *you*, being Bertrand Lowell, excuses that."

There was a sigh, the soft noise of breath blowing out between Bertrand Lowell's lips. "If you don't know what's wrong with everything you just said, I'm not sure I feel like telling you. I've had a very long day, and, frankly, I'm wiped out."

In the tent, Oliver would be looking for me with his sad eyes, Alex singing into the waiting crowd. It was Alex I'd heard, of course. I could have picked that voice out of a choir of thousands. I stood up. "I should get back to the party."

"Rebecca." It was the first time he'd said my name. "You don't actually think you have everyone fooled."

"Excuse me?"

"The only difference between you and me is that I'm honest about my ambitions."

"We're not even the littlest bit alike."

"Now you're saying things just to spite me." He sighed again. "Hardly playing fair, *Dr. Madden*."

Something cool slid across my chest, an ice cube tracing a damp arc across a countertop. "What's that supposed to mean?"

"Doctor, doctor," he sang, "I've got a pain in my ass."

"You had it right, you know. You're awful."

"What if I told you I got a look at your schedule last fall."

"I'd say you're lying."

"It just so happens I have my connections in Dean Richards's office. His secretaries can be quite, shall we say," he chuckled, "flexible."

"I can't for the life of me think why you'd care."

"I was intrigued," he said thoughtfully. "There you are, marching around campus with your friend the Queen Bee and the rest of her minions. But you and I both know you're nothing like them, not a bit. And I'm not talking about the question of filthy lucre here either." He rapped his knuckles gently against the table. "Nothing more common than money, for Christ's sake. No—you piqued my curiosity, which I'll have you know isn't so easy to do."

"I had no intention of doing anything of the kind."

"What I find fascinating is that you thought you could keep it a secret. It took me a while to see how deep the whole charade actually went," he continued. "Smart, the way you'd arranged things. Genius, really. Chem first thing in the morning this spring and calculus in the fall, like you were this idiot freshman or something, snapping out of bed at the most ungodly hours. It nagged at me, see, why you'd want to get up at the crack of, and then—" He clapped his hands together. "Well, let's just say I managed to put two and two together. You do it so no one notices you're gone. Slip out early in the morning, with no one the wiser for it."

"I don't know why it should be anyone's business whether I'm taking chem or not," I said hotly. "Least of all yours."

"Now, now. So long as you live in *this* town, it's everybody's business—you know that as well as I do. Which is why you did such a superb job of keeping it under wraps."

"This has been an entirely illuminating conversation—"

"God, no," he interrupted. "Please don't. The Miss Innocent bit makes my head pound. And you can't leave now, not when I've been so generous." He managed to sound genuinely wounded. "Invited you into my cave, given freely of my cigarettes."

"I really do have to go."

"Come on, have another finger of something. It's the imported kind, the good stuff."

I shook my head. "I've had too much to drink."

"Now you're being silly."

"I'm only saying what I think."

"What you think, my dear, is precisely what you just accused me of thinking."

"I've forgotten what that is," I said. My head had begun to spin again.

"You *are* drunk," he said kindly. "I believe you were accusing me of looking down on everyone in this town." Both our cigarettes had gone out by now. The sleeve of his pink shirt was so close I could have touched it by lifting one finger. "Kettle and pot, gorgeous. You're the one who thinks you're better than all of us. Always have. I've known that about you all along."

What was I supposed to do? I would have believed him if he'd said he saw the face of Jesus in my eyes. I was twenty-one, and listen: I knew nothing. All I knew for sure was what I loved. I loved the cool, dim halls of McCarren Hall, the building Oliver had seen me leaving. I loved the lab on the second floor, where Professor Potts taught chemistry. I loved the clean white countertops and the shining order of it. I loved the awkward, bespectacled boys I worked side by side with, the boys who peered at me and the lone other girl in the class—a Holly Stevens—on our first day as though we were unidentified specimens, before turning away and forgetting about us. I loved Holly Stevens a little, for her Martha Clarkson clothing— shapeless skirts, blouses two sizes two big and the wrong color for her complexion—and for her brilliant mind, which she used with the cool dexterity of someone uninterested in the everyday. I loved the night sky and the old telescope in the observatory, the way the youngish Professor Tinsley had shown me how to find Venus one night that spring, the smell of dried leaves and tobacco rising out of his coat as he moved around me in the dark, adjusting, until I saw it: a dot of light seared into the blackness above the horizon. I loved my evening hours at my study carrel—the quiet of the library, the books I pored over long after the floor had emptied of students. I loved the names for the bones of the foot—calcaneus and talus, the elegant, articulated joints of the metatarsals. I loved my father, who I thought must be the wisest man in the world; I loved my mother, despite the crease in her forehead when she came across me reading—*intellectual*, she told me, a label men found wholly unattractive; I loved her for her love of music and for the brisk efficiency with which she moved through the house, making everything shine. I loved what I had lost, those afternoons Alex and I spent down by the canal when we were girls, the light in my memory impossibly golden, impossibly bright. I knew I loved all of that. But beyond that, I was a fool.

"You don't know the first thing about me," I said. His hand when I reached for it already waiting.

Chapter 10

W E must have all driven back from the wedding in Betsy's car, exactly the way we arrived. The sky would have been that particular blue, the blue that runs the length of my childhood like some brilliant animal spine. Say the car was oddly quiet. Say the radio jangled in the background, the tin-can strains of a piano rattling out into the hot air. Say Betsy and Lindsey spoke to each other occasionally at first and even to me, that Alex snapped her glasses off at a certain point and turned to the window, that the car went silent then and that she did not look my way again, not even when I gathered my things and stepped out of the car, mumbling goodbye. The truth is that I don't remember any of it, only that by the end of the ride I knew. Everything had changed.

Not that you ever would have known it to see me that first afternoon. I went straight to the patio when I got home and spent the rest of the day in one of our old deck chairs, flipping through a stack of my mother's magazines and pouring myself glass after glass of lemonade. It was Sunday, I reminded myself. School was done. Summer stretched before me, a vast, uninterrupted vista of time with which I could do what I liked. I tried to remember how I'd felt at that thought just a day or so before, my joy at the prospect of being able to do as I pleased for three whole months. I reminded myself of the books I meant to study in preparation for the fall; entrance exams for medical school were scheduled for November, and I had a stack of practice tests to work through between now and then. There was a dress I'd planned on sewing to make my mother happy, the pattern clipped from the pages of her *Vogue*. I had plenty to keep me busy.

But the longer I sat in the deck chair and tried to read, the less I understood of the words running across the pages. I might blink and find myself trapped in a moment from the night before, turn a page and catch a flash of Lindsey's red hair across the circle of chairs. I put down my glass and there were Alex and Bertrand, laughing across the table. Sometimes it got so bad I had to get up from the chair and lean my head between the branches of the orange tree, breathing in the sweet air, or I'd go into the kitchen and stand in front of the refrigerator with the door wide open—something my mother had expressly forbidden me to do—as though the memory of that night was a fever I could cool. Mostly, though, I just sat, listening to the house sparrows chatter back and forth and staring down at the pictures of the models smiling up from the pages. The sun hung in the sky, the heat even in the shade stifling. I would have moved if I'd thought I could, but my body felt like something that hardly belonged to me anymore, my legs, when I glanced down, the legs of a stranger.

At a certain point late in the afternoon, my father came out into the garden with a drink. "She's home," he said, looking pleased. "The intrepid coed."

"She is."

"The report?"

"Favorable." I did my best to smile as he settled into the chair next to mine. "Clear skies for the happy couple. Champagne and ice cream. Dancing till all hours."

"Bride?"

"Blushing."

"Daughter?"

I felt my chin quiver unexpectedly. "Making do."

He was quiet a moment. "Your mother pushes sometimes."

"Do you think—" I stopped. "That is, do you ever wonder if we wouldn't all be happier somewhere else?"

He gave me a wry smile. "If only it were that simple. *Let us dare to read, think, speak, write,*" he recited. "Let us dare, in other words, to live however we please."

"Lincoln?"

"Adams." He tapped the arm of his chair. "I have always found him to be unparalleled when it comes to questions of personal freedom."

"We have the right to be here and therefore here we are."

"An odd sort of logic when you put words to it." He settled back and crossed his long legs at the ankle. "We're in the position of being able to choose, which is what our forefathers fought for, after all. The American dream. Whether it's a curse or blessing is open for debate."

"Both, maybe."

He looked at me over the top of his glasses. "Has it gotten that bad?"

I sank deeper into my chair. "I'm fine."

"That doesn't sound very convincing."

"Really, everything's fine."

He frowned. "You don't feel burdened by our life here?"

"No, sir."

"Weighed down?"

"No."

"Unduly put upon? Afflicted? Oppressed?"

I couldn't help smiling. "No, no, and no."

"I've always operated under the assumption that this is the best available option," he said slowly. "That despite certain . . . shall we say *disadvantages*, we feel ourselves to be living the fullest possible life under the circumstances with which we have been provided. Would you say that's an accurate description?"

"I would."

"Then you feel free in your everyday choices. Unencumbered." He waved his hand. "You feel you can do as you please."

"Belgium."

"What's that?"

"I'm Belgium," I said. "Sovereign of my own land."

"Belgium," he repeated. "That's my girl."

"Dinner, you two." My mother stood in the doorway, snapping her apron. Her cheeks were flushed from standing over the stove and her arms were bare, the sleeves of her dress pushed up past her elbows; she looked young, girlish almost. She might have been any one of my classmates, just another pretty coed busily ticking off the requirements for home ec. She caught me looking at her and winked. "And here I thought *I* was your girl."

"The one and only," my father said, a smile breaking across his face, and I thought for a moment I might weep.

W

Let me say first that when my period went missing—that was the word that came to me when I checked the calendar two weeks later, *missing*, as though it might still be found—my thoughts were entirely selfish. This is what they tell you about becoming a mother, that you forget yourself completely. But I was twenty-one; I couldn't have forgotten myself if I tried. I looked down at my flat stomach that night as I sat on the bathroom floor and dug my fists into my abdomen until I thought I might be sick. I had the wild thought that I could somehow still get it out of me. I sat on the floor, holding my head in my hands, and then—like a child—I waited: One day, two. Five days, a week.

I took the city bus out to Arroyo Seco one afternoon and walked the trails that ran back and forth along the edge of the canyon. I have always preferred being alone in nature, and as soon as I was old enough to go off on my own, I got in the habit of heading to the canyon on those rare occasions I tired of reading at home or felt, as my mother put it, like clearing my head. The bus stopped not too far from the entrance to the trails; I didn't mind the ride. In high school I often brought along a book or my study materials, lugging my beloved *Gray's* or *Grant's* in a shoulder bag and walking until I found a good patch of shade. But that afternoon, I simply walked—up past the first plateau and down into the open plain, where a pair of hawks circled above me, keening. Sunlight slanted down across the hills as I circled around a row of oak trees, their branches spread wide and crooked. By the time I turned on to the mouth of a trail that led up the side of the canyon, my legs had begun to ache in earnest. I stopped to rest on the edge of the lookout, next to the cheap telescope that wobbled slightly in the wind, and as I stood there, breathing hard, I thought about jumping.

You understand: In those days, to be pregnant and unmarried was the end of everything.

However. I did not jump. Not that afternoon or any other. I walked back to the stop and caught the last bus home. My mother was standing in front of the mirror in the front hallway when I came through the door, giving herself a critical glance; she winced when she saw me—my legs covered with red dust, my arms—and then smiled to cover it up.

"There you are!" She looked fresh and lovely in her cream-colored blouse and pleated skirt. "Don't tell me you've been out playing tennis in this heat."

"I went for a walk through the canyon. I thought I'd get a little sun."

"With?" She waited. "Betsy? She always does have such a nice glow about her."

"That's right," I said slowly. "Betsy and I. We made an afternoon of it."

"Isn't that nice." She hesitated. "Of course, you'll want to be careful you don't develop the muscles in your legs *too* much. Betsy's quite petite, but you've got your height to think about. Great-Aunt Beatrice used to tell us we should be able to close our hands around the widest part, like this—" She held both hands up, pinkies and thumbs touching so her hands formed a perfect O.

"Yes," I said. "I mean, no, I won't."

She looked at me thoughtfully. "You don't think you might want to pop on over to the club for a bit? It's been ages now since you went for a swim, though it's wonderful you're getting outside. You know I hate to see you cooped up." She stood there a moment longer, looking at me in that appraising way as she knotted a scarf around her neck. I was all at once gripped by fear—fear that I might bury my head in her shoulder and confess, not just Bertrand but everything: the envy I felt watching the other girls throw their new things carelessly on the floor, wearing dresses once, twice, before declaring them old; the joy I went around swallowing after mornings at the lab, telling my parents when we spoke Sunday nights that I was having an awful time of it in Bio, that if it weren't for Oliver or whoever I'd have failed by now for sure. *Stupid*, I told them. *You wouldn't believe how stupid I am at it.* "I thought we might have lunch together one of these days," she said finally. "Just the two of us. I think we deserve a treat, don't you?"

She pressed her blouse down over her trim waist. "My goodness—a senior! You'll be gone before we know it. Starting a family of your own."

My cheeks grew hot. "I have a little while longer."

She ignored me, fussing with her gloves next. "What in the world am I going to do with myself? I still remember Mother's face the day I got on that bus. One look at my suitcase and she burst into tears. And *she* had both my sisters to keep her company."

"You'll have Daddy, won't you?"

She brushed at my shoulder, removing an invisible thread. "It's not the same for men. They have their work."

"It's awful, isn't it?" I was horrified to feel a sob rising in my throat. "Daddy working so hard all the time."

"There now," she said soothingly. "You *are* tired. What do you say to a nice shower, hmm? A cold glass of juice?" I nodded as best I could. "What is it, sweetheart?"

"Nothing," I managed. "I don't thank him enough, that's all. Or you." I stared at her through the tears already blurring my sight. "You must think I'm horribly ungrateful."

"Hush." She patted my shoulder; I wanted desperately for her to stop. "You'll give yourself a headache."

"I really have had the most wonderful year."

Her hand went to her hair next, tucking a few invisible strands back behind her ears. "I don't suppose we have anyone in particular to thank for that?" I looked at her; now she was the one to color a little. "I happened to run into Frank Hinden the other day at the store. He mentioned that Oliver speaks very highly of you."

"Oliver?"

"Such a nice young man—polite. Beautiful manners. Of course, you've known each other all your lives. I thought perhaps—"

"We're just friends," I interrupted. "I don't see why that seems to be so difficult for everyone to grasp."

"I don't care for that tone, young lady." She gave me a look. "There are worse things than people thinking the two of you are paired off, but never mind. He'll make some lucky girl very happy one of these days. Frank told me Oliver hopes to follow in his footsteps," she went on, taking a compact from her purse and inspecting herself in it. "Seemed pleased as punch about it."

"I've never heard Oliver say anything about being a doctor."

"Perhaps it didn't come up in conversation—"

"He would have told me," I insisted.

She looked at me a moment, her expression unreadable, and then she dropped her compact back into her purse and squared her shoulders in that way that meant she was done with the conversation. "Alright, then, Rebecca." She sighed one of her sighs. "Lunch at the club. What do you say?"

"That sounds nice."

"Then run along and take a nice hot shower, there's a good girl." She straightened her jacket as she turned toward the door. "I'll be back in a flash."

Early the next morning, I borrowed the car under the pretext of a day at the beach, Mother giving me an approving smile from across the table as I left. The owners of the house a few doors down and across the street from Alex had planted a row of loquat trees along the edge of their property, and I drove around the block a few times before pulling over and nestling the car in beneath the branches. The car stayed cooler in the shade than the outside air, but even with all the windows rolled down I had to shift back and forth in the upholstered seat to keep myself from melting, peeling one leg off and then the other. The loquats barely smelled that time of year—it was too late for the little white flowers that appeared all along Pasadena's wide avenues and then dropped one day like a troop of synchronized parachuters—but every now and then an overripe fruit dropped onto the roof, landing with a soft thud.

Isn't it funny? I remember exactly what she was wearing that morning when she finally emerged, a little before noon: a thin blouse, pale, pale blue, a pair of sunglasses pushed high on her head, and red shorts that stopped so high on her legs her mother must have torn her hair out, watching her leave. She carried an enormous bag on one shoulder—headed for the beach, no doubt, the end of a rolled towel sticking out just behind one crooked elbow; she cradled a book against her chest as if it were a nursing child. *I'm reading*, she'd tell the boys coolly even as she crossed and uncrossed her slender legs, aware of how that small gesture undid them. *Higher learning— ever heard of it?* She ducked into her car. A moment later, the motor purred. She cranked the window down and leaned out, adjusting the mirror as she ran a lipstick around her mouth, the red of it bright as a poppy.

All those hours lurking in the shadows, and what did I do when she finally appeared? I watched her leave. The engine revved, the car disappeared around the corner. I sat there a moment longer before turning the key in the ignition. And then I drove as fast as I dared, heading west toward the water, past the cliffs that sloped down to the beach, past the ice-cream stands and the lines of cars stopped at the side of the road with the tourists lined up along the shoulder. I drove all the way to the exit sign for Malibu before I pulled over to the side of the road and turned the engine off. I sat there a long time. The sun was dropping toward the hills along the western edge of Pasadena when I came back off the highway; it was nearly dark by the time I turned into the driveway at El Molino and let myself in the back door.

I don't know that I can explain why I did what I did next. I must have felt there was nothing left to do, that desperate feeling I'd had as a child when I gazed up at the sky and tried to imagine it going on forever or thought about the fact that my parents would die one day, that I would die too. You will have guessed by now that I hadn't heard a word from any of them—not just Alex but Lindsey and Betsy too, Betsy the only one to come to the phone when I gave up and called around at the end of that first week, trying each of them in turn. She was leaving for Tahoe the next day, she said, sounding harried. She'd been so busy, *gosh*, sorry, but she'd have to call me when she got a second to breathe. Did I mind? Was that— she really did have to go, sorry, sorry, we'd talk soon. I don't know that I'd ever felt so lonely. Nor had I ever had so much to say, the words jamming up like fruitflies in a jar from one of Mr. Percy's experiments, the stopper sealing everything airtight.

But my mind was blank when I pulled out the sewing kit my mother had given me for Christmas one year—or that's what I told myself, anyway, the thing unzippered quickly enough as I sat with it on my knees. I drew the needle up the length of my arm three times: first the brachial, next the basilic, the cephalic. The shock was enough to keep the sting at bay, long enough that I didn't stop until I looked down and saw the blood springing up against my skin. That red, just as Alex had predicted, surprising.

Chapter 11

I told my parents on a Sunday afternoon. I didn't name any names. I said only that I was pregnant, that I was more or less six weeks along, and that I was sorry. The three of us sat in the garden with a pitcher of iced tea sugared to an aching sweetness. For the first few moments, neither of them said a word. My mother gripped her glass of iced tea as though it was the only thing keeping her upright; next to her, my father stared at the tiger lilies with an expression of faint bewilderment.

"I don't suppose . . ." my mother began. "That is—"

She got up and went into the house. Her words came out in a sharp staccato—*yes, no, I see, no, please.* Then came the click of the receiver, then another phone call. Her voice kept up a steady stream of noise like a typewriter. My father stayed where he was, his kind face pulled taut as a sheet. When my mother came back out, she lit a cigarette right away.

"Tuesday." She knocked the ashes into the heavy glass tray with a flick of her pinky. "Father Timothy says he thinks they'll take you as soon as a week from Tuesday. He's making a few calls. Only eight hours by bus, apparently, right through the Sierras, and he says the sisters are actually quite selective." She touched one palm to her right temple as though pressing something back into place. "As selective as they can be."

My father sat with his hands against the table, bracing himself.

"He was very kind about the whole thing."

"He is," my father said slowly, "an exceptionally kind man, Father Timothy."

"We'll tell everyone you're going abroad. Art history and language in—" My mother tapped her finger against the table. "Italy, there you are. That's what the girls at all the best New England schools do, isn't it? It won't be so bad." My mother smiled in a way that looked painful, as though the curve of her lips might crack her skin wide open. "Father Timothy said they do a wonderful job keeping everyone up on their studies. You won't even have to worry about falling behind. Seven, eight months? They'll pass just like that," she said. She was speaking very quickly now, almost eagerly. "He says everything will be fine. He says you'll be very comfortable up there, mountain air and all. Nice girls, he said, mostly from the area, but that doesn't mean they don't have manners. You might even make a friend or two. Father Timothy says you'll be surprised at how fast the time goes. He says you'll be back before you—" She held her cigarette next to her cheek, the glowing tip a tiny third eye, and then she put her hand over her mouth and went inside.

"I'm sorry," I said to the table, and my father nodded so slowly that for a moment I wasn't sure he'd moved at all. I wished desperately that he would look at me, that he would shake his head and call me *Queenie*, but he only sat there another minute or two, holding the edge of the table as though it might break if he let go, and then he got up and followed my mother inside.

\\//

I'll say this for my mother: When she set her mind to doing something, there was no stopping her. The story of my study abroad
must have burned through town like something fueled by kero-
sene. The phone began to ring the very next morning, the shrill
buzz stopping and starting until she picked up the receiver and
took it off the hook. From time to time, the front doorbell trilled. I
could tell by the way my mother's voice changed when it was for
me, which it mostly was. What mail came for me that week I threw
away unopened, the few times I let myself retrieve an envelope from
the wastepaper bin and open the invitation to a Phi Beta picnic or a
birthday party at the club more painful than I cared to admit. A
card from Betsy started off by saying formally that she was sorry to
have missed me, that she'd heard the news through so and so all the
way up in Tahoe and wanted to send a proper farewell, that she was
exhilarated to think of me *traveling!!!*—but that was as far as I could
go before dropping the card back in the bin.

There *was* one person who made it through the barricade. When
my mother said my name outside the bedroom door one afternoon,
I heard the slightest catch in her voice. I opened the door to find her
standing off to the side with a curtain folded over one arm, pincush-
ion balanced in the crook of her elbow.

"You have a visitor," she said, clearing her throat. "And he
doesn't have much time." She hesitated. "You might want to brush
your hair. Freshen up a bit." She turned away and then, abruptly,
turned back. "Rebecca."

I was struck in that moment by how young she looked. Of course,
she was no more than forty at the time—young by today's standards
to be the mother of a twenty-one year old—but in those days I
thought of her as a mother. Not old, I don't mean, but ageless.

"If you thought the identity of the person in question was important—" she went on haltingly. "That is, I assume if you thought it bore any weight—"

I shook my head so violently I felt as though it might snap right off my neck. "He's nobody. Nobody at all."

My mother stood there another moment; when she spoke, her voice was flooded with relief. "Go on down, then. You won't want to keep him waiting."

I came down the stairs slowly, still not understanding, and there was Oliver Hinden standing in front of the door, his dark hair buzzed close to his head. When he saw me, he put his hand to his forehead in a mock salute. The sun lit him from behind like a stained-glass saint.

"At your service," he said, clicking his heels. "Yours, God's, and the United States of America's."

"Don't," I said, rudely, and then I half-ran the rest of the way down the stairs to make up for it. "You're going?" I said it into his shoulder, the starched cotton of his shirt rough against my cheek.

"Looks like it," he said. I didn't have to see his face to know he was smiling.

We sat on the porch and talked, incredibly, about nothing. He said something about the weather and the threat of a storm the next afternoon. I asked if he'd heard about the forest fire that had damaged a few houses out by the canyon and he said he had. I remember I was holding one of the cloth serviettes Mother liked to put out with the cookies, and as I sat there I closed my fingers around the balled-up cloth and squeezed hard enough that I gasped from the pain when I finally let go.

"You're alright, then," he said at last.

"Sure I am." I said it with a cheerfulness that must have struck both of us as false.

Oliver frowned. "Because this study-abroad business . . ." He

cleared his throat. He was so deliberate with his words, so careful:
It was one of the things I'd always liked best about him, his unwill-
ingness to say anything he didn't mean. "I would have figured you'd
want to enjoy being a senior. Stick around for the celebration."

"I could say the same about you."

He pressed the tips of those big fingers together. "Rebecca—"

"It must be exciting," I broke in. My hands were shaking as I
refilled our glasses from the pitcher of ice water. I was so blind in
that moment, so sure of what he was about to say—some bumbling
confession of love, I thought, a soldier's last romantic stand. We'd
been friends all our lives. I didn't think I could bear the idea of one
more little change.

"Which part?"

"Vietnam," I said, surprised. "Defeating Communism."

He shook his head, smiling—in agreement, I thought at the
time. Of course I was saying all the wrong things, none of it what
he wanted to hear, none of it important in the least. "I've got train-
ing for a day or two," he went on. "Time enough to make a fool of
myself, fumble my way through the drills."

"But then you'll fight, won't you?"

"Sure I will," he said quickly. "Don't worry." He made a move
as though to cover my hand with his, and I flinched. I would have
done anything to take it back. But Oliver just shook his head again
and stood, brushing crumbs off the front of his pants. "I'll make
everyone proud."

Oh, I'd heard of dodgers. We all had. There was a boy who'd
grown up down the block who went north to Berkeley for college—
Peter Jacobson, the son of a chemist—and later I'd hear how he
painted himself green and showed up for his physical in nothing
but his underwear. He was thrown in jail for it: It was one way to
escape. In general, we held a very dim view of deserters. We pretended they didn't exist, mostly, the ones that ran off or made

excuses, the sleepwalkers, the lazy eyes, the sudden homosexuals. A disgrace to the country, we called them, a shame to their families. We didn't acknowledge the other ones either, the boys and girls who linked arms and circled the induction centers, the ones holding up their white placards—USE YOUR HEAD, NOT YOUR DRAFT CARD or, simply, RESIST. I didn't know the first thing about what might draw any young man to battle, but I'm sure I clung to some vague cliché of bravery—a swell of patriotism at the sight of the American flag snapping briskly in the wind, the boyish desire to win.

"It's good you're doing your duty," I said finally.

"What else am I supposed to do?"

"Loads of things," I said, surprised by his vehemence. "It's not like any of the other boys are signing on—"

But he'd stopped listening. "I'm not a brain, not like Buzz or Doc. You know that as well as I do. I'm not like the rest of them—headed for law school or medical school." He looked at me pleadingly. "My father keeps telling me I'm not buckling down. It's a question of diligence, he says. Strength of will. Guess I've proved the most awful kind of disappointment—"

"Oliver," I said sharply. "You're his *son*."

"I look like my mother," he went on, in a low voice. "Have I ever told you that? I look exactly like her. Sometimes I think he hates me for reminding him of her."

"He loves you—" I began, but he cut me off right away.

"I'm not even a decent athlete. No coordination to speak of. But I can move, can't I? You remember when we used to play kick the can? I was good at it—running and hiding. I was good at finding places no one would think to look." He hardly seemed to be talking to me anymore. He'd turned his face toward the edge of the back-yard where the hedges clustered close together, as though he was talking to them, to the dark spaces between their branches. "I'll be fine," he said.

"More than fine," I said staunchly. "You're going to make us proud, remember?"

He sighed, and I saw I'd disappointed him. "Sure I will."

We fell silent for a minute or two. I drank my water down like I was the one headed off to war, and then I pushed the crumbs from my sugar cookie around my plate with my finger, starting up again with something silly—a question about the yard or pointing out my mother's roses. It was a relief when the screen door banged shut and my father came out into the bright sun, blinking.

"An honor," he said, shaking Oliver's hand, "to welcome a man of duty. Serving God along with your country, bless you." His face creased into a smile, the first I'd seen in days. "Your father must be proud." My father didn't care to talk about the war—that one or this one—though it seemed to please him all the same to see the young men in coffee shops across town with their khakis and crew cuts, their faces freshly shaven, gleaming.

"Yessir," Oliver said, coloring. "I certainly hope he is, sir."

He left the very next morning. The local paper ran his picture that Sunday along with the others who'd enlisted that week, Oliver's face serious in the way of professional portraits at that time, his eyes looking off to some point beyond the photographer's left shoulder. But I prefer to remember him the way he was that afternoon, sitting across the table from me with his legs splayed out in front of him, one of my mother's sugar cookies resting on the rim of his plate as though he planned, at any moment, to pick it up and take a bite. We didn't speak of him after he left, my father and I. When I heard the Hindens' car start up early the next morning, I knew as I lay there, the heat of the day already turning my room too warm, that my father was hearing the same thing. He of all people must have known what that meant: the turn of the key, the motor stuttering to life, the silent drive to the train station, Dr. Hinden's eyes glassy as he waved goodbye to his eldest son. The unsteady hiccup of Oliver's heart under his army issue coat. My father knew better than any of us what lay ahead for a young soldier, and he might—had we been a different sort of family, had it been a different time—have said something in the days that followed Oliver's departure, offered some small consolation for the loss of my old friend to something as terrible as war. But by that point the war was just another thing that went unmentioned in my house. Something of little consequence, I mean, next to what I had done.

\|/

It must have been Friday of that same week when I heard Alex's voice floating up from the foyer sometime in the afternoon. I went straight out into the hallway and leaned over the banister, straining to hear. "Goodness, yes, it's a wonderful opportunity," my mother was saying. "She's just over the moon, though of course she'll be sorry to have missed you. She's been busy as anything these last few days." I tiptoed down as far as the third stair from the top. My mother's back came into view first, then Alex's shoes—a pair of low red heels I had always envied her terribly—pressed together so her ankles touched. I braved another stair, my heart pounding. But when Alex's gaze met mine, she didn't so much as flinch. Her eyes flicked my way and I—I froze where I was, half standing, half not. I kept waiting for her to raise her finger and point or smile or start across the hall, announcing in her marvelous voice that under no circumstances could I leave, that she would lie down across the doorway if she had to, sorry, Mrs. M., but Italy, my ass, she didn't buy that story for a second.

But she did nothing of the sort. Her eyes slid back to my mother; she smiled casually, pushing a piece of hair back behind her ear. I understood in that moment that she must have guessed the real reason behind my leaving, that she had come to my house in order to confirm her suspicions. If her hunch had been wrong and I had, as my mother claimed, decided to go halfway across the world on a whim, I would have rushed down the stairs to meet her, eager for reconciliation. It was a test; I'd failed. The truth, she would report back to the other girls, worse than any of them had dreamed. *Knocked up, no question*, she would announce, savoring the drama. *Exeunt, Rebecca.*

I did not go back into my room after I retreated. I went instead to the window in my parents' room and waited until Alex emerged, crossing our short driveway with her unhurried stroll. She'd almost reached the hedges when she turned. It was the strangest thing. I'd never seen what the other girls said sometimes, that the two of us looked alike—in certain lighting, Betsy might say kindly, to soften the obvious blow. I didn't see it any more than Bertrand Lowell had. But when she turned that afternoon and lifted her gaze to the front of our house, I saw my own face looking back.

It was fear that changed her face into something like mine. Like a veil thrown over her head, it dimmed her beauty, shaping her features into an expression I recognized right away. For all my careful work, I had never learned to mask the dread I felt at every turn—fear that someone would discover my mother's stitching in one of my dresses, fear that someone would catch me coming out of McCarren Hall, fear that any one of my many failings would be discovered and I would be sent, like an orphan from one of my childhood novels, back to the dull little world I'd inhabited before Alex came along. In all my years of knowing her, I had never seen her look afraid of anything. I waited—stupidly—for her to wave or smile or laugh. But she did nothing of the sort, only stood for a moment looking up at the window with that same awful expression before turning and disappearing behind the hedges.

She was halfway down the block by the time I reached her. "*Quelle surprise,*" she said as she turned, not looking surprised at all. "I was told the lady of the house wasn't home."

"It was all a mistake," I said determinedly, putting a hand on her arm; she glanced down at it with mild astonishment. "I drank too much. I'm not used to drinking that much—"

"Zip it, please."

"I never meant for anything to happen. This has all been a terrible misunderstanding—"

She pulled away. "Not in the mood."

"If you'd just let me explain—"

"Florence is lovely this time of year," she said in a loud voice. "I hear *Il Duomo* is magnificent."

I crossed my arms over my chest. "It's Nevada, for your information. And supposedly it's hot as hell."

She blinked. "I can't imagine what you mean."

"I said it was a mistake."

"A rather big one," she said pointedly.

I drew a line across the pavement with my toe. "You're still angry."

"I prefer *incensed. Lit on fire.* Speaks volumes, don't you think?"

"I'm sure the nuns will tell me I'll burn for my sins."

"Speaking of fire."

"Weren't we?"

"I don't know anymore," she said, drawing herself up to her full height. "I honestly don't."

A chipmunk chattered noisily from somewhere within the hedges; far away, a car horn blared.

"I've been busy as anything, in case you were wondering," she went on. "In case you think this whole thing has been all about you. Auditions start this winter for all the big shows—Broadway, et cetera—and I've been working like a dog. Speeches, primarily. High time I expanded my repertoire. Not to mention every so often you come across something really compelling."

She seemed to be waiting. "Oh?"

"*By the law, I am judged to die, and therefore I will speak nothing against it,*" she recited. "Anne Boleyn on the executioner's block—1536, I believe it was. Facing the ax, not the flames." She put her hands to her throat. "Speaking of incensed. She must have been angry as hell, but there she stood, waiting for the blade to fall. Preaching forgiveness."

My head had begun to throb lightly. "She must have thought she was being a good Christian. She must have—"

She stepped forward before I registered the movement and pressed her hand down over my mouth. Her palm was warm and slightly damp and smelled of cigarettes. "I have always found strength in the face of adversity," she said slowly, "to be among the most admirable of traits." She was so close now I could see the variegated greens of her eyes, the paler spots floating in among the darker tones so light they were nearly yellow. "There's nothing I like less than a coward."

"I'm doing the best I can." My voice came out muffled, the words garbled, indistinct.

She dropped her hand. "Who said I was talking about you?"

I shook my head, shaking off the pressure of her palm against my mouth, the sour taste of her skin. "I leave Tuesday."

"Nebraska, did you say?"

"Nevada."

"Quite the adventure."

"I'd hardly call it that."

"I don't know. A girl like you could get in all kinds of trouble on her way to Nevada." She shifted where she stood, foot to foot. "So this is *bon voyage* or whatever. *Buon viaggio.*"

"Something like that."

"Any parting requests?" She raised her eyebrows. "Come on, there must be something."

I bit my lip. "Tell me everything will turn out alright in the end."

"Everything will turn out alright in the end." She grinned. "How was that?"

"Spectacular, thanks."

"Sorry," she said airily. "Look, all I know for sure is that none of us knows a damn thing."

"And your Anne Boleyn?"

She gazed at me thoughtfully. "Bingo," she said. "She knew precisely what was coming. Fat lot of good it did her." She leaned forward and tapped her finger to my nose. "Watch your head," she said. "Afraid that's all I've got."

Chapter 12

I T was hot on the bus to the convent. By nine or so the sun burned
through the windows, the seat under my legs damp with sweat. I
would have liked to roll my stockings down right then and there,
never mind about the other passengers; instead, I sat with my suitcase tucked under my feet, staring out the window as we drove
through the Sierras. We climbed for what felt like hours, the bus
groaning as we came out the other side and began our slow descent,
winding down toward desert that stretched as far as the eye could
see. Heat shimmered in the air like a thin wash of mercury, the sky
liquid or nearly so, everything on the verge of melting.

The convent was just outside a town called Jackson, a town that
turned out to be an intersection of four roads and a row of low one-
story buildings that stopped as quickly as they began. My mother
had written down the directions from the nuns on a slip of paper I
took from my pocket and examined there in the dusty lot, my suitcase resting against my shins. *Look for Main Street*, the note read.
Take the street that runs perpendicular to it, LAGUNA. This she had
underlined, <u>LAGUNA</u>, and I stared at the word as I started off

across the lot, trying to pull from the letters some trace of the affection that had guided her hand to draw that line. To her offer to accompany me on the trip out, I had said no, no thank you. Better I should go alone, I said. Less attention that way. Though no sooner had I taken my seat on the bus than I found myself wishing I had answered otherwise or that she had seen through my protest to my desperation, the need for someone to hold my hand and chatter about nothing as we wound our way through the mountains.

Laguna turned out to be not much more than a trail that led off Main Street, a rocky path meandering up a steep hill I might have missed easily had I not been walking so slowly, suitcase bumping against my knees. I must have climbed a good ten or fifteen minutes at least before the walls of the convent appeared in the distance, the stones in the afternoon sun giving off a cold red light. I saw when I got closer that the walls were crumbling here and there, tufted in places with the straggling grass ends of what looked to be birds' nests. The sign that marked the entrance was covered with a fine layer of dust. I stood for a moment, breathless from the climb. I let my suitcase drop to the ground with a thud and went up on tiptoe to get a look at the building itself. There wasn't much to see. The walls were high and the convent built low to the ground. I sank back onto my heels, and then I did something I can explain only as a kind of desperation. I reached out with my index finger and dragged a line through the dust covering the black lettering on the sign, crossing it out. ~~ST. JUDE'S~~.

No sooner did I drop my hand than I turned abruptly and started back toward town. I went down Main Street and found a motel just half a block or so from where the bus had stopped. It was the kind of place people slept in only because they were passing through on their way to somewhere else, because they had to sleep or else they might die. The desk clerk hardly glanced up from her magazine as I counted out a few bills from the envelope my mother had given me and slid them across the counter. The light in the hall-way was dim, the paint peeling off the ceiling in strips. The room, needless to say, was dismal. I remember that the quilt covering the bed was a hideous green, bilious and stained in patches by God knows what. I dropped my suitcase on the floor and stepped out of my shoes, too tired to bother with my clothes. The last thing I remember before drifting off is a fly crawling up the windowpane on the far wall, its body like a spot of ink beading against the glass.

It shouldn't surprise you to hear that the appointment I called to make the next day was illegal. This was 1965; far less had changed than people choose to remember. I was dimly aware of how steady my hands stayed as I dialed information, how clear my voice rang as I navigated the operator's requests. She gave me the number and address of a hospital in Fresno and somehow I managed, alternately bullying and pleading with a strength anyone who knew me would have been astonished to witness, to get the information I needed. I lied over the phone as though I'd been doing it my whole life. I lied to that nurse or receptionist, whoever she was, and I lied to the driver on the bus I rode the next morning back through the Sierras, the sky an ominous swell of clouds. I lied to the doctor the next morning in Fresno; in retrospect I understand he must have heard a thousand stories just like mine. He must have had to bite his tongue to keep from laughing when I murmured something about a family friend, a married man with children of his own. The shame of it, I said, too much to bear.

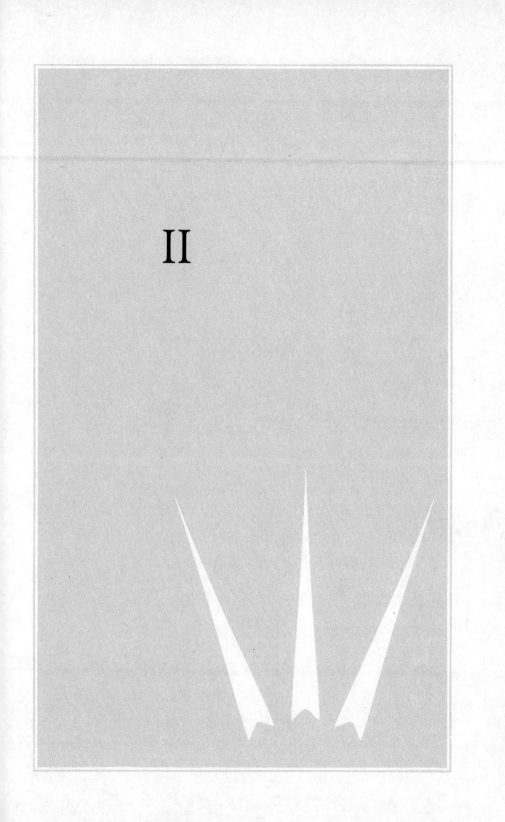

II

Chapter 1

E V E R Y evening that summer the local weatherman on the radio announced a new high: one hundred degrees, one hundred one, one-oh-two. We were advised to stay indoors and mostly did, the house noisy with the clicking of all the ceiling fans. Water was restricted across the city. As a result, the hedges that bordered the front of our property wilted and turned yellow, the narrow strip of lawn that flanked our front steps drying until it crackled underfoot. The heat kept the phoebes quiet until evening, when they started up a stream of whistles, a high, thin noise like the sound of children playing.

It came as a shock to realize I had never made my mother angry before. Oh, she'd gotten impatient with me—little things, when I was slow to carry out some task around the house or I forgot to do something she had asked me any number of times to do. But her anger that summer hit like strong weather: It was everywhere all at once. Remember that to earn a decent living in our community was not enough. To be kind and good, to work diligently and with integrity, was not enough. My mother's silk flowers *à la* Neiman's, her chicken paillard, never mind my father and all his years of work at the firm, his regular attendance at church—none of it was enough. We were holding on by our fingernails, my parents might have told me, if we had ever spoken of such things. We were only ever hanging by a thread.

But everything that hot, windless summer went unspoken. My mother's anger took the form of silence, a deep freeze that left the house echoey with all the small noises of the day—the water running in the sink, the thud of the mailman dropping his delivery through the slot, that *click-click-click* of the fans. Overnight, her sense of industry disappeared, her latest project involving the lamp shades abandoned, her sewing put away in a drawer somewhere. At meals, her hands lay still in her lap or else fiddled idly with something, rolling a fork or a pen or a scrap of paper against the table. The garden she left to the elements, her roses wilting within days and dying. Gone were the carefully prepared casseroles, the terrines, the recipes clipped and clothespinned to the cookbook stand; gone was the art of presentation, the smile, the *ta-da!* Dinner was invariably something cold—tuna salad or hard-boiled eggs with deviled ham, the vase on the table that had once held a steady rotation of flowers left conspicuously empty. Mornings, I often emerged from my room to find her sitting on the living room couch with a blouse or skirt lying untouched in her lap, her expression unreadable, or else I overheard her telling my father after breakfast that she had one of her headaches and not to bother her, to please be sure to pull the bedroom door closed behind him when he left.

She refused to speak to me those first few weeks, directing her requests instead to my father as we sat at the table, pretending to eat. She might ask him to remind me I needed to move my books from the staircase or put my shoes away properly in the closet. We

sat through meals like a trio of polite strangers, pinned to the table
by the glare of the overhead lights. It was, as a rule, much too bright
in that house, Mother insisting on keeping the lights on all day. *No
need for gloom*, she'd say briskly when my father suggested switching
at least a few of the lamps off, and then she'd go around the house
making sure all the rooms were lit up like department stores. The
curtains she kept drawn to keep out the heat, though from my seat
at the table I could make out a sliver of glass behind the heavy cloth.
I spent most of those meals watching the shiny leaves of the lemon
tree shift against the pane.

"There's a new house going up on Del Mar," my father offered
at lunch one Sunday. This a month or so after I arrived home—late
July, sweltering. "I drove past it the other day on my way to work."

"Is that so?" Mother smoothed the napkin across her knees.

"Seems a shame. It was a particularly nice piece of land."

"They'll spoil the view."

"Yes," my father said deliberately, as if the thought had never
occurred to him. "I suppose they will."

My mother sat up a little straighter. "I'll need the car later. I
have to pick up some things at the store, and I can't bear walking. I
have to go right past the Lindquists'."

"Now, Eloise—"

"*Directly* past. It's intolerable." Her chin had begun to quiver.
"We'll have to fix up the Ford, that's all. I went over the numbers
last night. We can manage it just fine."

"I'll take it in tomorrow. I—" My father coughed into his
napkin.

"Walter?"

"It's nothing," he murmured. His eyes were watering furiously.
"The chicken salad. It's a little dry."

She glanced down at where her food lay on her plate, untouched.

"The refrigerator hasn't been working properly all year. I told Marvin the last time he was here. I was perfectly clear."

The phoebes called from the lemon tree. *Tsee-tsee. Tsee-tsee.*

"We may as well start on dessert." She stood abruptly.

"I'll help." I picked up the plates and followed her into the kitchen, where a cake sat on the counter, round and yellow as a harvest moon. "That looks good."

She wiped a knife clean against the dish towel and began slicing. "I can't remember the last time I bought a cake." She still refused to look at me when she spoke. "I don't care," she said childishly. "It's been too hot to cook."

"I could give it a try."

"I don't recall you being particularly interested."

"I've been thinking I ought to take advantage." I shrugged before I thought better of it, but she wasn't paying attention. "It's not every day you get the chance to learn from the best." She took a carton of vanilla ice cream from the freezer and began spooning it out. "That's what my friends say, you know," I persisted. "They always say you're the best cook of all the mothers by about a million miles."

She sighed. "The other mothers have *help*, Rebecca. They don't have to cook."

"I thought you liked cooking."

"I do." She placed her hands on the counter and stood a minute. "I did. I've lost my taste for it, that's all. There doesn't seem to be the time. Or I can't be bothered to find the time. I don't know." She was gazing intently out the window over the sink, as though tracking something's movements—a squirrel, I thought. A vole in among her roses. "I don't know," she said again. Her hair was pulled back tight from her face, and what lipstick she had applied earlier must have rubbed off, leaving her face oddly colorless. "It used to be there was never enough time, and now—well, now I've got all the time in the world, don't I, and I can't think of a thing to do." Her tone changed again. "I'll be forty-one this fall."

"Betsy's mother is forty-eight."

"My mother used to say you could tell a woman's age by her hands." We both looked down at her hands, the fingers spread against the Formica. They were, I believe, very nice hands, freckled lightly but strong for their size, capable, though when I'd asked her once if she'd learned anything from Henry Girard, she'd frowned and said, no, her hands were too small and, besides, she was too stupid. "Well?"

"Well what?"

"How old?" Her voice was suddenly sharp. I believe it was the first time she'd looked at me directly since I returned. "Quick."

But I pretended to consider them carefully. "Thirty-three. Thirty-four, tops."

"I ought to have taken better care."

"You don't look a day over thirty-five."

She had that odd, distracted look on her face again. "It's not a nice feeling, getting old. There's nothing nice about any of it."

"You're not even close to old. You—"

"I find myself unwilling."

"Mother?"

"What?" She gave herself a little shake, standing up straight and brushing at the front of her apron. "Look at this mess. The ice cream's already melting—I swear, this heat will be the death of me." She handed me two dessert plates. "Take that in to your father, would you?"

We sat at the table with our cake in front of us, the ice cream pooling at the bottom of the dish.

"Isn't this delicious," said my father. "You don't care for it?"

"I'm afraid I've lost my appetite," Mother said.

"May I be excused?"

She waved me off; she'd gotten a little of her color back, but even so she looked exhausted, her eyes gone soft around the edges as though she'd taken an eraser to the skin there and rubbed. "If you wouldn't mind wrapping that cake up, Rebecca."

"I ought to be going as well." My father tucked his napkin under his plate.

"Did you need something from the store? I wanted to wait a bit, that's all. It quiets down after four."

"It's Sunday." He looked at her pleadingly. "I haven't been in weeks now."

She made a noise that was somewhere between a laugh and a cough. "And here I thought we'd all had enough of being stared at."

"Father Timothy says—"

"Father Timothy says. I can just bet what Father Timothy says." She stood up. "I'll be upstairs if anyone needs me."

"It's only this once," he began, but she was already turning toward the hallway, already at the bottom of the stairs.

"My head." Her voice came back over the banister, full of reproach. "It pounds."

We sat for a moment in silence, my father staring out at the hallway with that familiar expression of doomed adoration. At the time I had no idea how rare that sort of devotion was inside a marriage. It wasn't until I was married myself and saw how unhappy so many couples became over the years—the initial rush of joy fading beneath the slow accumulation of disappointments—that I understood my parents had succeeded at something where others so often failed, a delicate equilibrium held in place by the careful titrations of my mother's need for attention and my father's desire to meet her every demand. Not that his devotion ensured their marriage was a happy one. It meant only that it kept them intact in certain areas where so many marriages crumbled, those small fissures of unkindnesses and misunderstandings and deliberate cruelties mostly absent, I believe, smoothed over by my father's willingness to do anything—everything—to keep my mother happy.

"She doesn't mean it," he said finally, turning toward me. "They're fine people. Everything'll blow over soon enough."

"They shouldn't punish you."

"It isn't an easy business."

"Church?" I was speaking too loudly now, but I didn't care. "Or did you mean living in this good town of our Lord's apostles?"

He leaned toward me, his eyes fluttering behind his glasses. In that moment I felt certain he would strike me, though of course he'd never done anything like that before. But his hand only came forward to cup my chin—my mother's gesture; he held me there for a moment, tipping my face up so I couldn't look away.

"Love," he said finally. "I was referring to love, Rebecca."

\|/

I went straight up to my room after lunch, waiting until I heard the roar of my father's car in the driveway to take my *Grant's* and a glass of lemonade out onto the patio.

"You scared me." My mother swiveled around in her chair. Through the living room window came the sound of a piano: Rachmaninoff, I thought, by the crashing of all those chords, though the truth is I was never much good at telling the difference.

"I thought you were in your room." I slid my arm casually over the front of my *Grant's*.

"Too hot. I needed air."

"I'll just be inside." I turned toward the door.

"I've been meaning to tell you." She raised her voice. "We spoke with the school and you'll be staying here for the year. Your father and I agree it's for the best."

I turned back. "I'm not allowed to graduate?"

"Don't be so dramatic," she sighed. "There's no need for you to be in the dormitories, that's all. Not when you can sleep in your own room here at home. You'll have the old Ford to drive back and forth, once it's fixed up. I trust you'll find it sufficient."

"I think—"

"I can't say I particularly care to hear what you think."

"But it isn't fair."

My mother sat up very straight. "I suppose *you* stopped to consider what was fair."

"You didn't see what it was like there. It was the most godforsaken—"

"You do not have to use language like that." She cleared her throat. "Nor do you have to pretend you are incapable of following instructions."

"I did what I thought was necessary."

"And now that you've demonstrated your inability to determine exactly that, from this point forward your father and I expect to be kept abreast of everything you do." She nodded at me. "Your course of study, for instance."

My heart began to pound. "I don't know what that has to do with anything."

"Honestly, Rebecca." She gave me a wounded look. "You must think I'm blind. Animals this, cellular that. You've been leaving those books around the house for ages now. I assumed it was a hobby. Undesirable, certainly, but harmless all the same."

"So I've been doing a little reading."

She shook her head with what appeared to be genuine sorrow. "I spoke with your dean this morning."

"You called Dean Richards?"

"What have I said about that tone of voice, young lady?"

"I just don't see why you needed to involve him in any of this," I said, quieter.

"I had to tell him you'd be living here at home, didn't I? Imagine my surprise when he mentioned your course schedule this fall." She ticked things off on her fingers. "Biology, chemistry, organic something or other. All of them, he points out, *advanced*-level courses. Classes with prerequisites. Certain grade requirements."

"He had no right."

"Rebecca Ann." Her voice shook with indignation. "If anyone doesn't have the right in this situation, it's you. To think—we've given you every advantage. Provided you with every opportunity. And yet you seem determined to squander your chances at happiness." Her bottom lip had begun its familiar tremble. "What in the world were you thinking? Running off to God knows where and doing something so—so *deceitful*. So underhanded. Not to mention common. It's beneath you, the whole thing. Beneath this family. And now . . ." she swept on, ignoring my protests. "Now we find out you've been going behind our backs all these years. What is it you'd like us to do? Sit here twiddling our thumbs while you ruin your life? And for what, I might add—some ridiculous dream?"

"It's not a dream," I pointed out. "Medicine is a career. And I happen to love it."

"A *career*." She'd produced a handkerchief and was dabbing at her eyes openly now, her cheeks stained with tears; I felt a stab of guilt. "I suppose you think *I* never loved anything," she sniffed. "That *I* never had any dreams."

"I don't see what this has to do with you."

"No, of course not." She sat back as though all at once exhausted. "Why would any of this have anything to do with me?" I tried to say something again, but she held up her hand. "Enough. Your father and I are not the Gestapo. You're already enrolled for the upcoming year and we are not about to *bar* you from the classroom. I leave the decision to you." She took a cigarette from her case on the side table and held it between her fingers. "I'd only hope that your conscience might guide you away from spending your time and efforts on something of which your father and I so thoroughly disapprove."

My heart sank a little. "Then he agrees with you."

"You know perfectly well he does."

"And if I go ahead as planned?"

"Then I suppose you'll have to live with the consequences." She struck a match and lit her cigarette, inhaling. "Now, if you don't mind, I'd like to have some peace and quiet before it's time to start dinner. Horowitz." She waved toward the window. "There's very little that brings me solace these days like Horowitz playing the Nocturne in E-flat."

"If you could just listen—"

"Peace and quiet, Rebecca."

"I never meant to make you unhappy."

"Please." She shut her eyes tight. It was awful to see her like that, no bigger than a child folded into her chair, wishing me away. The nocturne began; she kept her eyes shut. I walked to the door and stood a moment longer, waiting to see if she might call me back, and then I turned and went inside, letting the door bang shut behind me.

This will be strange to hear after everything I've just said, but it was my mother I found myself wishing for that day in the doctor's office in Fresno. She would have known exactly what to do. She was, in the end, a strong woman, precise in both word and action. She would have put on her lipstick and combed her hair in her hand mirror, and then she would have told everyone, including me, what to do. But I was alone when I arrived on the overnight bus, and it was raining; by the time I found the building, my stockings were soaked through and my clothing was stuck to me all up and down my body like damp paper. I must have arrived looking like something thrown up by the sea.

Everyone in the office was very efficient. I was aware even at the time that everything seemed rushed, though I was the only one in the waiting room and I saw no one on my way out, still woozy at that point and half-numbed from whatever it was they'd given me for the pain. I remember that as I lay back against the table I spotted a cold sore blooming above the doctor's upper lip, that as I began to drift off I was gripped by the thought that it was all terribly wrong, the doctor with his cold sore and the empty waiting room, that I would die there on the table in a town hundreds of miles from anyone I knew. I believe I might have screamed had one of the nurses not finally smiled as she patted the sheet into place around my shoulders, the tranquilizers cutting the world off with a velvet curtain. It was hard to think of how many girls must have been right there where I was, spines flattened against the cold steel of the examining table. I could have kissed her for that smile.

Chapter 2

EARLY that August, a black man by the name of Marquette Frye was arrested in Watts, a neighborhood not twenty miles from where we lived. I would later learn that the policeman who made the arrest, a white man named Lee Minikus, claimed Mr. Frye had failed a sobriety test and grown belligerent when asked to cede his car, though what I understood from the papers the morning after his arrest was only the details of the aftermath. A mob had assembled, the article said, the crowd grown violent. The police officers feared for their lives.

The night after the riots over Marquette Frye's arrest began, I sat with my father in the living room after dinner, my mother already gone up to their room with one of her headaches. We had a small television set in the kitchen, but my father had always preferred listening to the news on the radio, saying he found all that moving around on the screen distracting.

The announcer was a smooth-voiced man named Marcus Thompson, who reported dozens of beatings and looted stores in Watts, cars set on fire. Through it all, my father's expression stayed perfectly, almost eerily, calm, his eyes like coins set deep in his skull. I remember that I tried to ask him something at a certain point— whether he knew anyone who lived in Watts, or if he'd ever driven through there before—but no sooner had I opened my mouth than his hand came up, shushing me.

The riots lasted five days. Every night after dinner I followed my father into the living room and sat there in the uncomfortable hard-backed chair, listening to Marcus Thompson report a thousand, five thousand, fifteen thousand National Guardsmen moving into the area to take control. A curfew of eight o'clock was set for everyone who lived within a certain radius. I tried as I sat there, tracing the silhouette of one of the Russian dolls my mother kept on the bookshelf ledge or pretending to read, to imagine what it must be like to be ordered indoors while the streets were burning with trash, while officers pushed men and women into patrol cars that vanished into the sweltering night. How strange to listen to the newscaster describe that scene as I sat in our quiet living room, the streets in our neighborhood silent, pristine.

Very little was said those evenings by my parents or by me. Despite the riots making the headlines every day that week, the three of us sat through our meals making our measured efforts at polite conversation. The weather, we agreed, awful. The new neighbors down the street of little interest, given their lack of children and their age (advanced). The click of our silverware ticked off the minutes, my mother sitting in her new, listless way across the table, me waiting for her signal to clear. When the riots ended later that week, the dead numbered somewhere in the thirties, the injured upward of a thousand. The night they announced the last arrests, my father stood and switched off the radio.

"A terrible shame." He took a handkerchief from his pocket and began wiping the lenses of his glasses clean.

"Yes."

"There is nothing more undignified," he said slowly, "than one man doing his best to take away another man's dignity."

I thought about that. The only colored people I knew were the cooks and maids who worked for the families in our neighborhood. The ones who didn't live in the houses themselves arrived by bus each morning in a cluster that fanned out as they walked down El Molino and disappeared, one by one, into our neighbors' homes; I'd passed them occasionally on my way to Windridge, their white aprons blinding even from a distance. "It doesn't seem fair," I said slowly.

"What's that?" My father peered at me, his eyes without his glasses oddly vulnerable.

"It's just—Ruby, the Carringtons' maid? Her father died a few years ago. He lived in Missouri, I think. The funeral was a few weeks before Christmas." I paused. "Mrs. Carrington was having a party and she said the timing was too difficult. There was too much to be done, what with the party and all. Alex said Eleanor—Mrs. Carrington—just put her foot down." My father slid his glasses back onto his face and blinked at me through them. "She wouldn't let Ruby go to her own father's funeral," I went on. "I remember thinking it was cruel."

"Cruel," he repeated. "Yes. We are, as a species, too often descended into cruelty."

I hesitated. "Then you believe they're right to protest?"

"I believe injustice eventually gives way to justice," he said. "Slowly, perhaps. With great effort, and too often through the unfortunate medium of violence. But I do expect it comes to pass."

"Then something like this has to happen," I persisted. "By your way of thinking. You believe change requires drastic measures."

"I believe," he said, "that there will come a time when we look back at the subjugation of the Negro class as one of the most shameful chapters in this nation's history."

"And the war?"

"Pardon?"

"Do you think it's shameful, what they're doing over there?" I thought of Oliver stepping down off the porch, the determined set of his shoulders. It seemed impossible that he might have killed a man by now, though of course chances were he had. I tried to picture him lifting a rifle and sighting down the barrel, his finger squeezing the trigger.

My father frowned. "War has its own rules."

"All's fair?"

"Something like that."

"So the dignity of the enemy is irrelevant."

"There is nothing about life and death that should ever be termed irrelevant," he said sharply. "Not to mention it's hardly within my jurisdiction to deem something that transpires on the battlefield fair or unfair. However, just because any given situation has not been questioned does not by any stretch of the imagination mean it does not warrant questioning."

I smoothed my skirt over my knees. "And yet somehow it continues to go unquestioned."

He looked at me warily. "I won't go against anything she's said."

"I wouldn't expect you would."

He stood a moment longer. "There is a good deal that is wrong with the world, Rebecca," he said finally. "But I choose to believe there is more that is right. I find a great deal of comfort in that choice."

I watched his back retreat through the door and then I sank back into the couch, drawing my legs up under me. I might have guessed my father held views quite different from the other fathers in our neighborhood—his hard-won success, as I have said, a story unfamiliar to the shipping heirs and oil tycoons whose houses lined our streets. But the truth is that at twenty-one I knew very little of what my father thought. Long before the events of that summer brought our dinnertime conversations to a standstill, we had spoken only in passing about politics or money or our beliefs about the world. In those days, parents did not speak to their children about such things, and in that respect we were no different from anyone else.

Besides, my father worked long hours at his firm, often too tired when he got home to do much more than eat the dinner Mother had prepared and retire to the living room to catch up before the next day; the few times my mother came in when he had the radio on, she excused herself from the room under one pretense or another. *Ugly,* she might say as she paused by the coffee table to straighten one of her vases. What was going on over there in Chicago or the riots that began in Hong Kong that spring. *So much ugliness,* she said, wiping a line of invisible dust from the coffee table with one finger. When there was so much else to look at in the world.

TOO soon, Labor Day came and went; too soon, I found myself driving the old Ford to school, my stomach clenching as I made my way down the familiar roads. I stood at the edge of the far parking lot awhile, watching the girls chatter and blow smoke into the morning air, the boys—with that touch of self-consciousness that always made them appear younger than their years—rumpling their own hair, the ends of it bleached close to white. I could have stood there forever, I think, an outsider allowed to remain on the periphery, where I belonged, to watch and observe without fear of being observed. But I knew if I waited too long I might be forced to enter the classroom late—the thought of everyone turning in their seats to stare too terrible, I'm afraid, for words.

"Land's sakes, Rebecca Madden, I'd thought you'd gone and fallen off the ends of the earth." Ann Knight, a girl I knew from freshman-year history, stopped me in the path. "Where in the world were you hiding all summer?"

"I didn't—" The words stuck in my throat and I tried again. "We were away. Tahoe."

"I looked for you at the pool." Ann Knight frowned. She had never been a particularly attractive girl, and over the summer she'd let her mousy hair grow long in a way that didn't suit her. "Now, who was it I was just saying to—" she began.

"Come *on*, Ann." Margie Capps was a junior with a pointy nose; she took Ann by the elbow and propelled her forward. "We'll be late for class." I could hear her clear as a bell as they headed down the path in the opposite direction. "What were you thinking?" Margie was saying. "Haven't you talked to a *soul*?" I started toward McCarren again, but now everything had changed. I could feel people's eyes attaching themselves to the back of my neck; a hush went over a group of girls sitting on a blanket as I approached; a couple on a bench at the edge of the grass stared down at their hands. I recognized the girl from my Lit class the year before. She'd come up to me one afternoon and asked me shyly where I bought my blouses.

"Do you have a minute?" The girl who stopped me outside the building couldn't have been more than sixteen or so. She had long brown hair that hung down to her waist and a tan, friendly face.

"Excuse me?"

"Hey," said the girl softly. "I just wanted to give you this. You have a beautiful day."

The piece of paper was pale pink, the script sprawling: *Peace.* I closed my hand around it as I climbed the stairs to Professor Potts's office, giving my hair a pat before I pushed open the door.

"Miss Madden." He looked up from his desk, where he was scribbling something on a pad. "Nice to see you." He was a small man, gray-haired and prone to an unfortunate tic in his left eye when he became flustered, which was surprisingly often. He'd been head of the natural sciences department for years, had recently published a paper on mitosis to wide acclaim. Of course I admired him tremendously.

"Sir." I sat and crossed my ankles.

He was frowning down at a piece of paper. "I received your note regarding organic chemistry. You need my permission?"

"Yes, sir," I said. "Professor Wilson said that considering it's an advanced-placement course, I need a department head to sign off. . . ." I folded my hands across my knees. I'd forgotten about the slip of paper, and it crinkled as I tightened my fingers. "I was also wondering if there might be something else I could take. Double up."

"What exactly did you have in mind?"

"That's just it," I said. "I'm not sure. I'd like to be prepared for the November exams, that's all. I've been studying like mad."

He frowned. "I apologize if I'm forgetting something."

"Medical school, sir." A drumming started up in my ears. "We spoke briefly about it last year? I've gotten behind with the reference letters, but I should still be able to squeak in under the wire. Provided you're willing."

"Miss Madden."

I smiled in a way I hoped was appropriately bright. "Sir?"

"I'm sorry if I let us get ahead of ourselves. If I'd fully understood your intentions—" He cleared his throat. "Medical school— well, it requires a certain head for numbers, an extraordinary sense of discipline I'm afraid only a handful of students exhibit each year. Now, nursing is a wonderfully rewarding occupation. You've done fine work these past few years." He uncapped his pen. "A program like St. Joseph's would be ideal, for example. Excellent reputation."

"I've got nothing against nursing," I said slowly. "Sir. But I really do have my heart set on medical school."

He coughed. "Allow me to—*hrrmpph*—clarify. Dean Richards went over this at some length just the other day. As I'm sure you know, each year I am permitted to pick no more than half a dozen candidates to recommend for graduate studies by official letter. University policy. I'm afraid I've made my selections for the year."

I sat stiffly in my chair. "The thing is, sir—"

"My hands really are tied."

"I happen to know for a fact Dean Richards spoke to my mother. I'm not sure you understand the circumstances."

"I understand perfectly." His voice was a notch louder. "To whom Dean Richards did or did not speak is hardly my concern. I am quoting him directly when I say—*as per university policy*, I might remind you—I am allowed no more than half a dozen candidates to recommend, and I'm sorry to say you're not one of those six. If you'd like to find someone else on the faculty to recommend you, you're more than welcome. However, I should mention that as head of the department I reviewed everyone's lists just this morning, and I'm afraid your name does not appear on any of them. As I said," he went on, more firmly this time, "I'd be happy to write any of the nursing schools on your behalf. You've taken more than enough credits already to qualify, and fortunately, there is no limit to the number of students I may recommend for those particular pro-grams."

I thought for one awful moment that I might cry. I fixed my gaze on the paperweight balanced on the corner of his desk. It was an ugly thing of glass and wood; I stared at it as though I'd never seen anything more fascinating in my life. "And Holly Stevens?"

"Pardon?"

"I'm asking if Holly Stevens is on your list. Sir."

"A fine mind." He tapped his pen against his desk and rear-ranged a few sheets of paper; his left eye had begun to twitch. "I'm afraid Miss Stevens is not on the list either, though of course I'll be recommending St. Joseph's to her as well. Unfortunately, she neglected to meet certain qualifications for the medical degree pro-grams."

"Which qualifications would those be?"

He sighed. "Of course you understand I'm not at liberty to dis-close that information."

"May I have an example?"

"Example?"

"I'd like to know who among us had what you'd call exceptional talent."

"Exceptional talent," he repeated. He rocked back and forth in his chair, his eye twitching madly now. "Eugene Price was in your class, is that correct?" I nodded and he brought the chair down with a thump, clasping his hands in front of him on the desk. "Eugene Price scored an eight hundred on the MCAT at the age of nineteen. His paper on James D. Hardy's work regarding live lung transplants was among the finest I've seen in my twenty years of teaching at this school. Dr. Price—senior—is himself one of the top neurosurgeons at Pasadena Presbyterian." He looked me directly in the face. "Eugene Price is the number-one candidate on my list. I expect him to matriculate to Stanford. Does that answer your question?"

I stood, lifting my bag to my shoulder. "Thank you for your time, Professor."

"Rebecca," he said quickly. "Miss Madden. You're a bright girl. Nursing really is—"

"Rewarding work," I interrupted. "I understand perfectly, sir."

He stood then as well, rubbing his eye with the palm of his hand. He was several inches shorter than me, and in his tweed coat and rumpled shirt he looked oddly elderly, fragile almost, some-one's doddering grandfather forced to deliver unwelcome news. "I expect to hear wonderful things about you down the line."

"I wouldn't hold my breath," I said, rudely.

I came down the stairs slowly, digging my nails into my palms; when I stepped outside into the dazzling sun, the girl with the long hair was still standing by the door. She turned toward me with that same expectant smile.

"Here," I said. I thrust out my hand and the girl stared as I opened my fist, letting the paper fall to the ground. "You have a goddamn beautiful day."

I don't believe it was more than a few weeks after my meeting with Professor Potts that Alex passed me on the path one morning— early October, no later than the second week or so. I remember that the heat had broken days before, the wind picking up one afternoon with an audible sigh. Cooler weather in that part of California has always seemed to me to have a particular effect on the light, a kind of tempering that fades the sun from glare to shimmer. That morning it hit some small pin or jeweled barrette in Alex's hair, and I looked up, distracted by the brightness. She was wearing a pale-green blouse and smart black heels, a sweater buttoned carelessly around her shoulders in a way that would have looked sloppy on anyone but her. I'd never seen the girl she was with before, a blonde with a glossy bob doing most of the talking while Alex listened or did not, heels clicking, the dark mass of her hair pinned back on one side with a clip. *Clack*-clack, *clack*-clack. I slowed as they got closer, clutching my books to my chest. The girl turned to watch Alex when she caught sight of me, chattering all the while. But Alex's face didn't change. She kept her gaze focused straight ahead, her red mouth set in a line straight as the horizon; it was the other girl who colored as they passed, her eyes carefully avoiding mine. We were both so engrossed in making a show of indifference, the other girl and I, I don't think either of us noticed when Alex reached for the end of my scarf. It was a small movement, no more than a twitch of her fingers.

"Hey." The word came out as a croak. But she kept walking, gone by the time I felt the air moving across my skin. When I stopped and turned, there it was in the distance—my favorite scarf, the only one I owned that was pure silk, fluttering behind her like a small orange sail.

But I'm wrong about the time of day. It must have been late afternoon by the time she passed me, the sun already beginning to sink down behind the row of gum trees that fringed the main quad. Five or six at least, long after classes were done for the day. I wouldn't have dared go into any building on campus otherwise, for fear of running into someone I knew, and no sooner had she passed me than I turned and walked over to McCarren Hall, the building where Professor Potts held his class and where I had sat crouched over my desk as recently as the spring before, working out a set of formulas. Where I had seen for the first time, my freshman year, the honeycomb network of a fly's wing under the scope.

The halls were dark and empty, the classrooms cleared of students. The door to the lab was closed but unlocked. The university held night sessions for high school students from time to time, and someone had likely left it open for that evening's class. I flipped on the lights and stood a moment in the narrow aisle between two islands, the beakers lined up in their drying rack at one end, the sinks scrubbed clean. I had always found the order in that room soothing, not to mention the quiet in which we worked, the silence broken only by the clicking of metal against glass and the constant hum of concentration. The whole thing put me at ease. In that still, cool room I forgot to slouch, forgot to worry about the cut of my dress or the look of my shoes, the small talk I found so tricky to navigate suddenly, blessedly unnecessary.

I don't know if I can describe what came over me as I stood in my old classroom that afternoon, fiddling with a bit of glass tubing someone had left out to dry. I was thinking, oddly enough, not of Alex or my mother or even Professor Potts but of Bertrand Lowell.

No doubt sitting in his father's office building at that very minute, I thought, reclined in a desk chair with a scotch and soda at the ready, his feet propped up on the windowsill as he let his cigarette burn down to a nub. I suppose in that moment I blamed him for all of it, for the great ruin I understood my life to be. I was surprised to see that my hand stayed steady as I swept my arm across the counter, the sound of glass breaking like the noise of a sudden downpour. I think I broke every bit of glass in the room. God knows I tried. I walked up and down the narrow aisles with rage shooting out from every limb—the beams of it, I imagined, extending outward until the entire room shone with the bright white light of every way in which I had been wronged.

\|/

She must have slipped in through the door right behind me. I don't know how else she would have found me in that building, McCarren a warrenlike configuration of rooms with which she would have been entirely unfamiliar. I walked right past her when I came out of the lab, my footsteps loud against the tile.

"*Brava.*"

Her voice boomed in the darkness, and I whirled around. "You scared me."

"That was some show." She came into focus slowly—her shoulders, her face, the gleam of her arms. "Really—*brava, bravissima.* I didn't know you had it in you."

"What do you care?" It was a shock to see her standing there in the hall, my scarf knotted loosely around her neck.

"*I* said it all sounded like a bunch of nonsense. French literature, that was your thing—I was sure of it. I said to Bertie: Listen, you don't know her like I do. You don't have a clue." She stopped. "What—haven't you heard? We're like two little lovebirds."

"But I'm still being punished."

"I don't know what that's got to do with anything."

"I thought that was the whole point."

She sighed. "And here I always said you were the clever one."

"Looks like you were wrong."

"Looks like it."

There was silence for a moment and then I half-turned away. "If that's all—"

"Did you ever stop to think how it might feel?" she said loudly.

"How what might feel?"

"Oh, I don't know. Being lied to, for starters."

"I don't know what you're talking about."

"Shut up." She said it almost affectionately. "Please, just shut up." She was squinting in the dim hallway light as though she could hardly see me: She'd been drinking, of course, though as I said it couldn't have been much past six at the latest. No matter. I could see right away she'd had more than a few—it was in the looseness of her body, the way she swayed side to side as she crossed her arms over her chest. "Honestly, I could care less. I'm just wondering what you did with it. Your *moxie*, darling." She arched one eyebrow. "Your so-called *spine*."

"What's the point?" I said sharply. "Apparently I'm not one of the top candidates. I fall well below the cutoff of extraordinary."

"According to whom?"

"Dr. Xavier Potts."

She put her hands over her mouth. "No."

I felt a smile tug at my lips in spite of myself. "He happens to be head of natural sciences."

"Xavier Potts," she repeated. "Head of natural blowhards."

"He's a brilliant man."

"Oh, I'm sure he is," she said airily. "They're all brilliant, aren't they? Still—seems a shame, you giving up like that. But then you always did lack what my dear departed grandfather called the strength of one's convictions."

I stared down at my shoes as though I saw something fascinating there. "I don't know what there is to have conviction in anymore."

"All the king's horses and all the king's men. The tale of a thousand important little men."

I glanced up. "Humpty Dumpty?"

"Aim high—isn't that what they always told us?" Her voice was tight. "Incidental breakage be damned. Be *great*, Eleanor said."

"*Per aspera ad astra.*"

"Exactly." She looked at me. "I expected more from you. I expected the goddamn stars."

"Sorry to disappoint."

"Not half as sorry as I am."

I rubbed my arms as though I'd caught a chill; the anger that had overtaken me in the lab had yet to disappear, and I felt warm from it, feverish. "I should be going."

"You're always in a hurry," she snapped. "I'd like to know when everyone started being in such a goddamn hurry." There was a brief silence and then she seemed to remember something. "I could have helped, you know. If you'd bothered to ask. Or did you think you were the first girl around here to find herself in a sticky situation?"

I stared. "You don't mean—"

"God, no. Not *me*, stupid." She lifted her chin. "I'm afraid I'm not at liberty to discuss the details. Let's just say you're not the only one to disappear for a few days and come back—how to put this?—*unburdened.*"

"I really do have to go," I said, turning. My hands ached where I'd hit them against the counter, the skin there itching like crazy, bits of glass no doubt buried beneath the flesh.

"It's called reality, Rebecca," she called after me. "You might want to acquaint yourself with it one of these days."

What did it mean to call something real? What was not real? It was 1965 and the world was in an uproar, but every day in Pasadena, morning broke on an exact replica of the one before. President Johnson had been reelected that previous fall, and under him the war in Vietnam began to escalate—the details of which I mostly learned later, understand, years after the events of that decade had come and gone. Oh, there were names that floated in and out of the classrooms at school: Operation Starlite or General Westmoreland. A handful of murmurs about the protests under way outside the White House. There were even a few among the younger students who left school for precisely that, boys and girls younger than us by no more than a few years but already angry, furious—their world, as it turned out, a different one entirely.

But they were by no means the norm, the ones who left or got themselves kicked out. They were, in a word, unusual. Unusual was Bobby Pierce, a Browning boy we all knew as Lindsey's younger cousin but who remained until that year otherwise unremarkable. I don't believe I'd thought twice about him before that fall, when he grew his hair long and dropped out of high school—simply stopped going one day, refused point-blank. Mrs. Pierce, it was said, at her wits' end. Unusual was Bobby Pierce and the crowd he began hanging around, boys with beards and girls in long dresses, who drove in from small towns along the coast to gather downtown and do God knows what. Unusual was Bobby Pierce getting thrown in jail for splashing red paint across the steps of city hall that next spring, his father leaving him there the full week before paying bail. He washed his hands of Bobby, he told anyone who would listen. He would not have a coward for a son, no, sir.

Chapter 4

J U S T before Christmas there was a scandal at school involving one of the English professors and a first-year; I'm afraid that sort of thing was just as common back then, though this case in particular attracted an unusual amount of attention. It seemed the girl had been discovered in the professor's bed, the wife returning home unexpectedly after a visit to an ailing aunt. The professor in question was a Shakespeare scholar. Of course, the headlines in the school newspapers made all the expected jokes: CAMPUS ROMEO'S OTHER NAME NOT AS SWEET. Or: OUT, DARN FROSH! Point being that in the aftermath of that scandal, I was more or less forgotten about. By the time we came back for the winter term, I found that most people simply ignored me, a few girls going so far as to give me vague smiles when I passed them on the path or sat down next to them in class, as though they remembered my face but couldn't for the life of them place it.

In retrospect, I wish I'd worked up the courage to speak to Holly Stevens. I spotted her on the path from time to time over the course of that year, her mud-colored hair held back from her face by a headband too wide for her narrow face; I might have stopped her one day and walked with her a ways or asked if she might like to sit down for a cup of coffee. We might have found we had more in common than our names gone missing from Professor Potts's list, though I learned later that Holly went ahead and applied anyway, that she was rejected by every school but Wisconsin—because, I can only assume, she lacked the appropriate references. I can't say we'd ever exchanged more than a handful of words, Holly and I. The truth is that I felt a greater sense of kinship with the boys who were in Professor Potts's class with us. They at least had shown a little enthusiasm for the work we did there, exclaiming and swearing under their breath while she went about her experiments with her unflappable calm, jotting things down in a black thick-tipped pen no doubt chosen to draw attention to the irreproachable accuracy of her notes.

I can only think now that Holly Stevens did what she could. She was brilliant, as I said, and it must have killed her to see the rest of us make our clumsy mistakes. She must have examined the lineup of students that first day and dismissed us immediately, even Eugene Price; we were all of us deadweight, mortals with faulty minds and slow fingers, scratching out our answers in pencil we promptly smudged. But now I'm just being cruel. No doubt Holly Stevens understood all along what it took me until that meeting with Professor Potts to discover: Both of us were working on borrowed time, a narrow window of years in which we were permitted to believe we might be allowed to do as we pleased. To be *great*, as Eleanor had said. Holly Stevens had simply chosen to use that time as best she could, to snap up knowledge so long as it was made available to her and tuck it away in her exquisite mind, before it was too late.

What else can I tell you about the rest of that long year? I spent most of it by myself, shut up in my room or out by the football fields, where I brought my lunch on the days I had to stay on campus for afternoon classes. I ate on the grass, one of my old novels spread open on the ground in front of me in case anyone happened to walk by. It was purely for show. I found I was no longer able to read—strange, because books had always been such a comfort to me, but at a certain point that year I became too easily distracted, the concentration required to follow one sentence to the next proving elusive, beyond my grasp. Classes proved a similar challenge, my notebooks remaining more or less empty well into the semester, my pencils often not so much as removed from their case by the end of the hour. Of course, I was taking hardly anything of interest by that point, but I'm afraid I can't blame my listlessness entirely on the subject matter—home ec or the history of Aesop's Fables. It was something far more simple: It had all just come to feel like too much effort.

I spent a certain amount of time driving. As the months passed, my mother lost interest in my whereabouts. She seemed hardly to notice whether I stayed or went, giving me a nod when I came through the front door or a distracted wave from the armchair where she had begun spending most of her time, embroidering stacks of pillowcases, none of which I recall ever seeing finished, let alone put into use. She appeared for all intents and purposes to have given up, to have—like Bobby Pierce's father—washed her hands of me. I'm afraid I took advantage of what I now understand must have been a great sadness on her part, spending most of my free afternoons out driving the Ford aimlessly along the back roads. It was a relief just to be out of the house and away from school, away from the sight of Alex or any of the rest of them cutting across the quad—enough so that I was happy to spend hours going nowhere, driving in circles, really. Winter brought rainstorms that sent water rushing down the gutters along El Molino, my father carefully folding that morning's newspaper into his shoes before he left for work, to keep his feet dry. The rain gave my drives a welcome feeling of urgency, as though I had no choice but to be out there navigating the roads in the downpour, my hands steadying the wheel.

What else? As the weather grew warmer, every day on campus brought some small reminder of our approaching graduation—a poster for a party or a sign reminding seniors to double-check the information for their diplomas. I tried not to think about how different those final weeks might have felt. Each dormitory arranged its own special celebration for the night before graduation, and occasionally I found my mind drifting to what minor task I might have offered to take charge of for Cullers—balloons, say, or refreshments, Betsy and I driving clear out to Santa Monica to track down some exotic ingredient for a punch. I might have baked a cake, something Mother would have clapped her hands over and declared *divine*. It hurt especially to think of how much she'd been looking forward to this time. She would have been in fine form— fretting over my selection of dresses for the dances, allotting a special column in her first-of-the-month finances to what she likely would have dubbed *Et Cetera: R*—a new lipstick, a compact, a pair of heels she would have taken me to Neiman's half a dozen times to deliberate over before purchasing, the triumph of the final selection enough to leave her in high spirits for days.

As it was, there was little talk of the upcoming festivities. My father asked one night at dinner if I knew the date for our commencement, and when I told him he drew out his calendar and marked it on the appropriate page. Mother said nothing in particular until she appeared in my doorway with my graduation dress the week before the ceremony, the heavy white muslin zipped carefully into its special bag. The dress she'd sewn herself the spring before, both of us unduly pleased with how it came out, her smile—as I turned to make the skirt flare—triumphant. "I thought we might need a final fitting," she said now. "If you have a minute?"

I stood in front of my bed while she pinned, her face pensive as she knelt in front of me. "You've lost more weight," she said.

"I haven't had much of an appetite."

She sighed. "You're just like your father, I swear. The slightest touch of nerves . . ." She reached into the pocket of her housecoat and drew out a handful of pins. "Hold still." She pinched the material at my waist with her fingers, and I held my breath as she stuck the pin in. "You're looking forward to it?"

"Graduation? I guess."

"Any word from the other girls?" I looked down at her, but she was frowning at one of her pins. "They must be planning something."

"I wouldn't know."

She wriggled the pin through. "Rebecca—" I waited. "I don't suppose you've given the summer any thought."

"Summer?" I pretended to think. "No, not especially."

"I saw a sign advertising for volunteers at the Ladies' Auxiliary downtown the other day, that's all. I've been meaning to mention it. Careful." She held the pin beside my hip. "Two more on this side and then one on the other." She frowned, using both thumbs to push the pin through the thick material. "Well? What do you think?"

I looked at my reflection. The dress had wide shoulder straps and a sweetheart neckline, which had gone in and out of style but was at the present decidedly out. A year earlier I'd admired the neckline, considered it elegant, even, but now I thought it made the whole thing look girlish, too young. "It'll do."

"Not the *dress*," she said, impatient. "The Ladies' Auxiliary. It's not our neighborhood, which I thought might be nice. New faces. A fresh start. Not to mention it would show everyone you're doing your best to make amends. And who knows? You might end up working on a few events with the Pasadena chapter. The Rose Parade, for instance. I happen to know that's a collaborative affair." She held her breath as she pushed the final pin in. "All done." I turned and she unhooked the back for me, turning modestly away as I stepped out of the dress and into my skirt and blouse.

"I suppose that sounds alright."

She sat down rather suddenly on the bed. "This hasn't been easy on any of us."

"I know that."

"It all came as the most enormous shock." She pressed the tips of her fingers together, the gesture oddly prayerful. "You were always such a good girl, Rebecca. Dreamy, maybe. Easily distracted. But I never thought for a minute I'd have to worry about you."

"I wish I could take it back. I really do—"

But she kept going. "I don't know where I went wrong. I honestly don't." She held up her hand. "Please let me finish. Your father and I worked diligently to make ourselves valuable members of this community. I'm not sure you fully understand the sacrifices involved, but you can imagine how painful it's been to watch our years of hard work come to nothing. Nevertheless—" She cleared her throat lightly. "Excuse me. What I mean to say is that I do realize this must have been difficult for you as well. I am not a monster. I am simply trying to do what's best for this family. I have only ever tried to do what is best for all of us."

I sat down beside her, laying the dress across my knees. "I'd give anything to make it up to you and Daddy."

"Then tell me you'll make an effort." She turned to me eagerly, her expression pleading. "That's all people need to see."

"I don't know what difference it would make—"

"But I do." She put her hand on my shoulder. "It's been nearly a year, after all." She gave me a small smile. "I think it's worth a try. Don't you?"

But I could hardly bear to look at her. I had already decided, you see: I would leave for San Francisco the night of graduation, my suitcase packed and stowed under my bed, what little money I'd saved from the odd babysitting job here and there over the years tucked into an envelope and knotted with a piece of string. "Ladies' Auxiliary sounds like a wonderful idea," I said at last.

"Do you mean it?" She looked genuinely happy for the first time in months.

I gave her my best smile. "Why not?"

"Then that's that." She gave my shoulder a squeeze as she stood, draping the dress over her arm. "I'll just run this through the Singer and we'll be done in a flash."

She was out in the hallway when I called to her. "What is it?" She turned, her face bright in a way that made me feel terrible.

"I really am so sorry," I said, my chest tight.

She came back into my room then and embraced me where I sat, her cheek cool against mine. "I know," she said. "Dear girl."

Chapter 5

GRADUATION day dawned hot and humid. I stood on the platform with the other *summa* students, one row down from Holly Stevens, needle-thin in a dress that hung off her like a sail. Alex and the others stood together in a cluster on the opposite side, Betsy catching my eye at one point and giving a little wave, though I'm sorry to say I pretended not to see. I was so desperate to step down off the platform I could hardly stand still, the sun too hot, the muslin sticking to my back. I found my parents standing off to one side after the ceremony, the lawn jammed with families and the faculty still lined up in front of the platform in their robes, the waiters making their way through with trays of champagne.

"To the graduate," my father said formally, raising his glass. "The second Madden graduate in a long line of Madden graduates."

"Isn't this nice?" My mother looked around, smiling at no one in particular.

"It's nice to have it over with."

"Hush, you," she said reproachfully. Her hair gleamed in its chignon, her ears—as usual—left bare; her only jewelry was the thin gold of her wedding band. I thought for the thousandth time how much prettier she was than all the other mothers, how elegant she looked in her plain navy shift next to all of them decked out in their jewels. "It's a beautiful day. Let's enjoy it, shall we?" She turned her appealing look on me, then my father. "Shall we just have a moment where we simply enjoy—oh, look." She nodded. "Doesn't Alexandra look nice!"

I watched as she made her way toward the stage. "She's making a speech?"

"Special Performance."

"What?"

"It says right here." My father pointed at the program. Sure enough: *Special Performance*, it read. *Alexandra Carrington, '66.*

"I ran into Eleanor earlier. Mentioned she hadn't seen me at the club." Mother put a hand to her hair, smoothing back the strays. "She said it had been ages now."

"She's speaking to you again?"

She gave me a little smile. "Looks like it."

"Here goes." My father gestured at the stage and I stood up very straight, as though preparing to salute.

But I haven't even told you yet what it was like to hear her sing. The best I can say is that it was like being told a secret, the thrill of it vaguely illicit. There was a small, precise tension to each note, the sense of something live contained within each phrase; on the few occasions I'd heard her sing, I felt her voice run through me as though that live thing had been released. It was unusual in those days to be a girl who sang in public like that, just her and a microphone; it was the sort of thing only a certain kind of woman did. *Common*, we would have said, had it been anyone but Alex, and even so, the whole performance carried an element of the daring.

She might as well have stood up in front of us and begun to unbutton her blouse, stepped out of her skirt, twirled one shoe on the end of a finger. I'm surprised, looking back, that anyone allowed it.

I have since heard singers with what must be far more beautiful voices perform many of those old songs she was fond of—Gershwin and Cole Porter, the show tunes of our parents' days—but I don't believe I've heard anyone match her for sheer intensity. She sang as though it was the only way she had of breathing, as though at any moment she might die. That day there was an added sense of ceremony to the way she looked out into the waiting crowd, the gold necklace looped around her throat catching the sun as she poured herself into each note like honey into a glass. I believe we all felt that those words were being sung directly to us, the cord of each line spun out like a fisherman's reel and catching us where we stood. The world gone to pieces for all we cared.

"Wasn't that lovely," my mother said, clapping enthusiastically.

"Lovely," my father echoed.

I murmured something about the ladies' room and my mother nodded distractedly, turning to ask my father about Mrs. Cromwell, did he think it was true about the house in Palm Springs—it must have cost a fortune, didn't he think? My father as he listened lifting his face to the sky, where a few clouds scudded back and forth across the blue. I made my way through the crowd, threading between families, the girls I'd passed on the paths between classes waving their diplomas high. I caught sight of Lindsey and her parents, the three of them planted in the middle of the crowd; I hurried on. I needed to be alone, away from the crush of people and the flashing camera bulbs, away from the families happily chattering about dinner plans, the newly engaged showing off their rings—away, away.

"Hey." Someone was calling after me with an aggrieved edge

to her voice, as though she'd been calling for a while. "Hey, you. Rebecca."

If it was strange to hear my name being called, it was stranger still to realize as I turned that I hadn't mistaken the voice. "Here I am," I said, turning. I gave an awkward wave. "Happy graduation, I guess."

"Cut it out, will you?" Alex leveled her finger at me. "I'd like to get something straight," she said. "I don't want you leaving here under any false pretenses."

"I wouldn't worry about that," I said bitterly. "Everyone's made themselves very clear."

"Look at you, *summa cum* everything. You make me so mad, I could spit."

I noticed then that the silk on my left shoe was yellowed around the toe, a spot like a watermark widening across a ceiling; it was the sort of detail that never would have escaped my mother's eagle eye a year ago. "What do you want?"

"World peace?" She gave me a flash of teeth, the crooked one in the front like someone had pushed it in. "Justice for all? Or maybe I've just been thinking. Imagine, today marks the first day of the rest of our lives." She said it grandly, biting every word off. I realized she was quoting our student president, a nervous boy named George who'd given a speech that morning and whom no one, so far as I could tell, remembered voting for. "Maybe I got a little sentimental."

There was a small silence. I could hear the sounds of the celebration going on without us, the shouting and the laughter, the click of all those cameras going off, one by one.

"It's over, Becky," she said. Sighed it, really, in a voice so flat and quiet I hardly recognized it as hers. "*Finis.* I find the whole thing too terrible for words." She turned away from me abruptly to frown across the quad in the direction of our old dormitory, the brick turned to orange in the sun, the windows shuttered. The rooms, I knew, emptied by now of everything that told of their former inhabitants: the photographs cluttering the bedside tables, the posters tacked up along the walls, the army of lipsticks lining the bureaus' edges. When she turned back, I saw that her eyes were red, though she was smiling now, shaking her head. "Look at us," she said, laughing. "We look like we're going to a funeral. We're supposed to be celebrating, for Christ's sake. We're supposed to be cracking open the goddamn champagne."

"I can't say I feel especially celebratory."

"Me neither." She exhaled loudly. "Pity. Most of the time, I'd kill for a glass of champagne."

We stood another moment in silence.

"I'm glad it's over," I said finally.

"Mine eyes have seen the glory?"

"I have my principles."

She produced a cigarette from her clutch and lit it. "Enlighten me."

"I'm sick of it, that's all. I'm so sick of everything I could scream."

"So now what?" She blew out a ring of smoke, then another, another, the O's loosening like lassos in the humid air. "What are your intentions for the future, young lady?"

"I don't see how that's any of your business."

She flicked her cigarette impatiently. "Don't be mean."

"San Francisco." There was a part of me that desperately wanted her to know—had been waiting to tell her, really, disappointed to think it might be some time before she heard the news. "Those are my intentions. Singular: I have exactly one intention." I'd learned the bus schedule by heart weeks ago. It left three times daily from downtown L.A. I would take the overnight in no more than a few hours, the note to my parents already written and sealed in an envelope I would slip under their door. *By the time you read this*, it began, *I'll be gone.*

"City on the hill—Christ, that's Rome, isn't it. Or is it Philadelphia?" She looked at me.

I shrugged, summoning a confidence I can honestly say I felt no part of. "Anyway, I'm going."

"As of?"

"Immediately. More or less."

"Parents?" I shook my head. "Good girl. They'd just make things complicated. We're twenty-two, for Christ's sake. You'd think at twenty-two they'd stop making things so damn complicated." She smoked another moment or two. "Listen," she said abruptly. "I know things have gotten a little dicey these past few months—"

"You can say that again."

She ignored me. "—But that doesn't mean I don't support the effort. I'm behind you on this one. One hundred percent."

"Oh," I said. "Well. Thanks, I guess."

She watched me a minute, arms crossed. "Just promise you won't go out there and fuck up your life," she said finally.

"I thought I already did."

"Don't be idiotic." I thought I heard my name: *Rebecca?* My parents would be looking for me. *Re-bec-ca?* "I choose you, understand? I get to say who, and I choose you." She smiled faintly. "I happen to be rather fond of you, dummy."

I looked down quickly to hide my blush. "And you?" I said. "What will you do?"

Another burst of applause broke out somewhere behind us; a man laughed, the sound of it so like my father's I startled. It occurred to me that I hadn't heard him laugh in some time now. "That's sweet," she said. "Don't you worry. I've got my own plans."

"Then I guess this is goodbye."

She nodded as though I'd done something right. "You won't forget," she said—declared it, really. "A promise is a promise is a promise." She winked. "God bless Stein, the old hag." And then she turned and walked away, and, because of her white dress and the bright afternoon sun, she seemed to half-disappear. There one moment and gone the next.

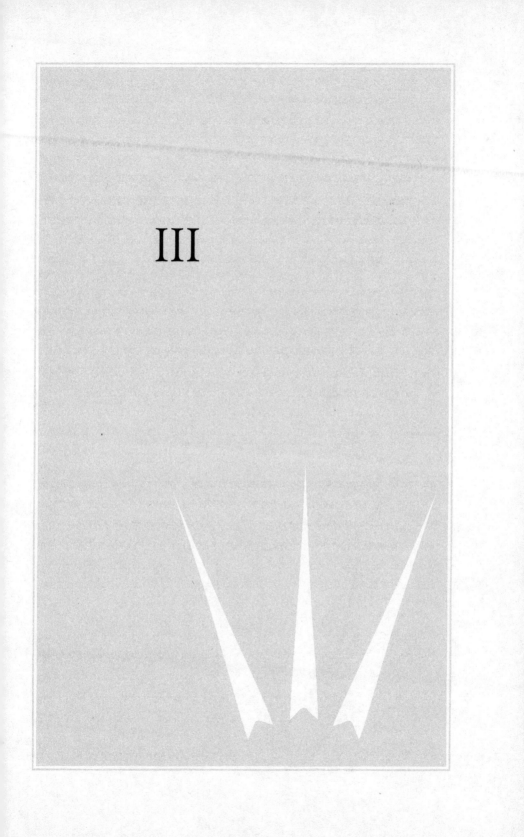

III

Chapter 1

I arrived in San Francisco during the summer of 1966. It will be difficult to reconcile what I'm about to tell you with what you already know of that time. I know what your history books say, that the streets of San Francisco were being stormed and the young people of that city and cities all across America were rising up against the old guard and tearing the country's idols to shreds. Maybe so. But I'm afraid what I saw hardly amounted to a revolution, no more than a few groups of girls and boys my age or younger standing around on the sidewalks here and there, smoking and leaning up against the storefronts along Haight Street, their laughter drifting through the cool air. They might have been the younger siblings of my Windridge classmates, fresh-faced and eager but with that restless look to their eyes. The Bobby Pierce look. I will admit to crossing the street to avoid them when I could, though they parted amiably enough when I had no choice but to pass. I don't suppose I would have been of any interest to them in my skirt and blouse, my purse slung over one shoulder, my hair clipped back from my face.

I was lucky in that I found a job easily enough. I worked as a waitress in an ancient Italian restaurant down by the Embarcadero, the kind with checked napkins and the tables set with old wine bottles choked with candle wax. It was a depressing sort of place, though at the time I believe I found it faintly glamorous, or I found the idea of it glamorous. me, a working girl with a pouch in my apron for keeping tips, the collar of my blouse ironed flat every afternoon before I came in. I'd never worked in a restaurant before, and I surprised myself with how slow I was to learn, taking notes as one of the girls explained, for the hundredth time, how to fill out the order tickets or fold the napkins into neat triangles, where to put the used silverware from the cleared tables, where to scrape the uneaten food.

In retrospect I wish I hadn't been so shy around them, the other girls. They were nice girls, all of them, from small towns with funny names like Altoona, Kansas, or Higginsville, Missouri. Towns they shrugged off when I asked them, their pasts old skin they'd shed and left behind with what appeared to be the greatest of ease. I can still see them all as though it were yesterday: Lana, with the round, sweet face that reminded me of Betsy; Elaine, the blonde with the lisp and the pert nose; Marcy, the black-haired girl I'd overhead discussing an affair she was having with her father's friend—*imagine*, she said, giggling; Anne, the small, less good-looking one who wore a constant look of mild agitation, as though she knew at any moment someone might come along and size up the group, find her wanting.

They were girls not so unlike the ones I'd left in Pasadena, the kind you might have found in any city across America at the time. They saved their tips in an envelope stashed under the mattress and called home every Sunday; they liked having a cigarette before service began and I joined them from time to time behind the restaurant, just to listen to them chatter, the smoke drifting overhead in a purplish haze. *Come out*, they called across the room at night after our shifts were done, the floors swept clean, the glassware polished to gleaming. *Come on,* one of them would say as they stood there good-naturedly pushing one another in front of the lone mirror, drawing on their bright mouths and sketching in those eyebrows that gave them a look of uniform surprise. *One drink won't kill you.* But I only smiled when they asked, saying I was tired or that my feet hurt. I went home instead to the sublet I shared with another girl, a tense, heavyset graduate student named Isabel who was writing her dissertation on Catherine the Great, as I remember it, and who seemed, quite honestly, hardly to notice whether I came or went.

But you'll want to know how I ended up with your father. I'm afraid it isn't much of a story, in the end. As the new girl at the restaurant, I worked all the holidays—Thanksgiving and Christmas, New Year's Eve, the last proving a particularly trying night, long and loud and full of big tables always needing this or that, all of them staying far too long. It was well past three by the time everyone cleared out. We were all exhausted, our aprons damp with God knows what, the floor littered with bits of colored confetti someone had thrown at midnight, our feet scattering it across the room as we ran back and forth from the kitchen to our tables until it looked, Elaine said, like a bomb had gone off in a rainbow. We brought the last of the dishes to the kitchen and wiped everything down, turned the chairs onto the tables, and went to work with our brooms and dustpans. I always liked that part of the night. The lights came up and everything that poor restaurant tried to be—a romantic place, a spot with a kind of old-world elegance—was exposed for what it was, the linoleum floor hideous, the bar worn and carved down by endless penknives, the wallpaper ancient, peeling.

"You." I looked up from where I was sweeping one last pile into the dustpan to find Lana standing over me. "You're not going anywhere tonight." She turned to the others. "Agreed?"

"That's right," said Elaine, snapping her rag. "It's New Year's, for crying out loud."

Lana smiled. "We don't bite."

I opened my mouth to protest and a vision of my room rose up in front of me—the drab walls, the light of my single lamp, Isabel shooting me a dour look from where she no doubt sat curled up in an armchair, thumbing through some treatise on one thing or another, her pen at the ready.

"One drink," I said finally, and Lana clapped her hands and cheered.

We ended up in a part of the city I'd never seen before, somewhere not far from the Golden Gate Bridge. The air when we climbed out of Lana's car was damp and heavy with salt; the breeze was surprisingly strong. I was glad to see the bridge through the fog, its shape distinct even in the dark. But then I have always loved the sight of bridges—they seem to me to be one of the great miracles of human ingenuity, testament to the kind of vision I attribute to nothing less than true genius. I remember reading once that the architect for the Brooklyn Bridge became paralyzed just before construction began, that he was forced to observe the goings-on from his home in Brooklyn Heights. It seemed exactly right. You would have to be trapped in order to pull off something as magnificent as that, to believe so deeply, with such absolute conviction, in the possibility of such freedom.

But I'm afraid despite the bridge I regretted coming almost immediately. I wrapped my scarf around my neck and hung back, watching the other girls stumble down toward the dunes, where a small crowd stood around a bonfire. When my eyes had adjusted to the dim light, I saw I was no more than a hundred feet or so from the water, the shoreline dotted here and there with birds glimmering palely in the predawn darkness: sandpipers, I knew the little ones were, their heads bobbing as they ran back and forth. Oliver had been a bird lover as a younger boy, the hummingbirds that came to my mother's garden to feed an endless source of delight. We'd sat on the bench together countless times while our fathers made polite conversation and watched them, Oliver pointing out how to identify the black-chinned variety and the one called calliope, showing me pictures once in the little book he carried around in those days—woodpeckers, grackles, robins, terns. I squinted through the dark now, watching as a lone pair of gulls skimmed out over the waves and dove toward the horizon, their sleek bodies disappearing into the water without so much as a splash.

I must have kicked off my shoes at some point, wanting to dig my toes into the sand. Or maybe I was all at once hot, or claustrophobic, or maybe I felt a sudden sadness steal over me at the thought of Oliver, how poorly I'd treated him. I know I felt that loneliness that comes when I am around too many people, that I wished desperately to be back in my drab little room, where I could pull the covers up around my shoulders and fall into a deep, dreamless sleep. When I felt my eyes begin to prick with tears, I looked up to where a few scattered clouds blocked the stars and searched in vain for the moon, the sun still no more than a faint glow along the horizon. The sand turned cold as I headed toward the shoreline, the tide working at the skin between my toes. Another gull veered down not a hundred feet from where I was, and I watched it skim the waves, wings stretched out to either side like fingers.

I don't remember where I read something about the idea of a vanished twin. It must have been in one of my biology classes, a lesson on the reproductive system or fetal development, or perhaps it was later, when I was pregnant with one of your brothers and read about it, the way women do, as though we might uncover some nugget of information to protect ourselves against the inevitable pain. I don't know. But I thought of her that night, as I stepped into the cold water: my vanished twin. How could I not? Faced with a crowd like that one, she would have *done* something. Snapped to life rather than faded as I did. I watched the gull rise up from the surface, wings beating hard. For one odd, suspended moment, it seemed to me that I saw her out there in the freezing water, the outline of her half-submerged body gleaming white in the moon. In that moment I felt the absence of her friendship as sharply as though the break were fresh. Or perhaps I missed being young and foolish, or maybe I was simply cold, the water now up past my waist. The truth is that some things, even with time, never reveal themselves entirely. I raised myself up on my tiptoes, tucked my chin under, and dove.

"What are you, crazy?" A wave caught me across the face and I sputtered, furious. I saw a cap of gleaming hair, a pair of blue eyes staring at me indignantly in the early-morning light. People gathered by the edge of the water behind him, their bodies silhouetted against the sky. They stayed until my rescuer waved and then turned away.

"Maybe," I said. "You?" I hadn't meant to laugh, but my legs were kicking underwater like mad and my head was light from the cold. I felt suddenly, giddily alive—hysterical, almost. It must have been the shock—of the water or of what I'd just done, I can't say.

"Jesus." He sounded disgusted. "That was quite a stunt." One hand broke the surface and rubbed at his eyes. I could see even in that dim light that he was extraordinarily handsome. His head under that golden cap was finely shaped, his nose aquiline; he looked, I thought as my arms began to numb, like a statue, something carved from stone. "Can we go in now?"

We paddled back a foot or so until we could stand. Goose bumps stood out all over my arms, my toes slowly prickling back into consciousness.

"I was just wondering," I said apologetically, rubbing my upper arms, "about the pheasants."

He shook his head, looking bewildered, but then he squinted into the sky. "Those are gulls," he said. "Plain old seagulls."

"Not here." I was speaking too urgently. "In Vietnam." I could feel him looking at me as we walked up the sandy incline; I was conscious of the way my wet clothes clung to me, my skirt wrapped around my legs like a second skin. "I heard the soldiers kill them for fun."

"Another radical, is that it?"

"I happen to know someone over there," I said stiffly.

"Everyone knows someone over there. One of my best buddies from law school shipped out just the other week." We stood next to each other, shivering.

"So you're a lawyer."

"Nearly."

"Aren't you supposed to care about defending life?"

He sighed. "I know this is when I'm meant to say something brave and all—"

"God, no," I broke in. "Honestly. I'd rather you didn't."

He stood there looking at me appraisingly. "I'm just glad it isn't me over there."

"Of course you are."

"We better get you warm—"

"Rebecca," I said.

He took my outstretched hand and I started to shake, the gesture oddly formal out there on the damp sand. But then he turned my hand over, palm up, and kissed me on the underside of my numbed wrist.

"Happy New Year, Rebecca," he said.

"Paul," he said, nodding gently. "Happy New Year, *Paul*."

It wasn't so uncommon back then, marrying someone you hardly knew. Of course, Isabel made a fuss over my leaving before the year was up, though she quieted down after I paid her the next three months' rent in cash and left her the small bureau I'd bought for the room. My suitcase and a few books were all I had to take with me. Another girl might have found that unsettling—sad, even, the fact that my life could be reduced to such an undistinguished heap— but I was glad for it. "I escaped," my mother always said, "I got *out*," and I thought of her as I left my key on the coffee table for Isabel and ran down the stairs to where Paul was waiting. I was free, wasn't I? In a gesture I found both surprising and touching, the girls at the restaurant threw me a going-away party. There was no need for me to work anymore, Paul said. We would live together in his apartment in Pacific Heights until we moved at the end of the sum- mer, Paul's family in New York and a position waiting, he said, at a prominent firm.

In retrospect, I wish I'd asked one of the girls from the restau- rant to serve as a witness. It would have been nice to have a familiar face there in the courthouse that June, someone to applaud when the justice pronounced us man and wife or to throw a handful of rice at our retreating backs. We'd decided to tell our parents after the fact, Paul declaring it would be a "hoot" to elope, that Bitsy and Jed, as he referred to them, would love it, love the adventure of the whole thing. Of course I was relieved to have an excuse to leave my own parents out of it, but as a result I'm afraid the only bit of festiv- ity to the day was the flower Paul brought with him, tucked into the inside pocket of his vest. He surprised me with it as we stood at the front of the room, waiting for the justice—an elderly, taciturn man— to shuffle his papers into order.

"To love," Paul declared, the cluster of yellow blooming in his hand. It was flowers, really, plural, a bunch of tansy he'd spotted on our way in and doubled back to pick on a whim. I stood in the dim cool of the courthouse, clutching the tansy in my hand, the stiff cotton of my shift gone soft against my upper leg where I kept pressing the palm of my free hand against my thigh. I felt strange: not myself, or as though I stood outside myself, looking in. I kept waiting for the thrill of it, the sparkle. I remember looking around the room knowing that I ought to be recording the moment, that later I would regret not having taken down every detail: the dusty lamp with its tangled cord, the lone chair in the corner, its seat cushion covered in cracked green leather. I fixed my gaze on a poster someone had tacked up on the far wall, a faded print of Rosie the Riveter in her blue shirt and polka-dot kerchief: *We Can Do It!* She looked not much older than I was, though it was hard to tell with all the wear and tear, one side of her face gone yellow and cracked in places where the sun had burned her skin away.

I'd written my parents the week I arrived in San Francisco, saying the apartment I'd found lacked a telephone, of all things. They could write me if they liked. My mother wrote back the very next week, saying formally that she was happy to hear I'd arrived safe and sound. The heat was killing the rhododendrons, she wrote, and last week there had been a terrible accident on 101 involving a truck full of chickens and a family of four—had I heard? Of course they missed me terribly, she added at the end. They had been worried, she said. Did I have the right sort of coat for the chill? The evenings in San Francisco, she had heard, downright cold. At the end of the page, as though it were an afterthought, my father had scrawled his signature. I don't have to tell you that hurt me more than I cared to admit at the time.

Now I could write to tell them I was married. *A lawyer*, I wrote that next morning. *Paul is studying litigation. He graduates at the end of the summer. We're thinking New York.* On the subject of our wedding I said only that it was very small, that my husband (I took particular pleasure at the look of that word on the page) had cousins with a house north of the city and we had been married there with just a few witnesses. Outside, I said, in the shaded grove of an old peach-tree orchard. *Paul's friends played Pachelbel*, I wrote. *A string quartet.* I wrote that last bit knowing it would please my mother to think of me walking down an aisle, however makeshift, to music, that at those words she would no doubt stand from the dining room table where she and my father sat with my letter and walk to the cabinet and put on a record of Pachelbel, her head tilted just so. I said nothing of the tottering old justice, the peeling walls, nothing of the strange sensation I had of looking in at myself as I stood next to the man who turned after those brief vows and kissed me chastely on the lips.

I'm embarrassed to admit I kept the tansy pressed between the pages of a book for years, the color of the bouquet fading from marigold to butter, the stems and buds drying to brittle but somehow miraculously left intact. I don't believe I've ever told anyone until now. I used to take it out from time to time and hold the dry little stem, as though the feel of those crisped petals might take me back to that afternoon, to that younger self who seems now little more than a bewildered stranger, a girl standing stiffly in a county courthouse wearing a cotton shift and a pair of Mary Janes, her hair pinned back behind her ears. As our marriage began to pull apart at the seams, I looked at those small, flat buds with the discerning eye of a forensic examiner, as though the dissolution of a marriage was something I might be able to trace back to its beginnings. As though I might have known all along we would come to no good end.

How do I explain your father? He appeared that night in the cold waters of the Pacific like the perfect solution, the final number to one of Einstein's beautiful equations. You've seen the pictures, those Polaroids from our old apartment in Pacific Heights, where we lived that spring and summer—me on the front steps in a shift and a pair of sunglasses I believed fashionable at the time, Paul holding a tumbler full of something. He really was extraordinarily handsome. A tall drink of water, my father called him once. Broad-shouldered but lean, with that shock of golden hair. The sun browned his skin until he looked half Indian, his classmates teasing him that he must have Navajo blood. "Christ, Bitsy would have kittens if she heard them saying that," he told me. "Her father's father's father—my great-great-grandfather—came over on the Mayflower, and she'll never let you forget it. She's an original, Bits. You'll see."

He was all of twenty-six when we met, but even as a student he dressed beautifully. He had impeccable taste, an unparalleled sense of what Mother called the art of presentation. I believe I fell for that as much as anything else. Every morning before he left for class, I watched as he shined his Italian-made black leather shoes with a little brush and a cake of polish; he combed pomade through his hair until it gleamed; he shaved meticulously in front of the mirror, clapping his cheeks with a hot towel and applying aftershave with even, synchronized pats.

"Are you happy?" This one morning not long after we married. He stood in front of me in his jacket and tie, his shirt freshly ironed, the collar turned down just so.

I wrapped the sheet around me. "I don't think I'll answer that question."

"On what grounds?"

"On the grounds that it may incriminate me."

He stood there looking at me: I can't tell you what that felt like, to have a man like your father look at me that way. "Bingo," he said finally, grinning. "Girl's got taste."

"The fifth?" I gazed up at him.

"My favorite amendment," he said, bending down to kiss the top of my head.

In early September, we went to Aspen on a belated honeymoon. It was all for me. Paul has never, as you know, particularly cared for the outdoors. He has always had what in those days I considered, on the basis of my own father's predilection for neatness, a lawyer's love of order, a certain impatience with anything that made a mess. Paul kept everything at a level that bordered on the fastidious—his golden hair, the collar on his shirt, the lapel of his jacket, the pen clipped to his pocket, his toothbrush placed at exactly the same angle in its little cup. Even, I'm embarrassed to admit, the sheets on the bed after we made love had to be stripped immediately, the bed remade with fresh linens before he could lie back down. I have often thought that was part of what drove him to drinking, the fact that it transported him to some other, more perfect place.

Still, in those early days of marriage, Paul's desire to see me happy eclipsed everything. The week before we left for Colorado, he bought me a pair of binoculars, tying the box up with a clumsy bow. *For Rebecca*, he wrote, *who deserves a better view*. The binoculars came with their own carrying case, black leather and lined with green felt.

Spectacular waterfowl! The Aspen guidebooks exclaimed. *Unparalleled buntings, red-tailed and chicken hawks, rosy-cheeked finches, buzzards, owls!*

We sat in our hotel room and watched the rain.

W E moved to New York in late October. Our apartment was on West 79th Street, a large, airy place on the twelfth floor of a building that must have struck me at the time as terribly luxurious, though what I remember of those first moments in our new home is the liquid way the sun poured down over the Hudson, a light clear and lovely as any California afternoon. Within days of our arrival the skies had sealed over, turning the view from our window into a wide, seamless stretch of gray, like wax that has been melted into a mold and left to cool.

I quickly found myself housebound. Oh, there were any number of things I might have done. Museums I might have visited, societies I might have joined. No sooner had we arrived than the invitations began pouring in, the wives of the other lawyers at the firm asking me to charity events and teas, cocktail parties, lunches, afternoons at the salon while our husbands were at work. I put on fresh lipstick and took taxis to strangers' apartments, where we went around introducing ourselves and then sat with our plates of melba toasts, the other wives turning to one another immediately to ask about teething, was it true about letting them cry it out during the night because, honestly, they were at their wits' end, and did anyone know of a really good hairdresser uptown? There were firm holiday parties and dinners at the partners' homes, which I attended with Paul, the men retiring to the study with their cigars and cognacs the moment the dishes were cleared, us wives left to chitchat over our tea. You can imagine how well I did with that.

That fall was when everything began to change. With Paul and me, I mean. Or: That fall was when everything began to shift. Like the fog parting around the Golden Gate, the truth slowly emerged, its own awful miracle. For a while there I remained deliberately blind, preoccupied as I was with my own unhappiness, the inertia I felt taking hold of me a little tighter each day like the torpor into which certain birds, Oliver once informed me, descend come winter. Snow fell that November in great, shining drifts, and I began staying home for days at a time. I was newly pregnant with your brother, ill and confined to staggering around most mornings as though I'd been dropped on a boat somewhere miles out to sea, the horizon dipping and rising with alarming speed. All at once the effort required to pull on a hundred layers and battle the crowded streets seemed too much. You'll recall that I had never lived anywhere outside California, the farthest my family had ever gone for a vacation a weekend we took in the Grand Canyon when I was very young, my mother later declaring the whole thing a disaster. In the absence of any concrete activity to occupy my hours, I spent far too long unpacking the boxes and setting up. The apartment was much bigger than our place in Pacific Heights, and I took weeks to pick out the rugs and draperies, arranging and rearranging the furniture—a project for which you must understand I had neither the talent nor the patience—and trying out small, colorful accents I found ridiculous but that *Ladies' Home Journal* assured me were *confident*. Paul seemed pleased to see me taking such an interest—"thatta girl!"—though in truth he'd already begun working long hours and hardly had time to notice much of anything, his mind already absented, focused on other, more important things.

\|/

Occupation: housewife. There it was on our tax returns that first January in New York, Paul's cramped black print marching across the cream-colored paper. It was on the kitchen table when I woke up one morning, Paul already gone to work, the apartment empty. *Sign here,* he'd written, taping the note to the table with an arrow pointing to the appropriate box. I stood for a moment, holding my breath. It was a trick I began playing at some point that winter, finding myself stopped all too often in front of the bureau in our bedroom with one of Paul's socks in each hand, distracted by a ray of sunlight that had escaped the curtain to run down the bed frame; or, if it was one of those days when I tried to make a go of it, to make what Paul at a certain point began to refer to as an *effort*, I might find myself frozen in front of a painting at a museum for far too long, aware that I wasn't seeing what everyone around me saw, that I was missing some small, crucial detail, the thing that would shift what I stared at from the inscrutable to the sublime.

But the longer I stood there that morning in our apartment, the more foolish I felt, just as I did those moments when the sun finally shifted behind a cloud and the light disappeared from the bed frame, or the painting failed to surrender its secret and I came to, holding a sock or a paper brochure proclaiming the genius of Picasso. I let out my breath and took up the pen and—turning the form over—began to write.

Dear Alex,

Was it Aristotle who said that the value of life ultimately depends on awareness? Contemplation? I am, in a word, surviving. I am only twenty-four. We vowed not to become our mothers—or you did, anyway, and I took it for granted. I thought it went without saying that we would make our own way.

I want to tell you it's nothing like we used to imagine when we were girls: New York. Life. The trees are bare here by November and everyone is cold as ice. There are too many pigeons, no sky to speak of. If there is excitement, glamour—if these gray streets are holding everything we found missing from our lives—they've hidden it well. None of it what we thought. I am beginning to think we went about our thinking all wrong.

I am writing because you claimed we were headed in a different direction. You trusted there was another path. You are the one person I have ever known who did not lack, as you once said of me, the strength of your own convictions. I am writing because I was always of the same mind, whether I admitted it or not. A different world, you said. I thought of it as a promise. It occurs to me now that that may have been my first mistake.

By this point, I'd covered the back of the form and moved onto the front, writing first in the narrow margins and then over the typeface itself, covering *housewife* with my determined script, the loop of my *l*'s girlish, fat. I knew even as I wrote that I would never send it, explaining to Paul that evening that I'd spilled coffee across the page, the form ruined beyond repair. At the time I must have told myself that was the end of it, that I would push that page deep into the trash and be done, wash my hands of the whole affair.

How little we know of ourselves, I should have said.

\\/

April 5, 1968

Dear Alex,

Chaos last night here—I suppose it must have been everywhere. By noon yesterday, the streets were crowded with people.
They stood right there in the middle of the road like they'd never
seen a car coming down Broadway. Stood and wept, holding on
to each other for comfort. All the restaurants had shut down or
else flung their doors open, handing out food and drinks. I'm
ashamed to say how little I knew of Dr. King. I know, of course,
that he was a great man, but I must admit to only having heard
bits and pieces. Those speeches, I mean. Everyone seems to have
memorized them but me. I've never had the mind for memoriz-
ing. Or I did once, but I lost it somewhere along the way. This is
one of those things that happens now: I misplace keys, I lose dol-
lar bills, I turn a corner and forget where I am. They say that's
what they do, the hormones. I'm pregnant: Did I tell you?

But last night. Is it awful to say that as I made my way toward
home, I found that sadness comforting? That I found the sight of
strangers crying in one another's arms moving in a way I can
hardly put words to? It seemed like such an enormous relief. To
cry like that, to be held by someone, to weep.

I find myself at a loss these days. I'm huge now, swollen. Big
as a house. A ship gone down. *A melon strolling on two tendrils*
(Plath?), and meanwhile the books all saying the same thing. I'm
supposed to be knitting booties or blankets or God knows what.
Sleeping all day. Eating nutritious foods. *Nesting.* I'm meant to be
a bird, not a boat. But I can't sit still. I feel myself sinking. I've
come unmoored, lost my anchor. At any moment, understand, I
might drift away.

June 26, 1968

Dear Alex,

Do you understand when I say something in me wants out? Not the baby—that part over, thank God. I barely recognized my body, the sounds it made. The way it pushed and groaned, the sheets wet ten times over an hour in and me still sweating like a horse. But I'm talking now about fear. The dark kind. Fear that sneaks up on you like a cat. I lie here on our bed while Matthew sleeps, Paul still at work or out in the living room, going over his papers, and somewhere in the back of my mind, beyond the shopping lists and feeding schedules, the naptimes, the reminders about the bottles being cleaned—somewhere it occurs to me that I will never leave this place. That the walls of this apartment will circle in. I feel the closeness of everything in this life, that's all. The way it binds.

July 2, 1968

Dear Alex,

Today I went down to the river and sat. Just half an hour or so, Gladys home with Matthew while I made up some excuse. It was the first time I've gone anywhere without him since he was born, and I swear to you, he knew. The way he clung to me as I put him in his crib! Those little arms reaching, the betrayal in his eyes as I drew the blanket up around his arms absolute. There was a moment as I stepped into the elevator and pressed *L* where I thought I might be ill.

But then—God, the freedom! To leave the building with only the house keys in my hand. To walk down to where the air blows clean and do nothing but sit. To be, for even a moment, just another anonymous stranger. The boats came and went, the lights along the shore of New Jersey blinking on and off. Every now and then someone passed by and I feigned a look of concentration, as though there was something out in the water I was studying—*amoeba proteus*, I let myself imagine. *Chlamydomonas*. The cells under the light of a microscope brilliant green. The colors jewellike, glowing.

July 16, 1968

Dear Alex,

I'd like to tell you that I tried. I did. I tried the way I tried with the wives and their afternoon teas, our wineglasses refreshed by Maria or Gabriella or whoever—the help is the point. Everyone has help. *We* have help. Gladys, for God's sake, and I don't know what I'd do without her. Point being, we are just like everyone else.

But, the *wives!* The wives are hell-bent on improving—what? Their minds, their skills in flower-arranging. Their sense of civic duty. They take French or Spanish and practice their conjugations diligently; they sign up for pastry classes, and our teas those weeks are filled with doughy pies, *mille-feuilles*, butter cookies with the jam thumbprint glowing at the center like stained glass. Then they find something new, the kitchen too hot come July. Butter everywhere, they complain, the children everywhere, butter in the children's hair, on their clothes. They find something else to stick themselves to. They get *involved*—orphans in Africa, illiteracy in China. Elderly racehorses.

One afternoon a week or so after Matthew was born and I was still delirious with fatigue, I called up and ordered the course catalog from NYU. I was half giddy when it arrived, the pages glossy and smelling of ink. Between feedings, I considered a class on French literature. I read about a course on the history of

Washington Square while I gave Matthew his bottle. I went so far as to leave him with Gladys just the other day and ride up to Barnard in the first set of clean clothes I'd put on in weeks, trembling with the strangeness of being away from him for that long. At one point I almost turned around and came straight back home. But one of the wives had mentioned a landscaping class. The properties of ferns, she said, fascinating. So I sat in the taxi and tried to concentrate—picturing something along the lines of botany, leaves mounted on a slide and examined under a microscope. But the class had very little to do with plants, in the end, concerned mostly with the colors of the flowers that bloomed on certain bushes come spring, the arrangement of tulips in a particular sort of garden. Did I prefer the British, the instructor asked that first day, or the French style of hedges?

Long after I knew I would never send a single one, I kept writing my letters. While Matthew napped or late at night, after Paul was asleep, I sat at my little desk in the bedroom and wrote until my hand cramped up and I was forced to put the pen down. Isn't it strange? I hadn't spoken to her in years. And yet when I sat down to write, it was always to her: my audience of one. From time to time I promised myself I'd throw the letters away. Better I should take up knitting, I told myself. Macramé. Something *useful*. But each time the urge to write her struck, it rose in me like something elemental, an uncontrollable itch. I took the pen in my hand and watched her appear on the other end, twisting her mouth in that way she had when she found something amusing, the smoke from her cigarette closing around her head.

You understand: I had no one else to tell.

Chapter 3

BUT all of this must sound horribly naïve. I should remind you that I was brought up to consider all questions concerning sex of an indelicate nature, that even as a married woman I undressed in the bathroom and blushed when movie stars embraced on-screen. At Windridge, we were given a single half hour's class as part of our "Home and Family Living" course, in which Nurse Salter took each of us by the hand in turn and told us she prayed for our souls. Remember that I was all of twenty-three when I married, that besides that one night with Bertrand Lowell, I had never done more than kiss a boy before Paul. There was, in those days, still so much that went unspoken. If weeks went by without more than a hurried peck on the cheek on the way out the door—well, that summer after we moved, Matthew was born, and then Lucas less than two years after that, and in the whirl of new motherhood I lost track, or I pretended I had. Remember that at that time a man who preferred men would have been labeled a pervert or worse. I believe at that time it remained a crime in every state across America, that he could technically have been arrested, Paul. Disbarred. Never mind the disgrace to the family name.

We believe what we choose. I don't expect that will come as much of a surprise to you by now.

We'd been married a little over three years when he came into the bedroom to tell me the truth. Or: He tried. I have never given him credit for that, for having had the courage to try. Perhaps I am wrong, but I have always believed that was what he came to say when he appeared in the doorway that night with his briefcase in one hand, a drink in the other.

"Do you have a minute?"

"Shh." I put a finger to my lips and nodded at Matthew, who sat nestled in my lap with a book, his head growing heavy.

Paul cleared his throat. "There's something I've been thinking we ought to—" he began in a quieter voice.

"Your mother called," I interrupted; I don't know why. I felt a wave of something pass through me where I sat, a touch of that vertigo I sometimes experience when standing under a tall tree—an elm or one of the old white pines that grows around the house here in Marblehead—the length of it a thing I all at once picture tipping to the side, crashing to the ground. "They're on their way to London," I said quickly. "They said they're sorry they didn't make it in this weekend but that they'll stop by when they're back next week. Sounds as though they're looking forward to it."

"London," he repeated. "Well." A quick grin. "Bully for them."

"Devon too, I think. Bitsy said something about an old Saxon church? She sounded very excited. She said they thought they might take a tour."

"Leave it to Bits to start frothing at the mouth over a pile of stones."

"It's nice they're taking a vacation."

"It is." He gave me a curious glance. "They've been talking about it for a while now."

"We should have them over when they get back, don't you think? They've hardly gotten the chance to spend any time with Matthew since Luc was born. I don't think we've had them over in forever now."

"No? I'd lost track. Everything's been so busy." He gazed at Matthew and I bent my head to your brother's forehead, breathing in the animal smell of his skin. I heard Paul take in a breath. "You know—"

"Lunch?" I was speaking in a voice pitched too high, too loud; Matthew stirred in my arms. "We could have them over next Sunday," I went on, quieter. "On the earlier side, before Lucas goes down for his nap. Gladys could run to the bakery on Eighty-Third, the one your mother likes."

"Sunday," he said slowly. "Why not?" He ran a hand over his face. "Rebecca—" But then he stopped. I believe that was the moment he tried to tell me the truth, that when he reached for his courage he simply found it gone. Like so many unhappy people, he didn't know how powerfully the vision of a happy life held him, I don't think, until he found himself confronted with everything he stood to lose. He was not a cruel man, understand, only weak like the rest of us. Under that golden exterior, after all—a heart. "He's getting so big," he said finally. He crossed the room and came over to where we sat, laying a hand on Matthew's head. We both watched our son for a moment, that small stomach rising and falling. And then my husband said very casually he guessed he'd try sleeping in the guest room for a night or two. *Guessed*, he said, shrugging— as though someone had put the idea to him. "I haven't been sleeping well," he said. "I wake up every time you go to feed the baby, and then I can't for the life of me go back to sleep." His mind drifted at meetings, he said. He was having a terrible time making it through the day. "A temporary fix," he said, leaning over to kiss me on the head.

He was at the door when he turned again, his pajamas folded neatly in the crook of his arm. "Rebecca." He smiled at me over our son's heavy body; it was an awful smile. "We understand each other, don't we?"

I don't remember what I said to him that night in the bedroom, his handsome face distorted by that smile like a pool of water ruffled by a strong breeze. I know that after he left I carried Matthew to bed, that after that I went straight to the bathroom and shut the door, running the water to cover the sound of the tears that never arrived. I know that after a little while I splashed cold water on my face and brushed my hair its hundred strokes before turning off the light and going to bed, that I only bit my lip when I came into the kitchen early the next morning and found him gone, Matthew already calling for me from his crib, Lucas's cries verging on frantic. It was only temporary, I reminded myself. Later, after Paul had taken most of his things from our bedroom and I started putting his clean laundry directly into the drawers of the guest room bureau, leaving his favorite toothpaste on the guest room sink, I kept turning the same lie over and over.

Continuing, in other words, to live as I always had. What else could I do?

Chapter 4

I'm sorry to say I saw your grandmother just twice before she died, both times on the occasion of one of your brother's births. We'd fallen into the habit of speaking every Sunday night not long after Paul and I moved to New York, Mother providing running commentaries about the state of the gladiolas or the new heated pool at the club, the cat that appeared on their doorstep one morning with a dead hummingbird in its mouth, depositing the body before it slunk off into the hedges. Occasionally my father picked up the extension in his study, the buzz of the radio giving him away long before his measured greeting—*hello, there*, or, simply, *well*. I wished desperately at those moments that Mother would give him a chance to speak, that she might pause her endless chatter; in retrospect I understand she was only doing her best to fill in what would otherwise doubtless have been a string of awkward silences, saving us from the weight of everything that went unsaid.

Strange, that first visit after Matthew was born, to find she was so much smaller than I was: I had not remembered that. But then that is so often the way with things from our childhood—they are never quite as grand or terrible as we recall. I remember, too, that the back of her skirt was wrinkled from the plane ride—the turbulence, she noted, *atrocious*—and her hand went there automatically as she turned from the window, smoothing the cloth flat before she lowered herself onto the couch. My father seemed ill at ease, his big hands resting on his knees as though unsure of what to do with them as he gazed around the room.

"All on one floor," he said finally. "Is that it?"

"It's a floor-through."

"A what?"

"A floor-through," I said again, my voice loud. "We were lucky to get one so big, not to mention the view. There aren't many places with a view like this."

They both turned to gaze at the windows.

"No," my mother mused. "I wouldn't think there would be."

"We had to fight off half a dozen other bidders. Paul was wonderful. Didn't give an inch."

My father nodded. "Sounds like a fine man."

"We're on pins and needles, as you can imagine." Mother crossed her legs at the ankles and smiled up at me, putting on her brave face to show she was still fighting the lingering effects of all that turbulence. "I feel sick we've let so much time go by without meeting him. Absolutely sick."

"Things have been so hectic," I began.

"No need to apologize to *us*, sweetheart." She picked up one of the throw pillows and set it back down immediately. "You've been busy as a bee. You've got the baby to think of, not to mention setting up this place. And Paul—well, it sounds as though they're keeping him on his toes."

"He should be home any minute." The elevator whirred as I said it; I hoped it was him, but it kept going, gears clanking as it rose.

"Isn't it funny, everyone living on top of one another like this?"

My mother glanced around the room as though she expected to see people emerging from behind the furniture. "You must get along famously with the neighbors."

"Everyone mostly keeps to themselves, actually."

"That doesn't sound so bad."

"Honestly, Walter," she said, reprovingly.

My father turned toward the window again. "Tremendous view."

"It's nice having the river so close by. And the parks," I said. "One on either side."

"Speaking of neighbors . . ." My mother sat up a little straighter. "I ran into Eleanor the other day and she told me the most terrible news: Ruby up and quit on her last week, just like that. Can you imagine? After nearly forty years with the family! All over the question of a little raise." She shook her head. "The whole thing's come as quite a shock. Ruby's always done terrific work, but Eleanor had every right in the world not to cave, I think. Why, there must be dozens of people like Ruby who would *die* for that job."

"Your mother," my father interjected, "has recently developed an allergy to the word *Negro*."

"It's not me," Mother sniffed. "They don't like that word anymore. Isn't that right, Rebecca?"

I ignored her. "Then you see them, the Carringtons?"

"We've been on the Ladies' Guild together this spring, Eleanor and I. Didn't I—? No? We've been having a marvelous time." Her voice changed almost imperceptibly. "Of course, she and Beau are just over the moon about the twins."

"Twins?"

"Alexandra. She's due in September." She paused. "I assumed—"

"Of course," I said quickly. "I'd forgotten."

"Strange-looking man, that husband of hers. I saw them at the park once—oh, it must have been ages ago." My mother coughed. "Tall as the day is long. Not particularly friendly, I must say."

"You know him," my father said. "She knows him, Eloise."

"That's right. A Browning boy, though I believe he's a bit older. Now, what was his name? Lundell? Labelle?" She clicked her tongue. "Lowell," she declared, triumphant. "Bertrand Lowell."

"Alex's husband." I had been standing and now I sat down. "Bertrand Lowell."

"Did you know him?"

"A little." I took the blanket from the back of the sofa and busied myself refolding it.

"A fine match, I think. Eleanor seemed very pleased. They have them over every weekend for dinner, she said." She looked at me. "I gather you're not in touch?"

"I've been so busy," I said slowly.

"It's such a precious time, isn't it?" My mother looked up at me, her expression wistful. "Why, I remember you as a newborn as though it were yesterday. Imagine—your father and I not even married a year, the three of us crammed into that tiny house up in the hills. I spent every minute with you. Up all night and on into morning. I saw the most marvelous sunrises—do you remember, Walter? Do you remember how much I loved sitting up with her while the sun rose? And here you've got this apartment, this view. You must be on top of the world." She reached out and touched her fingers to my arm. "Just look at this place. Look at you."

Paul came through the door not long after, shaking my father's hand and bowing as he presented my mother with a glass of champagne, which made her smile. I believe they both took to him immediately. He was charming and affectionate, kissing the top of my head before he sat down beside my father, placing a hand on my shoulder as I passed around the hors d'oeuvres. I served everyone shrimp cocktail from a silver bowl and pretended not to notice when I spilled sauce on the rug: My hands were shaking in that awful way they have. Not long after, Gladys came out with Matthew—damp and sweet-smelling from his bath—and my mother cooed over him, Matthew squirming a little until she handed him back to me, saying she must have lost her touch. I all but jumped at the chance to leave the room, taking your brother in my arms and murmuring something about feeding, though no sooner had I shut the door to the nursery than I found myself sinking into the rocking chair what felt like moments before my legs gave out. It was only when your brother began to wail that I realized I still held the bottle tucked into the crook of my arm, that I must have been sitting there for God knows how long with his little hands grabbing, my mind somewhere else entirely.

August 10, 1968

Dear Alex,

I'm writing to say I understand. Or I want to understand. I don't know that they're the same thing exactly, but I am doing my best here. I am making an effort.

It seems to me that the road to such-and-such is paved with delusions. Not heaven or hell, but the in between, the nowhere in particular. Where I find myself living. Do you understand what I mean by that? I don't mean to sound so dire about it. There are little things that nudge me out. Moments that lift the fog like a flap of skin. Matthew smiles his baby smile or the sun hits the river just so. A cardinal rises from one of the old elms down in the park, the flash of red as he wings north surprising. I have to think you have those, too, though given recent evidence I feel less inclined to imagine what they look like. I won't pretend to have a clue what form your happiness takes at this point, the shape it has assumed. Everything changes. I ought to have grown accustomed by now. And yet the change boggles the mind, as my father would say, the word just right, *boggles*, a word that shakes the brain, rattles it loose. The thought still stops me where I stand, Matthew feeding and that sour smell everywhere, the sound of his sucking loud.

Listen, the thought says. Eventually, you lose everything.

Chapter 5

M Y mother died in the fall of 1973, a heart attack due to blockage her doctor said must have been accumulating for some time. I spent most of the long flight from New York asleep, the damp heat as I stepped out of the airport at once strange and achingly familiar. I was something less than fully awake as I rode along the highway, the sight of downtown L.A. approaching oddly dreamlike as a result, blurred, a jumble of skyscrapers and billboards rising from the haze of smog. I had never taken a taxi in Pasadena before; that must have added to the strangeness of it all, the unreal quality of the scenery flashing by as we pulled off the highway and drove down those old roads. I asked the cabbie to drop me at the sidewalk in front of our driveway and then just stood there a minute, staring at the familiar façade before tucking my bag behind the front hedges and starting back down the street. I needed to walk around the block once or twice, I told myself. Clear my head.

I found myself in front of Alex's house soon enough. In one of our last conversations before she died, my mother told me that the

Carringtons had moved to Florida months before, some controversy over a large amount of money gone missing at Mr. Carrington's company. A *scandal*, she'd said. Meanwhile, the house looked exactly as it always had, its size impressive in a way even the other houses on our block didn't quite match, that high wall running all the way to the far end of the backyard that sloped down into the swimming pool. I would not have been surprised to hear a shriek from the pool as I stood there on the sidewalk, to catch a glimpse through the iron gates of my fourteen-year-old self disappearing into the blue water after Alex, our bodies leaving twin trails of bubbles.

I kept walking all the way to Swenson's, the little market where my mother had liked to do her shopping. I don't know that I thought much about what I was doing as I took a basket and walked down the aisle, stopping by the display of oranges. It was my mother who'd taught me how to pick out the best ones. She'd stood with me once in precisely the same spot and showed me how to run my thumb across the skin, checking the texture, the dimples meant to be of a certain size, the scent strong without being overpowering. I picked up an orange and held it to my nose.

Listen: It is a terrible thing, losing your mother.

There was a girl who lived in our neighborhood, Lucy Allen, who I was friendly with when I was young: Boots, her dog was called, his black coat set off by four white paws. Boots was supposed to be the family dog, but like all dogs he had his master, and in this case it was Lucy's father, Mr. Allen, a quiet man we might never have known was home until he came shuffling into the room. We might never have known, that is, if it hadn't been for Boots, who in an ecstasy of love would spring up from wherever he'd been sleeping minutes before Mr. Allen walked in the door and, lifting one boot, point his nose at the front door.

I can't say I had Boots's accuracy about timing or direction, but if I'd had a coat of fur, a strip of it would have stood straight up along my back when Alex came through the door. I stood there pressing my nose into the orange's cool skin and stared at that familiar profile as though it were possible I had mistaken someone else for her. I must have looked half mad. I actually went so far as to drop the orange deliberately to the ground, crouching there a moment—hidden, feeling absurd—before I forced myself to stand.

"Alex," I called, waving the fruit lamely in the air.

She really did have the most extraordinary eyes. The color that complicated green and wide as a cat's, the right one with that slightly startled look to it. "I don't believe it," she exclaimed, coming toward me. "For Christ's sake. Look at you!"

"Isn't this funny," I said. We embraced awkwardly, my head turned in against her shoulder so my nose was pressed into the crook of her neck; there was the overwhelming scent of cigarettes and strong, musky perfume.

She kept one hand on my arm as we stepped apart. "I'm so sorry about your mother. I only just heard this morning."

"Thank you. It was a shock."

"Is your family here with you?"

I shook my head. "We've got two young boys, and it's a long trip from New York." My voice came out oddly cheerful; I felt myself blushing right away. "And you? Twins, I hear?"

"Emily and Kate. They turned five last week." She looked at me closely. "God, you look terrific. I probably shouldn't be saying that right now, but you do."

"I don't know—"

"No, it suits you, wearing your hair down like that." She touched her own hair distractedly. She'd chopped it above her shoulders in a blunt cut that set off her features—that fine jawline, the delicate ears. "I've still never been, if you can believe it." She looked at me. "New York."

"You should come for a visit." My cheeks began to ache from smiling. "Really. We've got more than enough room."

"That's sweet."

"I mean it—we'd love to have you." I straightened up, aware that I had been slouching. "It would be our pleasure."

She smiled faintly. "You haven't changed a bit. No," she said quickly, "it's refreshing. Change gets old." I was struck in that moment by how tired she looked. I don't say it to be cruel; the truth is that exhaustion somehow became her, the area under her eyes bluish in a look vaguely Victorian, that dark hair setting her pallor off to striking contrast. I can't say I'd ever considered how tiring it must have been to be her: to be beautiful in the way she was, I mean, to find herself constantly navigating the demands of everyone's desires. "I used to see her in here sometimes, your mother," Alex went on. "Always made a point of telling me the latest news—did I know you'd moved to Manhattan. Had I heard you'd married a lawyer."

"She could be charming." I tried to keep my voice light. "Meanwhile, steel underneath, head to toe."

"Steel," she said approvingly. "I like that." There was a moment's pause. "It's the funniest thing. I was just thinking of you the other day."

"That *is* funny."

"Are you . . . ?" Alex gestured at the little patio outside the shop. The diamond on her ring finger caught the sunlight and scattered it; in some distant corner of my mind, I registered that it was strikingly large. ". . . in a rush?"

I pretended to check my watch. "My father's expecting me—"

"Please," she said, with that sudden intensity she had. "Let me buy you a cup of coffee. One little cup."

I smiled as though I hardly cared one way or another. "Why not? It's been forever."

Isn't it strange? If asked, I would have said my memory of her was like something preserved under glass, immutable and precise. But everything I remembered turned out to be no more than imagination and conjecture, a collection of blurred images like clouds reflected in a slick of oil. I'd forgotten all those small particular tics, the habits that turned her from merely attractive to extraordinary: A way she had of pursing her lips after she said something, as if every line contained a private joke; a tendency to move her hands expressively as she spoke, slicing the air to pieces. The amused look that crept across her face when she was only half listening. The color that rushed to her cheeks when she laughed—really laughed. Her smile, slightly crooked, displaying that odd bent-inward tooth. That voice.

She *had* changed. I was surprised to see it in the daylight, how dramatically her face had thinned through the cheeks, a fine latticework of lines creeping in around her eyes. She wore no makeup save a swipe of color across her lips, a red I thought too orange for her complexion. She'd always been slender, particularly those years at the U, but she seemed shrunken now, her features larger in contrast—her eyes, her mouth. When she shrugged, her shoulders jumped like a marionette's.

"Listen," she said suddenly, leaning forward so quickly her cup rattled. "I've been waiting for a chance like this. I owe you an apology. We all do."

"It was such a long time ago," I began.

"I don't care if it's been a goddamn century." She flicked her coffee cup impatiently where it sat in its saucer and it wobbled, spilling a little. "I'd want to wring my neck if I were you."

"At least you tried," I said. She frowned. "At graduation?"

"That? I couldn't bear the thought of a mind like yours going to waste. It made me ill. Positively ill." She brought her hand to her forehead and drew a small circle at the center of her forehead, no bigger than a dime. "The third eye. Do you—no? A friend of mine, that's all. Alfred. Involved with Hinduism. Higher consciousness, et cetera. Fascinating stuff." She thumped the table. "A travesty, anyway, talent like yours going to waste. Downright criminal."

I picked up the creamer and set it back down immediately. "And the others? Are you in touch?"

"Everyone's scattered to the four winds, as Eleanor used to say. Lindsey's been out in Santa Monica for years now. Husband sells something—plastics? Three kids, I think. Unless it was four. Let's see . . . Robin never came back, far as I know. Stationed in Monaco or somewhere around there, though to be honest I haven't heard a peep for years now."

"Betsy?"

"Bingo." She leaned in. "Dove's the one to ask about. Left some perfectly nice husband just a few months ago and up and hightailed it to Nebraska. Apparently she has family out there, the story goes, though there's a rumor going around she had someone waiting for her." She arched an eyebrow. "A woman someone. Don't say I didn't tell you."

"What about you?" I hesitated. "How have you been?"

She sat back, kicking the leg of the table as though she were no older than Matthew, a child restless at being made to sit still. "You know me—I'm like a cat."

"Nine lives?"

"I was thinking more of the always-ending-up-on-my-feet bit. Though lately I don't know." She made a face. "I've been feeling more like an elephant or a pyramid. Something ancient, is the point. Dusty."

"And Bertrand?" I forced myself to look at her directly. "Mother only just told me. I'm sorry I didn't have your number. I would have—"

"No, you wouldn't have. But that's alright." She squinted as though the sun was in her eyes, though we were well shaded out

194

there on the patio, the leaves of the banana palms thick overhead, lush and green and crowding close together. "Bertrand is . . . Christ, he's *Bertrand*. Come on, darling. We're old friends, you and me."

I tried to smile. "Old? Not us."

"Pyramids," she said with a hint of satisfaction. "Ancient ruins. Feels like it anyway. I blame all these college girls running around town. Place is lousy with them. You know the type: W-O-M-Y-N."

"Feminists, you mean."

"Is that what they're calling themselves these days?" She shook her head with what looked like disgust. "I don't know how anyone's meant to keep up. One day they're burning bras, the next they're jumping into bed with anything that's got a pulse. Terribly inconsistent." She tapped her cigarette against the edge of the table, letting the ash crumble to the ground. "We've got one next door to us—Alice. She's always gathering the troops for these evening discussions, raising consciousness or whatever. Married, Malice. You'd think the husband would put up a fight, but he's docile as a lamb about the whole thing. Suppose he comes home every night to a house full of girls chattering about free love and God knows what else, doesn't he. There are worse things." She stared at the ash. "I have to say I find it depressing—all of it, really. The whole thing. Movement with a capital M."

"They're doing some good, aren't they?" I fiddled with the sugar bowl, uncapping and capping it again. "Broadening our horizons?"

She let out a short laugh. "The only horizons they're concerned with are their own. Trust me, *us* they consider beyond saving. Oh, Malice is very nice to me and all, but you can practically see the pity oozing out of her whenever she catches me with the twins. Gosh, aren't I *busy*, she says. She can't for the *life* of her imagine how I do it all day!" She shook her head. "She's never so much as invited me over for one of those meetings. Not that I think I could stomach it," she added quickly. "All that shouting about taking back what's *ours*, protesting the so-called disintegration of American ideals. Constitutional rights, they claim. What—you didn't know? This whole thing's our fault, according to them. We didn't fight, they're saying. We just sat there while the years slipped through our fingers. Lay down and took it like a couple of kittens." She waved her hand. "As though we had a shred of choice. Can you imagine?"

But at some point during her speech I'd stopped listening. I was thinking of my letters, those pages locked up in my desk, each with Alex's name printed at the top. As she went on and on, they began to move. How do I explain? In the darkness of my half-listening mind, the letters began to shift and glow, the lines I'd written flickering like candlelight, the words burning faintly at first and then with growing intensity. Sheaves of paper glittered red and orange and yellow, the flames lying low before they leapt up, started climbing the walls.

"I should get back," I broke in. "My father will be wondering where I am."

"I've kept you too long." But she made no motion toward getting up, only sat and watched me from under half-closed lids. I shifted uncomfortably in my seat, clicking the clasp of my handbag open and closed.

"It really was so nice to see you—" I began.

"Oh, for Christ's sake," she interrupted. "Don't be like that. It's been awkward as hell, and there's no need to be polite about it. But I don't think it has to be so bad. Really, I'd like to keep in touch, if you're game." She took out a pen and wrote something on the napkin. "Here."

I took the pen and printed my number on my napkin—adding, inexplicably, my name: *Rebecca Turner*. "If for some reason you don't hear from me."

She folded the napkin into a neat square and tucked it in the V of her dress. "Wild horses couldn't."

"Sorry?"

She leaned forward. "I'm saying I plan to call."

"Terrific," I said. "Fantastic!"

"I really am glad this happened."

"So am I," I said, standing. "I couldn't be gladder."

We ate an early dinner together, your grandfather and I. Light shone down from the scratched chandelier, illuminating the surface of the dining table, the wood nicked badly enough that the lace runner my mother must have laid down in hopes of covering up the damage only seemed, instead, to accent it. The whole room appeared to have succumbed to a new fatigue: A water stain spread along the far corner of the ceiling, cracking it here and there; the sun had dyed the curtains a pale mustard yellow. Later, as I wandered from room to room after my father was in bed, I would see that the entire house had begun to slide into a state of disrepair—the eaves over my bedroom window sagging in a way I knew boded no good, a few hairline fractures here and there in the hallway ceiling that I remembered from my childhood now spread at what seemed an alarming rate, their lines interlocked like cobwebs. The furniture had worn down a few degrees from presentable to just this side of shabby, the fabric on a number of the seat cushions thinned to translucent.

You can imagine how awful I felt as I sat there at the table, the quilt I'd had at the U folded neatly across the back of the couch, its edges frayed despite evidence of my mother's neat stitching. I could have changed everything, understand. I wrote checks for perfect strangers, after all; month after month, I sent money toward saving dolphins or starving babies, when all along I could have been saving my own parents with nothing more than a scribble of my name.

But I was a selfish young woman, preoccupied with what I believed at the time to be a sadness I'd ended up in through no fault of my own. I shouldn't have to tell you it was a terrible thing to realize.

"Ugly business, getting old," my father said finally.

"They said it was unusual for someone so young—"

"I wasn't referring to your mother."

I had always thought of my father as a strong man, not overly large but tall like me and sturdy, as I have said, traces of his maternal grandmother's Bavarian roots visible in his broad shoulders. Now he seemed too easily contained in his chair; he sat off-kilter, one arm bent against the table as though it was all that held him up. "You're in perfect health," I said. "The doctors said—"

"The doctors said." He dropped his fork with a clatter. "You'd think they were God, to hear them talk. Men just like the rest of us, last time I knew anything about it. Bound by the same laws." He pressed his napkin to his lips. "I'm not myself. I apologize."

"You've had a shock."

"You wouldn't think it would have such an impact on a man, living alone a few days." He looked around him helplessly. "Suppose you grow accustomed."

"No need," I said firmly. "You're coming back with me on Friday. We'll have someone pack up your things and send them. Hush, I already decided."

He drew himself up. "I have no intention of becoming a burden."

"Nonsense. We'd love to have you—" But he was already shaking his head. "Will you at least think about it?"

"This is my home."

"It's too big for one person. The upkeep alone—"

"I'm too old to start over again somewhere new."

"You're not even sixty."

"Too old," he repeated. "Not to mention stubborn." He rapped his knuckles against the table. "We built a life here, your mother and I. Twenty-eight years in this house. Twenty-eight years," he said again.

"Please tell me you'll at least think about it."

He sighed. "I'll think about it."

It was quiet a moment.

"Unwilling to what?"

I looked up, startled. "Oh—nothing. Mother said that once. *I find myself unwilling.* I always wondered what she meant."

He twisted his napkin between his fingers; I recognized it as something my mother had begun to do that last year I lived at home, one of the many small tics she'd developed in the absence of her sewing. "She was a woman with a great many desires," he said slowly. "Some of which I was able to fulfill and others, regrettably, I was not."

I reached out impulsively and covered his hand with mine, the skin of his knuckles like a lizard's against my palm, cool and dry. "You did your best. Honestly, Daddy. She didn't exactly make it easy."

"Nothing worth anything has ever proven itself to be easy. I should think you'd have discovered that by now."

"You were a wonderful husband," I said firmly. "A saint."

He made a noise somewhere between a laugh and a cough. "I ought to have taken more care."

"You did everything she wanted."

"I won't dignify that with a reply."

"A saint," I repeated.

"That's enough—"

"You should eat something." I looked at his plate of food, untouched save a bite of mashed potatoes he'd pushed to one side. "You need your strength."

"There's too much food," he said, with a trace of irritation.

"Everyone keeps bringing food. They must think I've got an army hidden under the floorboards."

"They're being nice."

"I'd rather be left alone," he said forcefully, and as I looked at him bent over in his chair, brittle in that way people who have just lost someone always appear, breakable, as though their loss has drained them of something, some vital element that has otherwise kept them supple, intact, it occurred to me that he had not declined my invitation to come to New York out of politeness. He was simply telling the truth: He was no more capable of leaving that house than he was of flying to the moon. He would, I thought, likely die under its roof, in this very room, perhaps, in that chair.

"It's strange here without her, isn't it?" I looked around as though noticing for the first time that she wasn't there at the table, smoke curling up from her cigarette. "Quiet. We should play a record or something. Maybe one of—"

"No," he interrupted, and then again, quieter, "no, thank you."

"It was just an idea." I took my napkin from my lap and folded it into a square, smoothing the corners with the flat of my hand as though that had been the problem all along. I hardly knew what to say. It all seemed so difficult. Tricky, as though the wrong word might undo him, snap him in two. Of course, he was much stronger than I gave him credit for. People nearly always are during periods of duress, you know, though at the time I don't believe I'd experienced enough of those to understand.

My father cleared his throat. "It was your mother's wish that certain facts remain obscured from you while she was alive, and I respected that. However." He frowned down at his plate. "It seems important now that you gain a greater understanding. Suppose I held out the hope that she might tell you herself one day. I see now that was an erroneous supposition."

"Tell me what?" I looked at him. "What is it?"

He raised his gaze to meet mine. "The piano," he said gently. "She might have proven a real talent. There was talk of her playing professionally."

"But she turned pages," I said, genuinely confused. "She said her hands were too small. That she was too—"

"Stupid," he finished for me. "It was of the utmost importance to her that you not think of her as someone who had failed. I'm not sure you can appreciate the enormous pressure she placed on herself—"

"You're saying she wanted to be a pianist," I interrupted. "That she was talented."

"She had a number of mentors who seemed to think so. Older musicians who took her under their wing. Provided advice, the occasional lesson. Men, mostly. Of course, she was, as you know, quite beautiful." He cleared his throat again. "Never had the money for anything regular, though, and therein lay the problem. She would have needed a proper teacher to develop her talent into anything of significance. Regular coaching. She was entirely self-taught until she arrived in California, besides what little her father had passed along. There was no money for a teacher as she got older, and once the piano was gone—well, she had very little choice." He mimed running his fingers over a keyboard. "Played the dining table. And when they took that away too, she played the countertops. Incredible what the mind is capable of."

I remembered the feel of my mother's fingers tap-tapping that afternoon before I left for the U, the way they had run the length of my arm, light as air. "And Henry Girard?"

He looked at me. "Afraid he was getting on in his years by the time she arrived. He'd read her letters—found them pleasing, I believe. Flattering. Shame he didn't have time for pupils."

"I see," I said slowly.

"It's difficult to tell with these kinds of things." He fiddled with the edge of the runner. "Promise so often comes to nothing. Still, she might have had a chance."

"But what? She fell in love?"

He winced a little. "Something like that."

"She always said you swept her off her feet."

"I know what she said."

"And?"

But he sat there a moment without saying a word. "We took you to a recital once at the old town hall when you were very young, no more than four or so. You won't remember, I don't think. You might have been as young as two. Anyway, it was Paganini, if I'm not mistaken—fantastic piece. Big, thundering thing, orchestra and everything. I believe it was the only music I ever found myself truly moved by, not that I knew much of anything about it. Still, hard not to be moved by something like that. The young man who played it went on to become quite well known, I believe. A Russian. They often were in those days." He frowned. "I've forgotten his name. In any case, your mother insisted you were old enough. She bought the tickets as an early Christmas present—it was all she wanted, she said, and you know how your mother got when she set her heart on something. I thought for sure it would turn out to be a disaster." He shook his head. "But from the moment he started playing, you were at the edge of your seat. There you sat, still as a mouse from start to finish. Positively enchanted. Your mother told me later she felt if she hadn't been holding your hand, you would have run right up onstage."

I shook my head. "I don't remember."

"She considered lessons for you after that. Must have thought she saw something that night, a natural proclivity. She talked about it for a week or so—looked around for teachers, started drawing up a budget . . ." His voice trailed off.

"And then what?"

"She came down to breakfast one morning not long after and said she was looking into dance class for the following year. It was what all the other girls your age were doing, she said." He glanced at me. "She only ever wanted what was best for you."

My head felt overfull, filled to brimming. "What else?"

He sagged forward in his chair. "Rebecca—"

"The truth," I said loudly. "I think I'm owed at least that."

He bowed his head a moment. He was a man with no real friends to speak of, who had just lost his wife; I'm sorry to say I thought nothing of asking him all my questions, demanding answers. In retrospect I understand how painful it must have been, how everything he was saying must have felt like a betrayal. At the time, I thought only of myself. "Fair enough," he said finally. "The truth." And then he began.

\|/

"It wasn't a restaurant where we met. Your mother worked as a waitress in a bar—one of half a dozen jobs she held down to make ends meet. I'd only just recently arrived home—there was a crew of us who'd shipped back at the same time. The walking wounded, we called ourselves. Morale was pretty damn low. Afraid we took to drinking with perhaps more than the appropriate enthusiasm." He turned his fork over on the table, resting the tines on the wood. "In any case. One night we wandered into the bar where your mother worked. I noticed her right away—we all did. She was years younger than the other waitresses, face like an angel. She took her time coming over to our table. Straightened her apron, ran a rag over the counter. Stopped on the way to change the record on the player. I remember it like it was yesterday—she did it all so casually, as though she hadn't seen us sitting there, thirsty as hell in the heat, pounding the table with our hands . . . already drunk off our rockers, I'm afraid. And then this—this *sound*. I'd never heard anything like it.

And in a bar, for God's sake. Girard, of course, though at the time I didn't have a clue. Anyway. When she finally comes over to take our order, she sits right down at our table, bold as brass. Asks if any of us has a light. Says she's dying for a cigarette." He gave me a grim smile. "I thought she was after my friend Jim. Girls were always asking for a light from Jim."

"But she fell for you."

He looked away. "They called me Lieutenant. A joke. I happened to be the tallest, that's all. We were all privates, not a decoration among us. Soldiers with a handful of Purple Hearts and a few less limbs than we left with."

"And?"

"Afraid I allowed the illusion of grandeur to linger, that's all."

"She thought you were a lieutenant."

"Long enough to let me take her to dinner."

"And when she found out the truth?"

He let out a sigh. "She was angry. Wouldn't talk to me for weeks. Refused to serve me, sent over one of the other waitresses instead." He raised his eyes to meet mine. "Already too late, I'm afraid. She was, as I said, very beautiful."

"So then what? You up and proposed, just like that?"

"The heart wants what it wants, Queenie," he said slowly.

"She chose you."

"In a manner of speaking, yes."

"And the piano?"

He looked pained. "Things were different back then."

"I understand that."

"I don't know if you do." He coughed. "There were certain expectations."

"Meaning?"

"We were forced to make certain decisions."

"Marriage." I frowned. "But why?"

He squared his shoulders. "It was the honorable thing to do."

And then, of course, I understood.

I did not sleep well in my old bed. The mattress was soft and the sheets musty. There was the faint animal odor of dust. By the time light began to leak through the curtains, I'd been awake for what felt like hours. Outside in the orange tree, a phoebe began its morning exercises—*tsee-tsee, tsee-tsee*. They are, Oliver had told me once, particularly social birds, prone to congregating anywhere they can feed or roost, but that morning as I lay in bed, I heard only the song of a single bird sounding over and over again. *Tsee-tsee, tsee-tsee*.

The light was still dim when I got up and went out into the hall; in that last hour or two before the sun began to stream through the windows in earnest, I went through the house top to bottom. I don't know what I thought I might find. One of those letters to Henry Girard. A note. A diary, the pages opening to reveal my mother's round, looping script. *I find myself unwilling*, she might have written. *I find myself with child.* I imagined as I searched that my mother's life was a series of dark rooms, one leading into the next. I thought if only I could locate a clue, a lone beam of light, I could move through her past, illuminating all those dark corners: the old Georgian in Virginia; her father at the piano, fingers curved over the keys; that bus ride across America, Henry Girard glimmering in the distance, her North Star; the disappointment of those first weeks; the bar where she worked, the tables tacky with residue from the drinks the soldiers ordered, her hands playing hidden scales over the tops of the chairs. I went into my parents' bedroom and rummaged through the drawers of my mother's bureau while my father slept; I took the books out of every bookcase in the study, holding them upside down and leafing through the pages; I ransacked the old apothecary chest in the hallway; I ran my hands along the rough wood paneling until my fingertips were full of splinters. But my mother had been nothing if not relentless with her cleaning, and I gave up at a certain point, closing everything back up and dusting off my knees.

Downstairs in the kitchen, I poured myself a glass of water, pushing the old screen door open as I came out onto the patio. The sky was orange as I walked down to the roses, the Cressidas big and sunset pink, the Queen Elizabeths behind them, and the blowsy raspberry-colored Sophie's Perpetuals behind them. The last row was all American Beauties—these my mother's favorites, the Beauties, their bright red a color she'd deemed *heavenly*. I had always liked the Dark Ladies best myself, their blossoms close to purple and big as a man's hand, so heavy they bowed down nearly to the ground.

I'd never picked so much as a single rose before that morning; it wasn't allowed. When my mother gathered her roses to arrange for a friend or to sell, as she occasionally did, at a flower shop downtown, she did it with a pair of special shears, following a particular pruning technique whose complicated rules I had never so much as hazarded a guess at. But that morning I walked along the rows and took what I liked. Two in one row, three in another. My hands were scratched and bleeding a little by the time I'd collected a bouquet, but I walked over to the chair and sat down anyway, rubbing the petals between my fingers until they filled my lap with color.

I don't know what I believe about the dead—whether I think they inhabit a particular space or if I believe, as some religions do, that they are everywhere, or nowhere. It occurs to me now that I have never managed to come to any conclusion, that the morning in question I simply sat in my mother's garden long after the sun had risen over the far hills—the petals, when at last I stood, scattering everywhere. But then I have only ever looked for answers to those particular questions in the moment of losing someone. It is only when someone dear to me is dead and gone that I go sifting through the many possibilities—the what if's and the maybe so's. Searching, I mean, for something that might allow me to believe that he or she still remains, in one form or another, close by.

Chapter 6

October 3, 1973

Dear Alex,

I happened to read in the paper not long after we moved about a group of soldiers killed by their own platoon. A *tragic miscalculation*, the paper called it. You can imagine what I saw next: Oliver Hinden's name, listed beside ten others. My mother told me later he was buried in name only, the coffin empty save a lone handkerchief—filthy, it must be believed, flown clear back from Vietnam. It seems Oliver's lieutenant spotted the handker-chief on the ground not far from the explosion and sent it back to Dr. Hinden with a letter explaining that his son, Oliver, had been brave. That he had died an honorable death.

We are all allowed our stories—is that it?

October 10, 1973

Dear Alex,

My mother grew up with a fear of things disappearing. She watched her father disappear. She watched the life she had been born into vanish through the front door. She watched her mother disappear, my grandmother in later years sliding into a sadness from which I was led to understand she never emerged. She lived a life that stopped looking anything like the one she'd been promised, and so she left it: She *got out.*

Call it poor timing. Call it bad luck. Point being, it was not as she had imagined. She had certain expectations and they were not met. She loved the piano. She might, I believe, have played. She might have traveled the world like Henry Girard. I believe she thought she would. And yet she ended up living a life not so dissimilar from the one she left—standing on the outside, looking in. Or perhaps she was inside, looking out.

We must try twice as hard, she said. We must do our very best.

October 15, 1973

Dear Alex,

There are days I wish for catastrophe. Some natural disaster: a tornado, an earthquake, anything to bring the everyday to a halt. The boys howl. They throw their food; they destroy whatever is in reach. Lucas puts his hands into everything: He's at that age where he needs to touch the entire city, hold it in his hands. He flings himself at the world as though daring himself to die, and there are times I think I will simply turn away. Close my eyes, leave them both to certain destruction.

I would like the world to stop for a moment, that's all. For the din of the everyday to grind to a stop. I would like to speak into the emptiness of disaster. To speak my mind. To know someone— anyone—is listening.

Chapter 7

IT couldn't have been more than a week or two after I returned from Pasadena that Paul appeared in the doorway one night—drawn, no doubt, by my desk light, the sight of it at that hour unusual. I slipped the letter I'd been writing into a book and pretended not to notice him at first, casually unpinning my braid.

"Still up?"

I half-turned in the chair. "I haven't been sleeping well." I reached for my brush and started pulling it through my hair.

"Poor thing," he said, his voice softer. "You've had a month, haven't you."

"I'll be alright."

"There are pills for that, you know. The sleeping part."

"I'd rather not, thanks."

I said it sharply but he only shrugged, rattling the ice in his glass. "Suit yourself." He stood leaned up against the door frame, gleaming hair studiously mussed, that fine nose silhouetted by the hallway light. I thought, as I did whenever I saw him from across the room, that he was an exceptionally handsome man. A man you might spot on the street and smile at just because. "Poor Eloise," he said finally. "Poor old girl. Shame we didn't make a point of spending more time with her, in the end. I would have liked to have known her better. She had a way about her, didn't she?"

"Panache."

"What's that?"

I shook my head. "I wish I had too. Known her better."

He smiled his golden smile. "Family."

"Tricky."

"Speaking of." He let out a sigh. "Bitsy's gotten a bee in her bonnet about us coming out to the country house one of these weekends. The woman's relentless. I know the boys love it out there, but, Christ, it's a haul." Another sigh. "Not to mention they've got me working like a dog on this new deal. Another late Saturday, I'm afraid. And there's a good chance they'll need me in on Sunday as well." A pause. When he spoke again, his voice had dropped in pitch. "I haven't been a very good husband lately, have I."

I glanced at him quickly, but his face revealed nothing. "You've done alright," I said carefully.

"*Alright*." He clapped his hand to his heart.

I kept brushing, turning back to the mirror. "I meant to tell you . . . I ran into an old friend when I was back home. Alex? Alexandra. Carrington—well, Lowell these days. I'm sure I've mentioned her."

"Mmm." He frowned. "Can't recall."

"No?" My voice shook slightly and I jerked the brush through the ends of my hair. "God, this humidity."

"Hang on," he said, putting his drink down and crossing the room. "Let me give it a whirl. Come on, it's only fair. Give me a chance to claw my way up out of *alright*." He took the brush from my hand. I don't know that he'd touched me in months by then, our only contact the occasional kiss dropped on my cheek on his way out the door for the benefit of the boys. "Go on." He placed the brush lightly on top of my head and began to pull down.

"I invited her out, that's all." I sat very still. Of course the human body is built for affection: all those millions of nerve endings clustered up against the skin, a network of underground receptors waiting for someone's hand to run down your arm. I must have been starved for it by then. Those nerves suddenly clanging. "Not that I imagine she'll ever take me up on it. We're not even particularly good friends anymore. Or we haven't been for ages now, not since we were—*ow*."

"Sorry," he said absently. "Knot."

"Anyway, I haven't thought about her for years." I began to wish I hadn't said anything, though I'm sure I felt a certain pleasure at letting him know I was not without secrets of my own, that I had had a life before him, a past about which he after all knew very little. "We bumped into each other in the market, and she mentioned something about wanting to see the city. She has two little girls, twins. Matthew's age."

"You haven't been in touch?"

"Not since I left Pasadena. Or—before that, I should say. We had a kind of misunderstanding."

"Who was he?"

"What?"

"You went after the same man—admit it." His voice sounded amused. "That's the only kind of misunderstanding between girl-friends *I* know of that lasts this long."

"Don't be ridiculous."

"I have to say, I rather like thinking of you with a crush," he said happily. "There's something charming about the whole thing. A certain—"

"That's enough."

"Alright," he said, sounding hurt. "I didn't mean anything by it."

I was silent a moment. "It's a long story."

"I happen to have all night."

"I'm tired, and really, it Paul!" I turned, and he dropped the brush.

"Done!" he said, holding up his hands. "I surrender. Wave the white flag." He pulled a handkerchief from his pocket and shook it at me. "Sorry—today was absolute hell. Should have known I couldn't be trusted with a blunt instrument in my hand." He picked up his drink and turned on his heel, heading for the door. "I'll just leave you be."

I stayed where I was, my scalp smarting. "You're going to bed?"

"In a bit."

"*Your* bed."

He pivoted slowly. "Yes," he said warily.

"Of course you are."

"Rebecca—"

"Good night."

"We don't have to do this."

"What?"

"What's wrong?" He was looking at me strangely.

"What did you just say?"

"I asked if I'd see you at breakfast. What is it?" Now he looked concerned. "You've gone white as a sheet."

"Nothing." I tried to smile. "Yes, I'll be up early."

He stood there straddling the doorway in his easy way, one foot in and one foot out. He reminded me at times of the lion I'd taken Matthew to see one afternoon at the Bronx Zoo, a tawny majestic beast who sat blinking in the shade of an artificial cliff. There was something terribly depressing about the whole thing—the fake rocks peeling onto the asphalt, the way the glare of the afternoon sun reflected across the surface of the small pool, the attempt at trees. But the lion didn't seem to care. He blinked his golden eyes as though nothing lay beyond his own regal head, those enormous paws crossed daintily in front of him. "Funny business, don't you think?"

"What's that?"

"You never mentioning her before. A friend as close as all that," he said thoughtfully. "This Alex."

I turned back to the mirror again. "I suppose she never came up."

"She certainly didn't." He stood there a moment longer. I could see him watching me in the reflection, his expression—as it often was—bewildered, as though he had come home from work to find a stranger wandering through the rooms, folding blankets and feeding his children dinner, wiping their mouths clean. But then over the years we had become little more than that, really, two strangers who lived side by side and in the way of strangers continued to say nothing of what mattered. It must sound terrible to you, but at the time I believed my situation something closer to normal, one of those hard facts of adulthood we all grow, however unwillingly, to accept. The truth is that marriages involve all kinds of arrangements. You'd be surprised what people put up with.

Anyway, there was a part of me that was glad for the separation, the feeling of lines drawn through our lives, of lines within lines. It was the same part of me that had preferred to bury my nose in books all those years ago, the part that stood in Mr. Percy's classroom and lost myself in the complicated mechanics of a frog's digestive tract—the part that can still, to this day, simply drift, my mind slipping out of the present with the greatest of ease. It has always been in my nature to find ways of blocking things out, I mean, of losing myself in something other, a movie or a memory, surprised to recognize when I snap out of my reverie that the world waiting beyond the cover of the book or the door to the theater remains, of course, the strangest world of all.

I meant what I said to Paul: I would not have been surprised if I never heard from Alex again. But when the phone rang one afternoon a few weeks after I returned, I knew who it was before she said her name.

"Rebecca? Is that you?"

I sank down into the armchair in the living room. Through the window, the sky burned a clear, cloudless blue. "Hello, there."

"If I'm calling at a bad time—"

"Not at all." I cleared my throat. "I'm just catching up on a few things. Gladys took the boys to the park—the sun's finally shining for a change."

"Sounds divine," she groaned. "It's raining cats and dogs here. The twins aren't even pretending to eat their lunch. Not that I blame them. I got it into my head to try stewed prunes."

"Prunes," I said stupidly. "What a good idea."

"Don't. Do yourself a favor and just don't. No," she said sharply. "Do *not*."

"I'm sorry—"

"No, not you. Emily, *enough!* I swear, if I have to—" There was the faraway noise of a scuffle, a squeal. I heard Alex saying, *No, no, absolutely no.* Something clattered against the phone.

I waited. "I could call you back later, if that's more convenient?"

"No, I'm here, I'm here. Sorry. They just lose it this time of day. The witching hour, for Christ's sake. Me and my two little witches. They'll only sit still if they've got something in their mouths. American. The sliced kind, in plastic?"

She seemed to be waiting. "Sorry?"

"Cheese. The boys. Do they like it? It's all they'll eat. I'm up to my eyeballs in it."

"They're very good about their vegetables, actually. They like carrots. Matthew loves peas."

"Peas! Christ. You ought to be on a poster or something."

"Well," I said. "Thanks, I guess."

There was a brief silence.

"Look, I'm calling for completely selfish reasons. Escape," she said. "Mine."

I surprised myself by laughing. "Is it that bad?"

"I need a vacation." Her voice over the telephone was even deeper than I remembered, full of that old movie star's huskiness. "Just a few days. If the invitation still stands?"

"You're saying—" I stopped. "Here, you mean."

"I wouldn't want to impose."

"Not at all." I cleared my throat. "We'd love to have you. We could set something up for the New Year? January looks more or less clear—"

"Actually," she interrupted, "I was thinking sooner rather than later. I'm in a bit of a pickle, you see. It's nothing. The tiniest thing."

"Is everything alright?"

"Alright?" She repeated the word carefully, as though it were a word from an unfamiliar language. "Sure it is. Or it will be, any-way." The telephone wire crackled loudly. "It's just that I was thinking, you know, maybe end-of-next-week sooner. Is that too soon?"

I traced the outline of a lone cloud against the window with my finger, waiting until I closed the circle to answer. "Why not," I said finally. "End of the next week sounds exactly right."

The radiators, I remember, had gone haywire that afternoon. Heat hissed through the apartment, filling the rooms with a dry desert heat. I got into the shower after hanging up the phone and stood running cold water down my shoulders for what must have been the better part of an hour. When I finally stepped out, wrapping myself up in my bathrobe, I went into the guest bedroom and pushed one of the tall windows open, the air outside wonderfully cool. I took a cigarette from a pack tucked into the bureau full of Paul's things and lit it, sitting against the window ledge, my feet propped up against a chair. Oh, they knew just about everything they do now about smoking back then, and I was against it as a rule, but I didn't see the harm in one every now and again. I'd come to love the ritual of it— the weight of the silver lighter in my hand, the end of the cigarette tapped against the sill, the crackle of the paper burning as I inhaled. Besides, there was the odd pleasure of going through Paul's drawers, opening the half-full packs—all different brands, I noticed, an assortment of Dunhills and Lucky Strikes, skinny black Gauloises.

He'd made it a habit for years now to provide me with clues to his various affairs, little crumbs he left to mark the trail of his infidelities. He dropped names deliberately into the conversation: Tom from high school had stopped by the office to take him to an early lunch, or William over in litigation had sat up with him late in the cafeteria, drinking cup after cup of watered-down coffee as they went over a brief. A certain paralegal, Benny, had taken to bringing in some sort of fruitcake his grandmother sent him from North Dakota every week—*Lithuanian*, Paul had said, frowning. *That or Polish. Delicious, any way you slice it.* The evidence of his trysts he left scattered carelessly around his room—crumpled receipts itemizing lunches for two or expensive gifts I'd never see, rounds of drinks at a bar I'd never set foot in. All of it I understood he meant me to take as a series of kindnesses, a row of windows he built so I might see through into his other life.

But you know me too well to think I appreciated the gesture. The truth is that I found his honesty heartless. I would have preferred to see exactly nothing. I would, given the choice, have liked to live as though our marriage was one of those beautiful old buildings in the Village marked for demolition, the façade even as the wrecking ball descended remaining intact. In the face of that desire, his efforts at disclosure felt pointedly cruel, a deliberate unkindness I'm afraid I found unforgivable.

Every so often a gift appeared on my dressing table, wrapped and tied up with a bow, but those I left where they were, unopened, until he took them away.

Chapter 8

I don't know that I can explain what came over me in the days leading up to Alex's arrival. Why, after all those months of calculated detachment, I found myself overcome by a sudden tenderness for Paul, his strange and finicky obsessions with the squared edges of the stacked newspapers, the pencils on his desk lined up just so, the gleam in his eye as he took the wine bottle down from the rack at the end of the day. Who can say why, as I placed his folded undershirts in his drawer the afternoon Alex was due, I felt a rush of affection so powerful it verged on panic, the desperate kind of love one feels only for the dead.

Perhaps there is not much more to say about it than that. Perhaps all I need to tell you is that I sank down on the edge of his bed and put my head in my hands, that by the time I came into the kitchen to start dinner for your brothers, that tenderness had already begun to leave me and I became aware instead of a certain electricity in the air, a charge like the static that appears before a storm. Perhaps I need tell you only that as I made my final lap around the apartment, running my finger across the mantels to check for dust and rearranging, for the thousandth time, the stack of books lined up along the edge of the coffee table, I understood that passing affection had been no more than a temporary shield. The heart may hide its reasons, but it is a beast like any other.

You understand: The doorbell rang; my heart roared.

\/

The elevator doors slid open and there she was, her dark hair falling loose around her face, a wrap made of some sort of silvery fur pulled high and tight around her shoulders. "Pinch me." She pressed her mouth against my ear, breathing out cold. "I mean it." She stuck out her arm. "I won't believe I'm here unless you do."

"The infamous Alex." Paul came striding across the room to extend his hand, his face shining in that way a man's face has when it's just been shaved. "Welcome to New York. Look at that—you're every bit as beautiful as she said."

Which she was. Everything I'd seen that afternoon in Pasadena had disappeared, those small but perceptible markers of time I'd noticed from across the table replaced by that old remembered beauty. She wore a simple blue dress and plain gold earrings, her neck emerging from her wrap in a slim white column.

"I'll be one little minute." I gestured at the boys—both of them struck momentarily dumb—with a pot holder. "You're just in time for the feeding frenzy, I'm afraid."

"I couldn't be happier." Alex smiled at Luc, who was staring up at her with a look of wonder. "It's revolting how happy I am. Absolutely revolting. Hello there." Matthew reached out one shy hand to poke Alex's jacket. "Fox," she said, still smiling. "Go ahead, it won't bite."

She'd brought gifts for everyone: an art book for Paul, a board game for Matthew and a toy truck for Luke, a small bottle of perfume for me.

"It reminded me of your mother. The girl at the counter said it was lilac. Lilac plus freesia plus"—she frowned—"I don't know, something. But I'll be damned if it doesn't smell like those roses." She brought out a white baker's box and deposited it on the counter. "And the *pièce de résistance*, dessert."

"You shouldn't have."

"I couldn't resist. A Lady Baltimore, for God's sake. I haven't had one in about a million years."

"Wasn't that in a book?" A memory stirred somewhere in the nether regions of my mind: a cake, a spoiled girl, a tea room in— was it Charleston? "The cake. I thought I read something once."

"Owen Wister." Her smile was wide and startling. "The book was *Lady Baltimore* too, and the cake comes right at the beginning. Gosh—we must have read that ages ago. We were great readers, your wife and I," she said, turning to Paul. "Your wife especially—she used to eat books for breakfast. Absolutely devoured them." She rapped her knuckles against the box. "The cake, in any case, is delicious. I've got half a mind to slice a piece right this second."

I nodded in Paul's direction. "You'll have to fight him for it."

He smiled ruefully. "Someone's got to keep the dentist in business. Terrible sweet tooth, I'm afraid, and here I married the model of health. Off she goes on her walks, first thing every morning. Isn't that right, sweetheart?"

"God, you're good." Alex shook a cigarette loose. "I'm lucky if I make it out of the house before noon. You don't mind, do you?" She waved a lighter at me, flicking the little wheel.

"Go ahead."

"I don't believe it." Paul stared at Alex. "You wouldn't believe how I've begged for in-house privileges. Pleaded. Cajoled. What's your secret?"

She lifted her chin. "I knew her first."

He held up his hands in surrender. "Fork one over, please. Consolation prize."

I opened a bottle of wine and we sat together at the table and drank while Matthew and Luc ate their dinners. The boys were uncharacteristically subdued—intimidated, I thought, by the presence of a stranger at the table and confused by the smoking, not to mention the fox. Matthew asked for more potatoes and then sat, pressing them into his plate with the back of his fork. Luc stared at the gold bangle on Alex's wrist until she slipped it off and set it on the table beside him.

"Take it," she laughed. It was marvelous to hear her laugh like that, as though she could hardly have kept it in if she tried. Lucas held the bangle to his eye and peered up at the light, as if sighting through a telescope. Matthew watched jealously from under his fringe of eyelashes. "Aren't they gorgeous," Alex sighed. "You must be reading all the right books—Smith, he's the big news these days, isn't he?" She beamed at Matthew. He looked back at her—very solemn now, his blue eyes opened wide.

"We have a boy named Smith in my class," he told her. "Benjamin Smith. And he has a sister, Susan. Susan Smith."

"Is that right?" He nodded, flushing a little as he looked down at his plate; I have always felt bad for Matthew in moments of discomfort, his coloring so like mine I can feel the heat the moment it begins to rise under his skin.

"Matthew started kindergarten this year," I said quickly. "Isn't that right, sweetheart?"

His face was on fire now. "I like my new school," he told his plate. "They have better paints in art class. Also, they let us stay at lunch longer."

"He has a longer lunch," Lucas said excitedly. "I don't have lunch. I'm in little school. Little-kid school."

"Gorgeous," Alex repeated. "And here I am, not missing the twins the tiniest bit." She clapped her hand over her mouth. "Is that awful?"

After I'd taken the boys into their room and tucked them in, I brought out our food from where Gladys had arranged it on the counter. Paul carved the meat and opened a second bottle of wine. "To Alex," he declared. "After all these years."

I drank very little in those days, a few sips of a cocktail before one of the obligatory firm dinners, a glass of wine nursed through dessert. I'm sure I hadn't had more than two glasses when I felt myself sinking back into my chair, the weight of my body slippery against the wooden rungs. "You should have seen this one in college," I announced, doing my best to sit up. "The best Blanche the West Coast has ever seen."

"Hush." Alex rolled her eyes.

"It's true," I insisted. "Everyone said she was going to be famous."

"So you're an actress?"

"She has twins, remember?" I frowned at him. "Little ones. But you could go back whenever you felt like it."

Alex looked at me. "To?"

"Plays." I smiled uncertainly. "Films, whatever you wanted. Once the twins are a little older, I mean."

"Experience the pleasures of Greater Burbank's very own Regional Marquee, you mean." She took a sip from her glass. "Thanks, but no, thanks. I've got better things to do with my time."

"Well, it wasn't just about the acting," I said, trying not to sound hurt. "She had the most magical voice."

"*Had* being the operative word. Apparently the vocal cords thicken during pregnancy." She gazed meditatively at her cigarette. "I don't suppose these have helped."

"You don't understand." I turned back to Paul determinedly. "I'm not explaining it well, but everyone went nuts over her. Completely mad. She was that kind of girl."

"The Madden-ing kind?" His eyes had gotten that shine they got when he was drinking, their blue a few shades too bright. "A little joke. A pun. D'you know—"

"The kind who was going places," I interrupted.

"Oh, we were all on our way to *something*, weren't we?" Alex blinked. "Embracing Our Bright Future. Achieving Our Goals. Windridge Academy for Girls, Make Your—no, I've got it—Surpass Your Expectations, that's it." She eyed me. "Well, have you?"

"Have I what?"

"Surpassed Your Expectations?"

"It's funny about the two of you." Paul tilted his head to one side. "It's not one thing in particular, is it, but there's something similar. I can't seem to put my finger on it, exactly—"

"I've never seen that—" I began, but Alex interrupted me right away.

"To the dogs, she means. That's where I've gone. No"—she brushed off Paul's protest—"I've made my peace with it. I had my moment and it passed. They'll put that on my tombstone. Or: She had her moment and she passed it by. Your wife, on the other hand." She nodded at me. "That skin of hers is to die for."

I put my hand to my face. "Soap and water."

"It'll age you," said Alex emphatically. "No one tells you that part. Life with a capital *L*. Wears a girl out." She made a loop with her glass in the air, the wine sloshing up the sides. It occurred to me that she had eaten very little, that Paul had at some point already emptied that second bottle of wine and opened up a third. "I don't expect you to understand," she said to Paul. "It's not the same for men."

He glanced up to the ceiling. "My time at this dinner table is nearly up, isn't it."

"The Harpies have descended." Alex held up one hand, fingers curved. "Out come our tiny claws."

"There's dessert." I got to my feet unsteadily. Inside the box, the cake was large and white, voluminous. It sat on the plate like a deflated parachute.

"I've had a week." Paul stared at his wineglass, as though he'd only just realized it was empty, before filling it again. "My God, have I had one hell of a few days. And here it's only Wednesday. Can someone please explain to me how it's still only Wednesday?"

"He works very hard," I told Alex. "My husband's a workaholic."

She looked at him. "The brilliant attorney."

Paul waved his hand. "I do what I can."

"*Non compos mentis*," Alex declared. "Daddy's choice, not that it got him far in the end."

"*I am not a liar?*"

"*I am not of sound mind*," Paul corrected me. "Sorry to hear that. Anything I can do to help?"

She shook her head. "He's fine now. He and Eleanor are happy as clams down in Florida. The lawsuit did some damage, but we muddled through. Of course, Beau always was brilliant with investments, bless his heart. But thank you."

"Anything for an old friend." Paul glanced at his watch. "And now, speaking of old friends, I'm afraid it's time for me to leave you two to it. I should have been in bed ages ago."

"One more drink!"

He *tsked* his finger at Alex. "You're a terrible influence. I sensed that immediately." He stood. "Anyone for a refill before I turn in?"

"Just a splash." Alex leaned forward. "A splash. Only because it's so lovely."

"Nice, isn't it?" Paul tipped the bottle back upright. "Château Margaux '64, gift from a client. My kind of wine exactly—soft and plummy, easy on the acids." He glanced at her appreciatively. "We'll have to dig up something new for tomorrow. Rebecca didn't mention we were hosting a connoisseur."

"Hardly." Alex cradled the glass against her chest, cupping it with both hands. "It's just that we drink the most revolting swill *chez nous*. Husband prefers the strong stuff."

"Nothing wrong with a stiff drink every now and again," Paul said. "Take the edge off." He stretched his arms above his head in an extravagant yawn, the buttons across the front of his chest straining; he'd put on weight that year, his body thickening a bit through the middle, the way men's do. "I'll be sound asleep by the time you come in." He dropped a kiss on my head. "Should I leave the light on?"

"Sorry?"

"The bedroom light," he said softly. His mouth was so close I could feel his breath move across my cheek. "Shall I leave it on?"

"The light," I repeated. I'd done my best not to dwell on that particular side effect of Alex's visit, the guest room when I stopped in that morning to check looking perfectly innocent, the bed made up with fresh linens, the pillows smoothed flat, Gladys—with that imperturbably blank expression I could have kissed her for at times—announcing before she left that everything was in order. She had, she said, cleared out a few drawers, left a stack of clean towels by the sink. "That's alright," I said finally. "I'll find my way."

"I'll be asleep in about fifteen seconds flat," he said, straightening up. "Snoring like a chain saw, sorry to say. Guarantee it." He stopped where he stood, head cocked to one side. "Just look at that," he said appraisingly. "You two could be sisters." He held up his hands like a frame, fingers held in opposing Ls. "Click," he said. "American Wives."

"To the wives," Alex declared, standing to raise her glass to his retreating back. "To us." She walked a little unsteadily across the room to the couch and sat, patting the cushion beside her. "You come sit right over here by me, Becky."

I moved obediently, settling into the crook of the couch's arm. It was dim in the living room and pleasantly warm, the lamps spilling pools of yellow light across the dark windows. The scent of roast meat hung in the air.

"What's that?" I picked up my head.

"I was just saying, you outdid yourself. Look at this place." She waved her hand. "Look at this view. It's like something out of a magazine."

"It does the trick. Though sometimes . . ."

She leaned in. "Spill it."

"I'm adjusting, that's all." I forced a laugh. "Six years in this city and I still have to make an adjustment every now and again. Like a car after going a certain number of miles. A tune-up."

"Recalibration." She nodded. "Go on."

"I'm not making much sense." I stared out the window at the lights sliding into the river, the slow-moving barges trucking their cargo up and down the Hudson. "It's just that sometimes I feel like something's gone missing." I tried to laugh again, but the sound stuck in my throat. "That's not right either. It's more the feeling that I've forgotten something. Like when you walk out the door and realize you've left the keys on the kitchen table." I stopped, thinking—prompted by the look on her face as she watched me from her corner of the couch—of those letters locked up in my desk drawer. There was something dangerous about them being in such close proximity to her, the twinning of them and Alex a thing I thought might break me, shatter us both into a thousand pieces. I gave myself a shake. "Listen to me. I'm talking nonsense."

"Hush. You're marvelous."

"I've had too much to drink."

She made a dismissive gesture. "We're having a conversation, that's all. I can't tell you how nice it is to have a little adult conversation. Not that I don't have anyone back home," she added quickly. "We've got a whole gaggle of neighborhood girls, really. The anti-Malices. They come by every Friday for drinks and backgammon or whatever. A round of cards. Not bridge—Jesus. Rummy, usually, though sometimes I manage to coax them into a little poker."

"That sounds nice."

"It's smashing." She lit a fresh cigarette. "And you? What do *you* do for fun?"

"I keep busy."

She looked at me sideways. "You ended up doing just fine in the husband department."

"He's very good to me."

"Good?" She stared. "He ought to be stuffed and mounted on a wall somewhere, for Christ's sake."

I ran my finger around the rim of my glass. "And what about yours? You and Bertrand. How is he?"

"Gorgeous. Perfection." She crossed and uncrossed her legs. "That's not going to be awkward, is it? Because it was all about a million years ago."

"It's just you said you were in some sort of trouble."

"Did I?" She put her hands on her knees. In the warm light of the navy lamp shade, the skin on her forearms looked blue. "I don't remember."

"Isn't that funny," I said, leaning forward. "I hadn't seen that before, with the light."

"What's that?" She pulled the sleeves down over her wrists.

"Hang on—"

"Those flights," said Alex, getting up and stretching extravagantly. "Absolute murder on the old bones."

But the next day at lunch when she reached for the sugar bowl, the thin material of her sweater fell back from her wrist. The marks weren't all blue. They were green and lavender too, half a dozen shades of purple fading to yellow. On the underside of her right forearm, three indigo stripes came together in a clasp like a bracelet. It took me a moment to identify their odd shape as the long lines of fingers, the pressure that must have been exerted in order to leave a bruise immense. Of course he was a strong man, Bertrand, and Alex's skin that particularly bruisable white.

"It's none of my business." I reached across the table and touched my fingers to a mark just above her left wrist, a finger-size whorl of yellows and greens. Though the restaurant was cool, I saw she was sweating lightly. "But I hope you know you can tell me whatever you like."

Alex's hand went to the bunched material of her turtleneck, worrying the edge just under her chin. "As if I need to tell you a thing."

The room was white-linened, hushed. "Things are different now," I said. "We're not girls anymore."

She laughed; it was not a kind laugh. With one swift gesture, she pulled the turtleneck down.

"Everything alright, ladies?" A waiter paused beside the table. "Another glass of wine?"

"We're fine," I said quickly, before another sound escaped me. "Thank you." I stared down at my plate. The greens were sickening under their slick of oil, but I would have taken anything over looking at those marks—long and slender, ringing Alex's neck like the tail of a raccoon. "I suppose you'll tell me there's nothing to worry about."

"Let's see." She cocked her head to one side. "You married a jellyfish. I find that incredibly worrisome."

"Paul wouldn't lay a finger on me."

"Of course not." She smiled at me from across the table. "I'm curious, how long did it take?"

"How long did what take?"

"Before you disappeared completely."

"I feel sorry for you." My eyes were hot; I drank the rest of my water down. "What you're going through, it must make it hard to think clearly about anything. You must feel utterly—"

But she was laughing noiselessly, her head thrown back like a woman in a silent film. I got us out of there as quickly as I could. I left far too much money; I would have emptied my purse rather than sit there a second longer. We came out of the restaurant to clear blue sky, though it must have rained while we ate. Scattered puddles silvered the asphalt up and down the street, the rows of parked cars gleaming in the sun like beetles.

"There are people you can talk to," I said finally. "Trained professionals."

"How about you lay off the Mother Teresa act?" She was already veering toward a storefront. "How about that? And let's get back off the street, for Christ's sake. It's too goddamn bright."

We walked through the door, a chime sounding somewhere overhead.

Alex staggered. "*Watch* it," bracing her arm against my shoulder. Her cheeks were flushed, her eyes too damp and reflective, like shards of sea glass glinting up through shallow water. I tried to remember how many times she'd gone to the ladies' room during lunch, each time carrying her soft suede bag.

"Listen," I began. The saleswoman glided out from behind a rack of blouses. "We're taking a look around, if you don't mind."

"Not at all." The saleswoman wore her thin hair tied back in a blue ribbon. She had a face like a doll's, smooth and pink. "We just received a new shipment in for spring yesterday. Please," she said.

"Please *what?*" Alex put her finger to her lips, shushing me. "Look," she breathed. "Isn't this just what you need?" She held out a long black dress, a monster of a thing. Yards of taffeta and lace with enormous shoulders, the collar stiff with ruffles. A line of brocade ran down the center from the neckline to the waist; the buttons were gold and white enamel, big as half-dollars. "I bet you go to shows all the time." Her voice was suddenly wistful. "Paul probably takes you every month. Opening night, like clockwork."

I stared. "Not exactly."

"I haven't been in years. Theater's a bore, according to the husband. An exercise in self-indulgent exhibitionism, he says, and thank God I stopped wasting my time."

"I don't think we've been more than a handful of times. Paul's so busy—"

"Busy, busy," she interrupted. "They're all so goddamn busy." She lowered her voice to a whisper. "I'm stuck, Becky. Rock and a hard place."

"Nonsense," I said briskly. "You're going through a thing. Everyone goes through a thing."

"*Non compos mentis.*"

"You're fine," I insisted.

"Say that one more time," she said quietly, "and I scream."

My eyes had begun to burn again in a dangerous way; I turned to face the dresses. "This is a lovely pink." I pulled out a light rose-colored dress with a sequined trim, a billow of white lace spilling down the bodice.

"Hello," Alex called toward the front of the store. "Yoo-hoo? We'll just slip on back there ourselves." She held her dress up and the saleswoman nodded, looking relieved. "In here." I followed Alex into the dressing room and shut the door. When I turned around, she'd already started pulling her sweater over her head. She twitched her shoulders; the sweater fell to the ground.

I lost my old interest in astronomy somewhere along the way, but I still remember sitting in front of the television with Paul in our apartment years ago when the cameras caught Armstrong and Aldrin landing on the moon, the screen mostly gray and fuzzy with static. We ate our dinner and watched them come down off their rocket, big as polar bears in their enormous suits. They said their lines and planted the flag; all the while, I kept waiting for the moon. I wanted to see it brought to life—the moon I'd squinted at through the telescope all those years ago with kind Professor Tinsley, the valleys and plains I'd pored over on the page made real. But it was the men the cameras wanted to catch, their moment of triumph; all there was to see of the moon was a vague impression of colorless backdrop, mottled white shifting across the bottom of the screen.

"Goddamn zippers," Alex muttered, yanking at her skirt.

"Here." I reached my hand out, but she shook me off.

"Got it," she said irritably. "Goddamn *got* it."

I didn't know it at the time, but I read later that Armstrong and Aldrin came after a string of failed attempts, the number of unmanned rockets already launched close to incomprehensible. We'd sent so many into the stratosphere in hopes of landing on the moon that I was surprised the detritus from all those failed attempts hadn't blocked out the sun, the broken pieces drifting down to settle around the earth like a blanket of volcanic ash. It seemed the trick they kept failing to master was the deceleration. They could make the rockets fast enough, but they couldn't perfect the art of slowing down, and so the rockets kept battering the surface on all sides with these small explosions, leaving the moon pockmarked and littered with debris.

I understood that afternoon why they'd shown the men

instead of the moon, that's all I mean to say: There is nothing beautiful about the conquered. Alex's legs were crisscrossed with greens and purples, long zippers of bruises deepening in color as they approached her knees. An ugly mark the size and shape of a hand stood out just below the line of her underwear, the white lace along the hem edging the top half like a frame.

"Can I get you something?" She stepped into the dress and straightened up, pushing her arms into the sleeves. "Popcorn? Candy? You seem to be enjoying the show."

"It's awful." I thought for a moment I might be sick. "He's an awful man."

She smiled faintly. "I prefer 'the Sears Roebuck of men,' actually. One-stop shopping."

"You've lost any shred of perspective."

"Perspective is one thing I happen to be an expert in." She turned to appraise herself in the mirror, touching one hand to her face. "Which is more than I can say for the situation *chez vous*."

"I have everything I could ever want. A beautiful home. Two healthy boys—"

"You have squat, understand?" She was suddenly furious. "Zippo, zilch. *Nada*."

I looked down at the floor to avoid her gaze, the rug a dirty gray and shedding. "Next you'll say we don't have a chance at any of it. Happiness. Fulfillment. Love."

"*Love*." She drew the word out in a dangerous way as she turned to face me.

"Forget it. Just forget I said anything."

But she clicked her tongue and pulled her hair off her neck, laying one finger against her throat as though checking her pulse. "Love." She touched her finger to one slender bruise, then to another, another. "Love, love, love." She took a step forward. We were close enough that I could hear the rustle of her dress as it moved in and out with her breath. "I asked for this. What about that don't you understand?"

The room was small and smelled of mold and I was suddenly afraid. "I don't." I backed up. "I'm sorry, I don't."

"The funny part is, I had to beg him to do it the first few times." Her face in that light looked ravaged, the hollows of her cheeks dark with shadow. "Isn't that hilarious? Imagine, a big bully like him."

I felt the wall behind me and pressed my hands against it—hard, as though that pressure was all that kept me from falling. "I don't know why you put up with it."

"How else are you supposed to make it stop?"

"Make what stop?"

"The disappearing, dummy." She turned back to the mirror and I saw my own face reflected behind hers, pale and worried. "Just get me out of this, for Christ's sake, will you? I can hardly breathe."

I watched her reflection now, the long taut line of her back as she bent forward.

"It should have been you." I pulled the zipper down slowly. "At the wedding." Underneath my hands, I felt Alex's ribs expand and collapse. "I wish to God I'd never set foot in that room."

She straightened up and turned around, resting one hand on her belly. "So you got knocked up that time and now it's my turn. You, me, same difference."

"But it isn't." I stared at her stomach, still perfectly flat. "We're not the same at all."

"Tomato, to-*mah*-to."

"Next you'll tell me you asked for *that*, too." I was speaking loudly now, my voice filling the small space. "That thing that happened back at the U? The night the two of you—"

"Oh, God, really? You poor thing." She looked at me with an

expression of wearied tolerance. "I thought rape would give me a nice air of the tragic, that's all."

"You're joking."

"'Fraid not. He didn't lay so much as a finger on me. Of course, I was terribly disappointed."

"And the agent?"

"Christ, Rebecca—*Freddy*? A little credit."

I just looked at her, the pale skin of her chest above her brassiere, the dress caught loosely around her hips. "I'll take some of that," I said finally, gesturing at her purse.

"There you go." She said it kindly, as though she were speaking to a little girl. She handed me a flask and I took a long sip, the whiskey biting all the way down my throat. "Your turn."

"What do you want me to say?"

"Something with a touch of the truth might be nice."

"Oh, sure," I said, half-laughing. "How about, you're killing yourself?" I gestured at her stomach. "Killing your baby. Not that I think it matters in the least what I say." I took another sip just to feel the burn again. "Look at you. Pregnant, for God's sake, and drinking like this. Smoking. How can you be so selfish?"

"Easy," she said sharply. "If memory serves, you lost your chance to play that card years ago."

The whiskey had become something warm and loose in my chest, and I laughed from that looseness. "You don't know the first thing about me."

She looked at me, and now her eyes were a little sad. "If only that were true."

"I give up," I said tiredly. "We should go."

"God forbid we're still out when his lordship returns to the manor."

"He's my husband."

"I love the way you use that word as though it means something.

Really, it's adorable." She pulled on her sweater, running a leisurely hand through her hair. "I'd like to fill a book with words like that. Ones we seem to keep coming up with to refer to absolutely nothing. Husband. Wife. God. Love." She looked up at the ceiling as though the words were written there across the chipped white paint. "Dead. Alive. Child. Adult—"

"I'll be outside."

"Real," came her voice through the door as I shut it behind me. "Unreal. You. Me. Them. Us."

She didn't bother hiding a thing at dinner. She tucked the bottle of Dewar's between her plate and the candlesticks, tipping it into her water glass often enough that I lost count: once, twice, six times, a dozen. We ate late, your brothers already in bed. I let Paul pour me glass after glass of wine; I tore my bread into pieces and pressed them against the plate with my thumb. I laughed and laughed. I would have done anything to stop that laughter.

After dinner we took our drinks over to the couch, while Paul excused himself to take a shower. A plate of chocolates I'd put out earlier on the coffee table sat between us in their small brown papers, untouched. We were both what my mother would have called, quaintly, *fizzy*. I remember thinking, with what I believed at the time to be enormous clarity, that I needed to be careful, that if I knocked something over or spilled a drink, it would be the end of me. Alex had sunk down into the cushions at the other end of the couch, disappearing far enough into them that her voice seemed to rise out of thin air. She was speaking with an air of great delibera-tion about the desert, something she'd seen in the night when she'd been out late for one reason or another, a coyote or a cactus, she couldn't say for sure. She raised her head to make a point and I caught a flash of her eyes, flat and silvery, like tiny fish suspended in her face. We both startled a little when Paul came out of the bedroom, wrapping his robe around him as he walked.

He gave a low whistle as he sat down. "Ladies, I salute you." He picked up the Dewar's and examined it with a look of intent concentration. "You might find this difficult to fathom, Alex, but my wife is usually quite a respectable young woman. Quiet. Well-behaved."

"We're celebrating." I had to concentrate on each word, rounding my lips to sound out each vowel. "Something."

"So I see." He looked genuinely amused.

"Refresh me, please," sang Alex. "I'm in need of refreshment." She pushed her glass across the table toward him and he poured. "Just a smidge, thanks."

"Everyone take one little minute to look at that sky. Drink it in—I demand it." Paul leaned back in his chair. "I'm going ahead and giving you full credit for the turn in weather, Alex. It's been pouring all week, and here's tonight, clear as a bell."

"This view is disgraceful." Alex waved her hand at the window.

"It's why we took this place."

Paul frowned. "It was a little more than that."

"It was loads of things." I was laughing again.

"You'll have to come visit more often, Alex. I haven't seen my wife like this in ages." Paul smiled at her from his pool of lamplight, the white of his robe crisp against his skin. He looked particularly handsome as he sat there that night with his wet hair fitted to his skull—boyish, almost, though he was already getting that drinker's veil, the tint like red lace draped across his nose and cheeks.

Alex shrugged her elegant shoulders. "Maybe you don't take her out enough."

"Darling?" Paul raised his eyebrows. "Is that it? Have I been neglectful?"

"I have loads of fun," I said. It felt like the hardest thing in the world to speak. "Scads."

"Of course you do," Alex said soothingly.

"She's done tremendous work with the parks," Paul said. "Preservation and so forth. Didn't she mention it?"

"She didn't, actually." Alex looked at me. "What is it you preserve?"

"Grass."

"Oh, my," Alex clapped her hand to her mouth. "Is it endangered?"

"Poor," I said thickly. "Impoverished."

"Chinese, is that it?" She let out a peal of laughter. "Orphan-girl grasses. Good for you."

"I stopped last Christmas." I looked at Paul. "Remember?"

"I didn't." He tipped his glass back. "Christ. Someone in the donations department has been having a terrific time at our expense."

"And what was it you volunteered?"

"Time," I said. "Hours required for stuffing envelopes, planning benefit dinners, et cetera."

"Et cetera!" Alex cried. She'd disappeared into the pillows completely; all I could see were her feet—stockinged, stacked one over the other, like clasped hands.

"It really is a worthy cause," Paul went on. "I can't imagine raising boys somewhere where there wasn't a little green for them to run around on. They need their freedom."

"*That,*" Alex announced from the pillows, "is precisely why I had girls. Stick them in one of those fold-up pens with a doll and they're pleased as punch. Honestly, you can leave them there for hours."

"For the time being," Paul said. "They're still young, aren't they? They'll be chomping on the bit soon enough."

"I don't know." Alex raised her head to look at me. "You seem perfectly happy, Rebecca."

There was a small silence.

"My, my," Paul said mildly, rubbing his hands together as though the room had taken on a sudden chill. "It's gotten late, hasn't it? I've got to get myself to bed, tempting as it is to burn the midnight oil with you two. Honestly, I can't." He waved his hand at Alex's protest. "I've got an early morning tomorrow. Ad executives, eight o'clock on the nose." He made a wry face. "I'll need my wits about me."

"I'll just be a few minutes longer," I said.

Alex winked. "One more drinkaroo."

Paul stood, brushing his hands against his knees. "She's going to miss you, you know."

"I'd kill to stay here." Alex's face turned serious. "I mean it. I think I'd pay about a million dollars to stay right smack-dab here."

"You'll have to come again soon, that's all." Paul bent and pressed his lips against my forehead, the smell of his aftershave lingering as he straightened up. "Bring that husband of yours. Promise? You're both welcome here anytime."

Alex stared at her drink as he disappeared down the hall, smiling a little, as though she saw something mildly amusing in her glass. "Charming man. Must be popular with the secretaries."

"Don't."

"I'm just having a little fun."

"But it isn't," I said. "Fun. Any of it. He's too busy for fun, my husband." The laugh tore out of me before I could stop it. "He's so busy he's forgotten all about me."

"You poor thing."

"I'm drunk," I declared. "Again. Still."

"Hush." She put her finger to her lips. "You're perfect."

I shut my eyes; the room began to spin. "Do you think it's

awful? Paul and me, I mean." I opened my eyes. "Quick, before I change my mind."

"I'll say this much," she said thoughtfully, "and then I'll zip it. I stopped off at the Plaza on my way from the airport—oh, it's always been this thing with me. Schoolgirl fantasy, I suppose. I'd sit there in the stinking August heat with the goddamn lizards crawling up the walls. Or I was crawling. We were all in the same boat, is the point. I'd picture myself sweeping up those front steps, wearing some sort of spectacular gown. Jewels up to here. God knows how I came up with the Plaza—Audrey Hepburn, must have been."

"And? How was it?"

"Crap," she said, but her voice was sad. "Third-rate. The martini was warm, the food a complete disgrace. There was this very ugly little woman sitting by herself at the next table, drinking a Manhattan, who about broke my heart. But it looked terrific, the whole thing. You never would have known what a bust it was to look at it." I waited. "That's you," she said gently. "You and Paul. You're the goddamn Plaza."

"I don't know why I asked." All at once, I was furious. "You of all people. Someone who likes being tortured. Stockholm syndrome or whatever, but it won't go on like this forever. One of these days, he just might kill you."

She rolled her eyes. "*Quelle horreur.*"

"Don't," I snapped. "It's your *life.*"

"You're starting to sound eerily like Alfred."

"The Hindu friend?"

"Who?" She stared. "Alfred's my shrink. Try not to look so shocked. Bertie put his foot down. Said I could no longer be termed, quote unquote, *rational.* Anyway, Alfred says I'm classic. He told me to try swimming laps. Apparently water cures are back *en vogue.*"

"Classic what?"

"That's all he says. Classic."

"So he's aware of this, your doctor." I hesitated. "This abuse."

"One hundred percent aware. He's a closet smoker—the brilliant ones always are, you know. He must smoke half a pack at least during one measly forty-five-minute session. Not exactly enlightened to be so dependent, I told him. To which he said precisely nothing." She eyed me. "Happens to be educated up the wazoo, Alfred. PhD from Columbia *and* an MD. Between the cigarettes and the degrees, he's probably the most goddamn aware person I've ever met."

"Do you think he's any good?"

"Good?" She made a face. "Christ, I don't know. I do all the talking, so it's awfully tricky to say. The most he'll give me is that I've got to kill the shadow and liberate the self. Freedom vis-à-vis happiness being of integral importance. As though this is big goddamn news." She sat up a little. "What about you?"

"Me?"

"Do you ever think about it? Because you could tell me if you did." She was sitting with one leg crossed over the other at the knee, and as she spoke the foot that swung in the air began to jiggle a little, up and down. "I wouldn't breathe a word. I'm saying if you could be sure the children would be taken care of," she said impatiently. "Somebody there to feed them, change their diapers, rock them to sleep. They'd be looked after, not one bit worse for the wear. Are you saying you wouldn't pack your bags and go?" She leaned in, the space between us shrunk down to a cushion of air. "Be honest, Rebecca." Her voice was taut. "You wouldn't just make a run for it?"

There was a moment of silence.

"I should make us some tea," I said, getting unsteadily to my feet. "I'm not feeling well."

"Oh, for crying out loud." She gave a little wave. "It's me, Alex."

"It's getting late, that's all."

When she said what she did next, she spoke so quietly I thought

I had misheard: "It's his." She rested her hand on her belly. "The baby. It's Alfred's. *Herr Doktor.*"

"Alex," I breathed, sinking back down onto the couch "What will you do?"

"Don't look so shocked, please. Let's start with that."

"Does he know?"

"Alfred?" She raised her eyebrows. "God, no."

"I meant Bertrand."

She shrugged. "Maybe. Maybe not. I've been sick as a dog."

"I suppose you've considered—" I hesitated. "That is, you didn't—"

"I tried." Another shrug, smaller this time, as though the energy was draining out of her with every passing moment. "I couldn't go through with it. Isn't that ridiculous? A brave old goat like me." She gave me her most brilliant smile, but it was hollow now, a flash of teeth. "I read this book when I was pregnant with the twins that put everything in terms of vegetables. At eight weeks, your baby is the size of a pea. At twelve weeks, the size of a bean." Her face grew grave. "The place stank, mind you. It was out past Anaheim—I mean, it was in the middle of goddamn nowhere. Run by a bunch of bra-burners or whatever. A women's clinic, they call it. As though that takes away the smell of blood." She looked at me. "I had an appointment and everything. I really did mean to go through with it."

I shifted my gaze to the window, the hands reflected there—my hands—pleating the corner of the cotton throw, folding and refolding. "Yes, of course," I heard myself saying. "Of course you did."

"I must have sat there in the car forever," she said. "Dressed up in my suit and heels like I was headed to some sort of meeting—the PTA, for God's sake. Ladies' Auxiliary of Greater Who the Hell Cares. All I could think about was that lima bean. I was nine weeks along and I kept trying to remember what it was: A potato? A turnip? It's a vegetable, I kept telling myself. It's just a goddamn vegetable. But it didn't make me feel better. It made me so goddamn sad I wanted to die."

I waited a moment. "So what will you do?"

"Do?" She gave herself a little shake. "I can't leave him, if that's what you're implying. I wouldn't get a red cent."

"What about Alfred?"

"*Alfred.*" She threw me a look.

I said it again: "What are you going to do?"

"Enough about me," she said curtly. "Let's talk about you."

I looked down, pretending to scratch my forearm. "What about me?"

"Christ, you're not going to make me say it, are you? Look," she said, peering at me from under her lashes. "I'm not saying it doesn't have its convenient moments. I'm not saying it isn't cozy as hell most of the time. No one pawing at you under the covers, no shaving the legs every morning and tending to the dry spots, plucking the gray hairs. Or maybe you do all of that anyway. Maybe you've got your own little something on the side."

"Shut up." It came out as a whisper, my teeth clamped down. "Please, shut up."

"I wonder," she went on calmly. "Really, I'm genuinely curious. Does the female body even interest him? There are the boys, obviously, so unless they were both acts of immaculate conception, it must not be a matter of complete repulsion. But then the urge to spread the seed is purely evolutionary, I suppose. What I want to know is if he's the tiniest bit intrigued. Does he feel *anything* for the womanly form? Or have these last few nights with the two of you shacked back up together been like, I don't know, lying next to dead meat?"

I stood. "I'll go see about that tea."

"Oh, for Christ's sake." She pulled at my hand. "I'm sorry.

Please, let's not fight. Pretty please with a cherry on top? I'm being a monster, and here you've been so lovely. I won't say another word—I mean it. I'll be quiet as a mouse." I waited a moment, two, her expression as she stared up at me entreating. "Let's sit a minute. Can't we just sit here a minute?" I sat down reluctantly, and she beamed at me. "That's better, isn't it?"

We were both silent. I felt—as I so often did with her—that I had somehow disappointed her, that I had failed to recognize the significance of what she was saying, the words behind her words. I wanted desperately to say the right thing. Something comforting, something to smooth over everything she had revealed those past twenty-four hours, but everything that came to mind struck me as the most awful sort of platitude—words you might offer as consolation to someone you hardly knew.

"Eleanor's going to have a cow," she said finally. "She was always telling me to stop after the twins. Tie my tubes. She worried I'd take after her—dead babies, et cetera. Though sometimes I wonder if she isn't angry I haven't."

"Haven't what?"

"Had my dead baby," she said. "Everyone has one, according to her."

"So I'm in the club," I said. "Lucky me."

"Lucky you." She smiled, a little sadly. "Lucky duck."

I ran my hand along the edge of the pillow. "Do you think she was happy?"

"Eleanor? God, no," she said. "Yours?"

"I find myself unwilling." I shook my head. "Never mind. It's just—I was wrong. I thought I was the one who kept letting her down. Proving a disappointment. But it was life that did it, wasn't it? Capital L, like you said."

"I said that?" She frowned. "Christ, I've turned into the most awful bore."

244

"It isn't easy, any of it." I was horrified to feel tears sliding down my cheeks. "I'm sorry." I wiped at my eyes. "I thought it would take at least a few months for it to sink in. A year wouldn't have been too long. She's my *mother*. But it already feels so normal." My voice trembled on the last syllable. "That's the worst part—how normal it all feels."

"The difference between the sane man and the insane." She gave me a wry smile. "The sane man thinks he's crazy. The insane man thinks everyone else is. You're in shock, darling. Perfectly understandable. A natural part of the grieving process—think of it as a form of protection. Takes you out of the indefensible present and deposits you somewhere nice and neutral." She leaned forward and put her glass in my hand. "Now, drink that down like a good girl."

I tipped the glass back and did my best not to choke. "I am present," I declared, my throat on fire. "I am in the here and now."

"The question becomes where." She tapped her fingers against her knees. "And how. Where is the here and now. How the hell did we get here."

"Do you think they knew?" My mind had begun to whirl. "The mothers. Ours. Do you think they knew it would be like this?"

She sighed. "Everybody knows, dummy—it's a matter of who says what. Or doesn't. Which is the point, really. No one says a goddamn word."

"But what did they do?" My voice sounded desperate even to my own ears. "How did they make it, in the end?"

"God knows." She looked at me curiously. "Of course, there *are* the lucky ones. Your mother, for instance."

"Lucky?"

"I don't know that everyone gets one, that's all."

"One what?"

She spread her arms wide. "Great love. The love to end all other loves. I always admired that about your parents."

"Oh." I looked down at the carpet, prodding it with my toe. "Except she didn't—that is, I don't know that Mother thought of him quite like that."

"Ah," she said knowingly. "But *she* was *his*."

"It takes two." I was having trouble focusing. "Doesn't it? Two great loves. Two people believing it's a great love, I mean."

Alex's mouth was cool, chilled by ice. She pressed her lips against mine and moved back, her face barely an inch away. "That depends," she said. "What do you believe?"

Paul was gone by the time I woke up the next morning, the sheets on his side pulled taut, the pillowcase smoothed. I could tell by the silence of the apartment that I'd slept late, Gladys already come and gone to deposit Matt and Lucas at school, breakfast long served and cleared. I slipped a pair of slacks on and pulled a sweater over my head and then I went into the bathroom, splashing cold water on my face.

"You're fine," I told my reflection. I might have been fifteen again the way I stared, my palms damp against the countertop, my forehead beginning to perspire. "You are present and accounted for."

Embarrassing to say now how my heart pounded as I stepped out into the hallway, my throat dry long before I reached the living room and found it empty, the pillows placed just so. In the kitchen, the morning sun shifted through half-drawn shades, the paperwhites on the counter bluish under the lights. I must have known long before I spotted the envelope on the kitchen counter that she was gone.

"Hello?" My voice echoed back at me. I picked up the envelope and crossed the room toward the guest bedroom, edging the door open with my foot. The linens were stripped and stacked at the foot of the bed, the blankets pulled flat, tucked beneath the pillows.

The Mr. & Mrs., the words slanted upward across the envelope.

Thank you, the card read. *I had a lovely time. Come visit us in Pasadena! Love to the boys.* There was no mention of the early departure, the missing hours gone unexplained, only that card—signed with a series of little black X's, her name with that familiar flourish to the A. *Alex.*

Chapter 9

November 12, 1973

Dear Alex,

It was never my intention to send any of these. I don't believe I would have even if I'd had your address. What would you have written in reply? Exactly what you said. That I have been a fool all these years. That I turned a blind eye and now, I suppose, I am paying the price.

You would be correct, of course: I chose to look the other way. But if I landed myself into this mess, I ought to be able to get out. Only—to be honest—I don't know what *out* is anymore. What it looks like. In what direction it might lie. Sometimes I stand here in the middle of the mess, the toys and the dirty socks and the jackets, the discarded pants, the dirty spoons, the lone shoe, and it seems to me that my body is mere accident. That I might inhabit it by sheer coincidence. I may be no more than cardboard, I mean, a trick of paper and shadows. One of those dioramas Matthew brings home from school—you know the kind: Indians on Covered Wagon. Pilgrims Landing on Plymouth Rock.

I would call this Woman Stranded in Manhattan, or Woman, Stranded. Or maybe just Woman.

You understand, don't you?

Chapter 10

THOSE next few weeks felt interminable. Every time the phone rang, I jumped up from where I was sitting and dropped whatever book or magazine I'd been pretending to read, sometimes moving so quickly I answered before the second ring. I was more foolish in those days than I have ever cared to admit. I thought everything had changed, you see. That to wake up after a night like that was to wake up to a world made new, that from that day forward my life would bristle with that odd electricity I thought of as hers and hers alone. I thought myself on the brink of—what? Revolution. Disaster. *Something.* But days went by and it was never her on the other end. A week passed, two, the silence agonizing; after that second week had come and gone, I tried the number she'd given me—once, then twice, three times, half a dozen, dialing each time with a little shiver of trepidation—but the phone simply rang and rang, until I gave up and put the receiver back down.

Three weeks went by before she finally called, her voice when I picked up breathless. She'd been busy as anything, she said. She was sorry, but, gosh, all hell had broken loose while she was gone.

Wasn't it something trying to get kids to sleep at night at a regular time? Did I follow Dr. So-and-So's advice about schedules? Did I have anything to say about teeth, the losing of? Ears, infections in? I sank down into the armchair beside the phone and rested my head against my knees. No, I said, bedtime wasn't easy. Yes, the cold had really settled in now. We'd been to the playground that day and Matthew had climbed the monkey bars. When we hung up, I went straight to my bedroom and locked the door behind me, ignoring the racket of Lucas's small fists pummeling the wood. I sat down on the bed and pressed my palm against my teeth so hard they left a row of indentations in the flesh. Perhaps you already guessed that her visit would come to nothing, that anything she said or did should never have been taken as a promise. And yet I'd taken it as exactly that. The smallness of my life a thing I had allowed myself to think I might not have to encounter again.

We began speaking regularly after that first call, falling into a schedule with an ease I was grateful to observe—I called Monday and Wednesday evenings at ten, she took Tuesdays and Thursdays at the same time. The weekends we left mostly alone, though more often than not one of us ended up calling the other at some point— Saturday night after the children were in bed, or Sunday morning, early, before anyone else was awake. I came to rely on those talks more than I can explain. They were the spot of light my day bent itself toward, like a plant seeking out the sun. Despite the fact that our conversations continued to orbit the everyday subjects of child care and housekeeping, despite the events of her visit going unmentioned, the topics of Bertrand and Paul left more or less untouched—despite, in other words, the relative mundaneness of our conversations—it still sent a little chill down my spine every time I picked up the phone and heard her voice on the other end. I would have agreed to an hour of silence if those had been the terms.

I can't say for sure when I began to tell the other stories, the ones I made up because I knew instinctively they would please her—the candlelit dinners with some handsome lover (my something on the side) we both knew perfectly well never took place, the operas Paul never took me to, the charity balls I had long stopped attending, gala events where women wore dresses that glowed in the evening light like beaten gold. I know only that no sooner had I begun telling my stories than she fell silent, prompting me when I paused for too long.

"And then what?" she'd say immediately. "What happened next?"

I don't know what proved the stranger part of my new role as a Scheherazade, the fact that she seemed content to listen to my lies or the fact that I never ran out of things to tell her. All I knew for certain at the time was that as each new story came to a close, I could simply start over again from the beginning and she would never say a word, that I could continue to tell her lie after lie without so much as a word of protest. In retrospect, I see I should hardly have been surprised. The truth, I mean, never having been the point of any of it.

The heiress Patty Hearst was kidnapped later that winter—February, I believe it was. The day the story broke, her face stared up from the front page of every newspaper on the stands wearing an expression of mild consternation, as though surprised to find itself so prominently displayed. I bought a *Times* on my way home from the store, drawn in by the headline: GRANDDAUGHTER OF HEARST ABDUCTED BY 3. The article said that Patty Hearst and her fiancé had been beaten. Witnesses had seen her body carried off and stuffed into an unmarked car. Later that same day, I would hear on the news that a band of radical soldiers from a group called the Symbionese Liberation Army were claiming responsibility, demanding millions of dollars in ransom be paid to the needy from Santa Rosa all the way to Los Angeles. Of course, it was even bigger news in California—the entire state, according to Alex, in an uproar.

"Everyone loves a missing woman," she declared the next night. "Especially a good-looking one. You want to know what I think?"

"They're radicals. There's no telling what they—"

"*I* think she's no dummy, Patty. Ten to one, she did it on purpose."

"You can't be serious."

"Dead."

"Now, why would anyone go and pull a stunt like that?" I asked in my most reasonable voice.

"She's an heiress, not a saint. For Christ's sake, Rebecca, don't be such an elitist. If pricked, doth she not bleed?"

Somewhere outside, a siren was wailing. I'd been standing by the window when she called and I sank into the armchair now, folding my legs under me, pulling a blanket over my knees. "I don't see what that has to do with anything. She's been abducted."

"Gone *missing*. There's a distinction."

"And?"

She exhaled noisily. "Do I really have to spell it out for you? She gets the front page while the rest of us sit here and rot. Honestly, they have some nerve."

"Yes," I said, because she said it with such vehemence I felt afraid, as though she might crawl through the phone line, ready to put her hands to my throat and shake her point out of me if she had to.

"They're all the same, these girls. The Pattys of the world. Strutting around town with the same goddamn *bravado*. God, do I hate bravado." She was quiet, the click of the lighter over the telephone wire loud. "You should have seen them at NOW the other day—Nagging Old Whores. The husband's nickname—clever, isn't it!" I could hear the ice moving in her glass. "There was a job opening for treasurer. Malice let it slip one day, the snake. She does that sort of thing all the time—pretends not to know she's twisting the knife. She didn't think I'd be interested, she said. Gosh, she wouldn't have thought in a million *years*." She made a little noise of disgust. "Of course, they turned me down in two seconds flat. Apparently my math skills are subpar. One of the girls going over my test actually snickered—this one couldn't have been more than twenty, twenty-one. *Working for empowerment*, her button said. So I asked her where the empowerment was in turning *me* down."

"What did she have to say to that?"

But she seemed to have moved on already, skipped ahead, the conversation turned from dialogue to monologue. "At least in a compound somewhere, everyone would leave you the hell alone. I'd kill for some peace and quiet, I swear." She fell silent again. "Sometimes I think it's just a matter of time before I do something, I don't know, *irretractable*. Though I'd go for something quick, myself— quick and easy."

"Stop that," I said sharply. "The girls depend on you."

"So much depends on the invisible woman . . . How's that for a punch line?"

"Not funny."

"Sorry," she said, not sounding sorry at all.

I plucked at a thread coming loose from one of the pillows. "Should I be worried? Because when you say things like that, it makes me worry."

She sighed. "I'm feeling blue, that's all. Sunday bluish. It's only talk," she went on. "People say all kinds of things."

I waited to see if she would go on. "You shouldn't be upsetting yourself like this," I said finally. "You're in no condition."

"My condition happens to be impeccable, thanks."

"What I'm saying," I said slowly, "is that maybe we should try concentrating on the good parts. Look on the bright side every once in a while."

"That's about enough out of you, Pollyanna."

I wound the thread around my finger, pulling it tight. "You said it yourself. Look at my mother—lucky, remember?"

"Lucky?" She laughed, and I wished immediately that I could take it back. "Gosh, I'd forgotten. That's right, you and me and Patty, Eleanor, Eloise—we all hit the goddamn jackpot."

According to my rough calculations, she was due sometime in April. I knew she'd gone into labor only because she didn't call one night at our usual time. I waited a few hours before dialing her number, letting it ring and ring before I finally gave up. It was late at night there by then—early morning in New York—but as soon as I placed the phone on the receiver I picked it right back up. I had to fight before the nurse at Pasadena Presbyterian would even admit there was a patient by that name on the maternity floor. There'd been some small complication, she finally admitted. "Baby refused to turn around," the nurse said briskly. "She's still in there. Afraid that's all I can tell you for now."

I spent the rest of the week in a constant state of agitation, walking my route down along the river each morning with more than my ordinary speed, sending the boys out with Gladys nearly every afternoon so I could sit in my chair by the window and stare at the river traffic while I waited for her call. When the phone finally rang that Friday at our usual time, her voice was flat and buzzing with fatigue. Yes, the baby was fine. No, she didn't want to talk about it. It had been a nightmare, she said. *Der albtraum*—did I know the word? German, she said, not actually *nachtmar*, as most people thought, German the right language for it, though, because they had been Nazis in there. Absolute Nazis. She kept speaking fast, faster. Her voice ran over words so quickly, I thought she must be afraid to stop. Was it . . . ? A girl, she said tonelessly. Six pounds, so-and-so ounces.

"When they told me it was a girl," she said in that strange, buzzing voice, "I asked if they could put it back. No one even cracked a smile. Everyone looked so goddamn serious I wanted to scream."

"They must have been worried."

She was silent for a minute. "They sliced me open, Becky. Carved me up like a Christmas goose."

"I wish you'd called."

"Are you kidding? I was knocked out cold. They gave me something that landed me flat on my back. If that isn't irony for you." She laughed a little. "First they won't give me so much as an aspirin and then they put me down like a dog." It sounded as though she was breathing unnaturally hard. "I'd like to see the handbook that calls for no anesthesia during something like that. I'd like them to show me where it says—"

"They must have given you *something*. A cesarean, for God's sake."

"I'm telling you," she snapped, "I felt every little cut. Meanwhile, they just stood around with their knives, looking like they'd swallowed a room full of canaries. They strapped me to the table like a goddamn lunatic."

"You're both healthy. That's the important thing."

"That's what you're supposed to say." She sounded disgusted. "That's exactly what they tell you to say."

"Is your mother there? Because someone needs to be taking care of you. Do you hear me?" I tried to sound very firm. "Someone needs to be helping out with the twins. This is no time for you to be worrying about anything. You should be resting."

She was quiet again. "I thought maybe we'd come out for a visit."

"Who?" I said stupidly. "You?"

"Try not to sound so shocked."

"I'm just wondering if it's wise."

"You wonder all you want." She coughed. "We're getting the hell out."

"You mean you and—"

"Bertie, yes. And baby makes three." Her voice flattened, drew itself smooth as a sheet. "Fit as fiddles, all of us, so you can stop sounding so mother hen-ish. I want a vacation, that's all. A little time away from the twins, once I heal up and get out of this goddamn bed. I want to walk around somewhere that's not a god-damn sauna. Go to the opera. See a show. We'll have dinner, the four of us."

"The four of us," I echoed.

"Four and a half. Four and one screaming little quarter."

"It won't be that bad. Will it?"

There was another small silence. I pictured her raised up in her bed by the dingy hospital window, the Pacific foaming somewhere in the distance. "It'll be perfect," she said. "I can't think of anything more perfect."

She did write me once, a postcard sent no more than a month or so before she gave birth. I didn't mention it earlier because it hurt me terribly at the time to read. She was at the beach, she wrote. Hot as hell. *Shades of Flaubert—or is it Rimbaud? I've forgotten it now. I've forgotten it all. It's gotten tricky,* she wrote, *the remembering.* Each time I tried to read the first few lines, I couldn't help but see her sitting there cross-legged on a towel with a book spread open beside her, her belly big enough by that point to cast its own shadow. Of course I understand now that she must have written it from her house, that she no more picked up and drove out to the ocean than I went to any one of the hundred museums I claimed to frequent. We had settled into our lies by then, she and I; we wore them carelessly, coats we threw around our shoulders to counter the chill.

In the postcard, she wrote that she'd managed to escape for the day, that she'd left the twins with a neighbor and packed up a picnic basket for one. *Divine,* she wrote. I remember the look of that word in her angular handwriting, the way the *i*'s sliced through the page. *The waves are spectacular, Becky,* she wrote. *Carpe goddamn diem.*

Chapter 11

I T was late May by the time they came to visit. I took a taxi across the park to their hotel for dinner, Paul's secretary calling to say he was stuck in meetings and would meet me there. It was warm that evening, one of those New York spring nights that drives everyone half crazy with hope. People were out in droves, filling the cafés along the sidewalks and lining the benches along the park's periphery, the sound of their voices through the open window surprisingly loud. There looked to have been a parade of some kind on Fifth Avenue. The remains blew up in the wind, paper cups skittering along the pavement, clouds of confetti funneling toward the sky. A few balloons, partially deflated, went limping along the curb. The cab stopped at a light and I watched as a car pulled around the corner, passing close enough to one of the balloons that the drag pulled it up into the air where it fluttered, hovering, before drifting back down.

I'd asked Paul to recommend a hotel for them and of course it was very nice, the front opening up to a view of the park, the entrance flanked by gargoyles gone green around the eyes with age.

When I came through the revolving door into the lobby, I found myself blinking, the darkness inside after the bright sunlight momentarily blinding.

"May I help you?" The woman behind the podium smiled at me inquiringly.

"Mrs. Turner." I pressed my fingers to my eyes. "I'm meeting three others."

"Bertrand Lowell, party of four?"

I looked behind me into the street one last time. The light that evening was so beautiful I thought for one desperate moment I might turn and march right back through the door out into the spring air. Sit down at a little table outside one of those cafés. Order a drink, something celebratory: champagne, maybe. A kir royale.

"Ma'am?"

"Thank you." I settled the strap of my purse against my shoulder a little more firmly. "That's the one."

"If you'd like to follow me?"

I could have stretched my hands out like divining rods and pointed straight at her—Boots lifting his paw. The room was filled with people, the ceilings high. Alex sat in the middle of it like something on fire. She wore a cherry-colored blouse, her mouth a matching-red O. She was positioned halfway behind one of the partitions that divided up the room, the baby wrapped in white and resting against her chest.

"Becky," she called, waving. "Over here."

I came around the edge of the partition and there was Bertrand Lowell, his long body folded into the chair like an accordion. I was struck in that moment by how ordinary he looked, just another man among the many men sitting with their drinks. I must have been expecting some hint of that old thrill; instead, I felt only the piercing disappointment I have experienced countless times when something fails to live up to my expectations, like the time I rode the ferry to Ellis Island not long after arriving in New York and found myself gaping at the Statue of Liberty, crushed by the ugliness of that face up close—those hollow eyes, the cruel spikes of her crown.

"Hello there," Bertrand Lowell said, raising one big hand in greeting.

Alex got up immediately and put her cool cheek against mine. "Here she is," she said, beaming. "My lovely girl."

"She's beautiful." I touched my finger to the tiny forehead, the skin smooth as a petal.

"I meant you." Alex sat down hard. The baby's head bobbled awkwardly against her chest. "Whoops-a-daisie."

"It's been a few years," said Bertrand. He held his napkin to his waist and bent across the table, extending his arm. I grasped at his wrist. "Rebecca."

"More than a few." I was surprised to find that up close he looked exactly the same—his black hair untouched by so much as a single gray, his eyes that ghostly blue. "I'm afraid my husband may be a few minutes late. Stuck in a meeting—he sends his apologies."

"We don't mind, do we?" Alex appealed to Bertrand. "We get you to ourselves for a bit this way."

He looked at me from under heavy lids. "Rebecca Madden," he said. "Tell us all the news."

"Turner now," I said brightly. "Afraid there's not much to tell. I've got two boys at home. Matthew will be six next month. Lucas is four." I met his gaze and gave him my best smile. "They're good boys."

"Please ignore the tinge of green to his skin," Alex said. "He's had it up to here with girls, haven't you, Bertie? Says we're living in a henhouse. Getting pecked to death, he says."

"It's wonderful you could make it out." I tried another smile.

"Three days of freedom, thanks to Saint Eleanor." Alex's eyes were lined heavily with pencil; a smudge just below her left eyebrow had colored the skin gray. She looked, I thought, oddly disheveled, her blouse skewed to the right, her hair tousled in a way that might have been intentional but I thought was likely not. "She flew all the way back from Florida, bless her. Said she missed her grandchildren, and God knows we weren't coming to visit anytime soon."

"You must have your hands full." I glanced at Bertrand, who was examining his wineglass as though he expected to find something fascinating in its depths. "I can't imagine what it's like with three."

She squinted at me. "It's hell," she said. "If you're asking my honest opinion. Are you?"

Bertrand ran a finger around the rim of his plate. "Some people find motherhood quite rewarding."

"*Some* people," Alex announced, "are assholes."

I tried to hail a passing waiter. "More water, please, when you get a chance."

"And one more of these," Alex said. She waved a hand at her glass. "Speeds the recovery process," she said, catching my glance. "I read a study on it somewhere."

"I'm sure," I murmured. I was trying not to watch Bertrand, the way his mouth moved as he scanned the menu, opening and shutting like a fish's. The way, every so often, the tip of his tongue pushed forward between his lips and I caught the flash of it, pink as an ear.

"We should order a few things to start," he said. "Whet the appetite."

I rubbed the thick paper of the menu between my fingers. "The shrimp sounds nice."

"Isn't anyone going to say how funny this is?" I glanced up to find Alex looking at me again. "Or are we all just going to sit here and pretend it isn't the most hilarious thing?"

I feigned absorption in the menu. "Maybe the crab cakes?"

"It's not like it was all that long ago, when you get right down to it," Alex went on doggedly. "Seven years? Eight?"

"Is that it?" I willed myself to look at her; she was smiling that odd smile of hers, the corners of her mouth pointed down. "Gosh, it seems like forever ago."

"I might try the soup," Bertrand said. "Steak sounds good."

"They're known for their béarnaise," I told him.

Alex leaned across the table. "You can have him, if you like."

"Excuse me?"

She cocked her head in the direction of Bertrand Lowell. "The husband," she said. "He's all yours."

"Alex—" I glanced at Bertrand, who was gazing intently at the ceiling. "We really should get you something to eat. A nice cold soup, maybe? Vichyssoise?"

"All I'm saying is, *Je ne regrette rien*," she said, looking amused. "But maybe you do."

"Apologies, everyone." Paul came around the corner as though on cue, briefcase under one arm. "Gosh, I'm sorry. Meeting ran late and then traffic was hell—anyway, drinks on me. Just keep them coming. Where's our guy? Has he been by yet?" He stooped to kiss Alex on the cheek. "And this must be the latest addition. Isn't she a beauty," he said admiringly. "Hello, darling." He kissed the top of my head. "I *am* sorry. There must have been some sort of accident in the Midtown Tunnel. Police cars crawling all over everything and First was jammed up like you wouldn't believe. Forgive me? Sweetheart?"

I squeezed his arm. "I'm glad you're here."

He gave me a distracted look. "I came as fast as I—but where are my manners? You must be Bertrand." He stuck out his hand. "Hello there."

"Pleasure." Bertrand half-stood.

Paul shook his hand and sat down. "Don't let me interrupt."

"I was just about to ask Bertrand about his work," I said quickly. "Real estate, isn't that right?"

Bertrand nodded. "Something like that."

The waiter arrived with Alex's drink; Paul motioned at his empty glass. "Scotch," he said. "Rocks, splash of water. Just a drop."

Bertrand raised his finger. "One more."

"Anyone else?"

"I'm fine."

"Oh, don't be such a dishrag," Alex announced. "Take the edge off. It's a special occasion, for crying out loud." She smiled up at the waiter. "Two more, please." She gestured at her drink. "Doubles, both of them."

"Bertrand, you were saying." Paul closed his menu.

"What I do is basically a glorified version of buying and selling." Bertrand rested the tips of his fingers on his bread plate. "I find buildings run to shit—excuse my French—and I buy them at rock bottom. I fix them up, turn them around." He lifted his fingers and spun them in the air, rotating an invisible cylinder. "Quick, easy profit. Taking candy from babies."

"He's awfully talented at it. They call him the Jackal at work." Alex leaned one elbow on the table, resting her chin on her open hand. "A champion at picking out the weak member of the pack."

"What is it that you turn around?"

"Houses," Alex said brightly. "Places people were living before he spotted them."

Bertrand's eyes lifted slowly toward his wife. "It's the business," he said. "You have to know what will sell."

I was beginning to feel faint.

"Here," said Alex. She pushed her glass into my hand, jiggling the baby absently with her knee. "You've gone pale as a ghost."

"Not expecting yourself, are you?" Bertrand folded his lips into an imitation of a smile. "My wife claims it's contagious. Spreads like wildfire, she says."

The rim of the glass was so thin I could have snapped it with my teeth. "I'm a little tired, that's all."

He sat back in his chair and watched me. "Alex was just reminding me you used to have a keen interest in medicine."

"Our resident girl genius." Alex nodded. "Our own Marie Curie."

"You're exaggerating."

Bertrand kept his gaze on me. "Quite popular with the gentlemen too, if I remember correctly."

"Now you're confusing me with your wife," I said sharply.

"Is that right?" Paul took a sip of his drink. "And here she's always led me to believe she was a plain Jane. Bookish." He looked at me with an expression of mild appraisal. "Sweetheart. You're too modest."

"Could be I'm remembering wrong." Bertrand shrugged. "We didn't know each other all that well."

"Selective memory," Alex informed me from behind her hand, cupped as though she was whispering. "He's blocked most of high school and the U. Hard for him to remember his glory days, considering. Fall from grace and so forth."

"So what happened?"

"Sorry?"

"Medicine," Bertrand said, a little impatiently. "It's coming back to me now. You were rather hot under the collar. And then, what— you met this handsome guy?"

I looked down into the glass where a single hair, black and fine as a wire, curled around an ice cube. "Something like that."

"Christ, we all used to be on our way to *something*," Alex declared.

"That's right." Paul smiled. "The actress—our very own Rita Hayworth."

"I always preferred the 'Katherines' myself," she said. "Hepburn, Deneuve."

"She was terrific," I said quickly. "Really. Phenomenally talented."

"Can't say I recall that particular description being used in reference to *moi*." Alex pressed her fingers briefly to her temples. "Though you've reminded me. I've got a bit of good news—I've been invited back, can you imagine? Tiny little theater, right down the street. Hardly anyone pays attention to it, but it just so happens they've got this brilliant director in from London. I don't have the faintest how they lured him down there. Anyway, he's got it in his head he's doing *Medea*."

"Euripides?"

She gave me an impatient nod. "Who else? I happened to bump into this director at the store a few weeks ago, in any case. We were both wandering around the dairy aisle like lost lambs and we got to talking. He told me I'm born to play her." She looked around the table. "Medea," she said. "Absolutely born."

"Alex!" I clapped my hands. "That's terrific news."

"Isn't it?" She took her drink back, and I saw that her fingers were shaking. "Isn't it the most terrific thing?"

"Except I'm going to be gone for business most of next month," Bertrand said ponderously. "So, as we discussed previously, the timing's impossible. The twins are out of school in a few weeks. They'll be needing you."

"Don't forget baby," she said quickly. "You're always forgetting about her."

"There must be a good sitter in the neighborhood—" I began, but she cut me off immediately.

"That's the thing about children, isn't it? They need their mothers. There's no substitute for the real thing—central maternal figure providing warmth and comfort, see Harlow and the baby monkeys."

She was still speaking too fast, one word running into the next. "It's not enough that we provide food. We're meant to give actual, honest-to-God love and nurturing on a twenty-four-hour-a-day basis or else they die. Shrivel up into little husks. Never mind if you happen to be one of those mothers made of wire rather than terry cloth. Never mind if you don't happen to have been born with one nurturing bone in your body—"

"I don't know if that's exactly—" I interrupted, but she barreled on.

"It's in the way they glom on to you, isn't it? The way they grab, their sticky little hands. You can *feel* the need pulsing through them. It's like the umbilical never fully detaches." She looked around the table at us. "No one tells you that. Why doesn't anyone ever tell you that? Wouldn't it be nice if someone sat you down and said, now, look, darling, I'm going to give it to you straight. You've got to understand you're getting these things for life. They're not going anywhere, and frankly you might as well tie the goddamn cord around your goddamn throat for—"

"Hormones," Bertrand broke in. "Sometimes she says these things. I've found it's best to ignore—"

"Christ, Bertie, *they* know." She appealed to me. "Becky? You understand, don't you? Paul? Everyone gets it sooner or later. The bug, the itch. Just because we're not midlife doesn't mean we aren't entitled to our crises. Not to mention, God only knows how long any of us is going to live. Technically, you could be midlife at ten and not know it. *Technically*, we might all die tomorrow." She smiled brilliantly. "Some of us certainly go around screwing everything in sight as though we think we will."

There was a small silence. Bertrand sighed, a long exhalation that left him seemingly deflated, all the bluster knocked out of him.

Paul waved at a passing waiter. "Can we order? Somebody?"

Alex pressed a finger to her lips. "I'll shut up now. Promise.

I'll button it up. Boundaries, et cetera." She lowered her voice to a whisper. "I've been getting that kind of thing horribly mixed up lately."

"You must be exhausted," I began.

"What I *am*," she said loudly, "is bored out of my skull."

"In L.A.?" Paul gazed at her inquiringly. "I'd think it'd be just the place for a modern girl like you. Mind you, I've never been—"

"You have no idea," Alex interrupted. "It's completely vapid. Beige."

"Beige?" I looked at her.

"B-e-i-g-e." Alex put her free hand on the edge of the table and gripped, her knuckles gleaming white. "Everyone there is an f-u-c-k-i-n-g i-d-i-o-t."

Paul frowned at the baby sleeping peacefully in Alex's arms. "Do you two follow those new-wave shrinks, the ones who think they absorb that kind of thing?"

"We follow ourselves, actually," Alex declared. "The World According to Family Lowell. We're a bunch of geniuses over here. Ask Bertie. We're a house of regular i-n-t-e-l-l-e-c—"

"Cut it out," said Bertrand sharply. "I mean it, Alex."

Alex smiled. "O-K—"

"Bertrand," I broke in. "Let's hear more about this job of yours. How did you end up in real estate? How fascinating."

He turned his head and gazed at me as if he hardly knew who I was. "Any number of reasons."

"Money?" Paul toyed with the edge of his napkin. "Thrill of the chase?"

Bertrand waved one large hand. "Family business, honestly. Path of least resistance."

"Honesty's one of Bertrand's best qualities," Alex said quickly. "Why, just the other day—"

"Alex." Bertrand's tone was warning.

"Come on, darling, it's funny." Alex covered her mouth with her hand. "God, it's downright hilarious."

"We really should try to get something to eat." No one was paying me even a bit of attention.

Bertrand shifted in his seat. He bowed his head and put one hand to his face, cradling it in his palm. I was surprised to see how tired he looked in that moment, as though the years had physically worn him down, leaving not much more than bones and a draping of skin.

"It's the Sunday before my birthday," said Alex, "back in March—no, never mind," she dismissed my apology, "and this handsome man," she gestured at Bertrand, "calls me into the garage. He's got a surprise for me, he says. So in I go and there's my Bertie standing in front of three boxes. Gift-wrapped, all of them, bows and everything. The whole nine yards."

The only person to move was Bertrand. He dropped his hand to the table, where it lay next to his napkin like a dead fish.

Alex sat up very straight, tucking a stray piece of hair behind one ear; a thin loop of vein began to shiver just above her jaw. "Here's the deal. He throws out multiplication problems and I've got to give him the answer. Ten seconds for each. He's timing." The baby's head twitched from side to side; Alex glanced down absently. "Fair enough. Except I'm an idiot with numbers. Which is a shame, because Bertie here has been having a rocky time of it at the office and, honestly, it would have been swell if someone could have kept a tighter rein on our numbers." She leaned in closer. "Turns out some people, when kicked out of their homes, tend to sue."

Everyone around us was eating and drinking and moving their silverware up and down. They were doing all the things normal people do when they go out to a meal at a restaurant, discussing the movies or the weather, the latest bets on the baseball season. I found myself staring at Bertrand Lowell's hands, the marks on Alex's neck those months earlier thin dark rings, I remembered, one stacked neatly on top of the next like the necklaces those women wore to stretch their necks—where? Namibia? Botswana?

Alex was looking across the table at him, one hand fiddling with the buttons on her blouse. "But he scraped something together for me, anyway. Didn't you, my love?"

"What's that?" Paul swiveled his head in one direction and then the other, a spectator watching a game of tennis. "Sorry—diamond ring?"

Alex smiled brilliantly. "Not quite."

"You'll have to excuse us," said Bertrand formally. He took out his wallet and left a few bills on the tablecloth. "My wife hasn't been herself lately." He looked at us. "So nice to see you both."

"Nonsense. Stay and have some dinner," Paul said magnanimously. "My treat."

"Please," I said. "Alex."

"Goddamn it, Bertrand." Alex stood up, fast. There was a low squeal like the last gasp of air escaping a balloon as the cocoon of blankets rolled down her legs and under the table, then a beat or two of shocked silence as we all stood, none of us moving a muscle. The baby started to scream. Alex stayed where she was; I was on my knees and scooping my arms under that little body before I stopped to think, the baby's face already purple with rage, her mouth wide open, wailing.

"For Christ's sake." Bertrand started around the table toward where I knelt.

"Don't you dare," Alex said shrilly, stopping him. "Don't touch her, you brute. God only knows what you want to do to her. She'd be better off." She pointed to where I crouched, the baby's face eggplant-colored now, spotting white. People were staring. The whole room had turned to gawk in our direction. "Damn it, Bertrand. She'd have a better shot if I left her right here."

"There, there," I whispered, the baby's body cool and slightly damp. I shifted her up against my chest to get a better grip and she squirmed, desperate to get away. Alex finally knelt down next to me and I pushed the baby into her arms, those tiny feet kicking. For a moment it was just the three of us—Alex, me, the baby. Above us, the men kept talking.

"If everyone could please sit down," said Paul.

"I'd like to apologize for both of us—" Bertrand began.

"Bullshit, all of it." Alex put her free hand on my wrist. Her skin was still cold from the glass, the feel of her fingers like ice. The baby was shrieking, and she glanced down at her distractedly. "No one ever asked me a goddamn thing."

"Listen to me," I said firmly. "You're not well."

But she was looking at me with that gleam in her eye. "Dear Rebecca." We might have been fourteen again—fingers pressed together, eyes squeezed shut.

"Please," I said. "Sit down."

"Poor Medea." She ignored me. "Poor sweet girl. She must have felt just like this, don't you think? Like no one was listening to a goddamn word." She passed one hand wearily over her forehead, and then all at once her tone turned coaxing, intimate. She brought her face so close to mine I could feel the puff of breath with every word. "Except it doesn't have to be like this."

"Alex." I felt desperate to stop whatever she was about to say. "I'm begging you—"

"Come on, Bex." She'd never called me that before. No one had. "You and me. What if we made one goddamn choice for ourselves?"

And then she puts you in my arms, Violet—your wrinkled face furious, in the clutch of a rage.

"Empowered, my ass." Alex looks at me one last time before

she stands up, and now her eyes are clear, her expression serene. "I set the rules around here."

"Come on, you two." Paul coaxes. "Can't we convince you to stay?"

Bertrand shakes his head. "Embarrassing, all of it."

Alex raises her chin an inch. *"If it were done when 'tis done,"* she recites, her voice surprisingly strong, *"then 'twere well it were done quickly."* I stand up just in time to watch her wave at Paul. I can't move. I can hardly breathe, my arms full of you, your wriggling limbs. "I would have made a fabulous Medea, you know." Her smile is sudden, dazzling. "I would have brought the goddamn house down."

"She has become," Bertrand declares to no one in particular, "someone beyond the realm of comprehension."

"Sit down." Paul speaks with the imperious authority of a drunk. "We'll get something to eat."

"Stop," I manage finally. "Please."

"You know me. Never much for goodbyes." She glances down at you one last time. "Toodle-oo," she sings, waggling her fingers. And then she is gone.

Paul stands with his glass in his hand. He looks at us foggily and a frown creases his brow as he finds you, focusing, and then raises his arm.

"Cheers," he says, toasting me, you, everyone in the room.

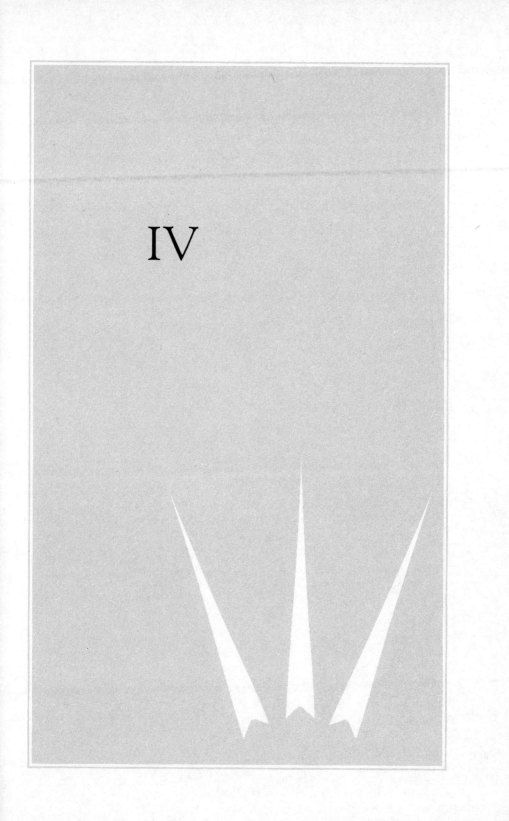

IV

Chapter 1

WHAT next? I left late that night. Escaped. *Got out.* I went back to the apartment and packed up a few things and then we drove north along the highway, the moon trailing us overhead. I watched you in the rearview mirror as I drove, your small face bathed in silver. You slept, Lucas beside you, Matthew in the passenger seat and restless once he woke, feet kicking the glove compartment until I asked him to stop, please. He was sitting in the passenger seat and he had certain responsibilities, I said. He was old enough, he insisted. He was soon-to-be six and I had promised, he said. He was too excited, he told me, for sleep.

We drive through the night and into the next morning, though the ride is not long enough, not nearly. Too soon we are through Connecticut. Too soon the sign welcomes us to Massachusetts— the name, I tell Matthew, from the Indians, the fact making its way to the surface of my mind like a bubble rising up from the murk of dirty water, signs of lost life. Massachusetts, I say, meaning *at the great hill*. It has been years since I drove and I find I've missed it, the thrum of the engine, the loaded spring of the gas pedal under my foot. Dawn shoots webs of sunlight across the sky, webs that shatter and spread—not webs at all, then, but something live, their insides leaking crimson. We drive and drive. We barrel down the highway until we hit ocean and can go no farther. The water gold by the time we get to it, the sun draining into the waves. I have never been to Massachusetts, I tell you, lifting you into my arms. I have never, truth be told, been anywhere, but the moment you came into my life I promised I would go.

Where? Somewhere, is the point. Anywhere.

Listen, I tell you. I promise to do the best job I can.

Then what? I baptize you in the freezing Atlantic while your brothers shuck their clothes and run screaming along the beach, their skin gone goose-pimpled within minutes and bluish from the chill. The air is thick with salt, shockingly cold. Though you don't seem to mind the cold. You bring one arm down against the water, splashing and splashing long after I have wrapped you up in your blanket and am holding you—too tight—against my chest. You splash and splash, your arm moving with such enthusiasm it occurs to me that you may well never have made that motion before. You may never, quite truthfully, have felt that particular freedom and you are having the time of your life with it, your eyes—when they turn to gaze at me—already your mother's, that same luminous green. I tie a scarf around my head and brush the sand from your blanket. I suggest breakfast. Pancakes, I say. The boys shriek with delight; they turn giddy cartwheels down the beach. It is morning and they are somewhere new and the fatigue, the strangeness of this all, has not yet set in. They spin and spin until they fall down on the sand. You kick your little legs. We begin all over again.

But the truth is something less extraordinary. I rode home with you from the restaurant that night in a daze, the bag of formula and diapers your mother had left behind resting at my feet. There were enough of both packed away to make me wonder. Beside me in the taxi sat Paul, his patrician face inscrutable as a painting. He didn't say a word until we were all the way through the park. He was, he said finally, confused. Just—he pulled out a cigarette and lit it with that great sense of intention drinking gave his every motion—well, to put it bluntly, he didn't understand. What was it that he was supposed to understand? Was there anything about any of this that made any sense at all? His eyes as he glanced at you focusing, unfocusing. Was I really going to sit there and say nothing? His words slid back and forth as though oiled. And I—I stood somewhere far from that humid taxi, the stink of cigarette smoke rising from the cushions. I stood—where? Down by the canal with your mother, the bullfrogs loud enough to drown out any thought at all. In the middle of Arroyo Seco, with the hawks spiraling above me. In darkest Brazil, where smooth-chested women wheeled and banked like schools of fish. I stood, I mean to say, far from anywhere, as far as I could get from that rocking taxi and Paul beside me, still talking, talking. *Think*, I told myself. *Dammit*, think.

We lived together one more month like that, our odd little family. Difficult to imagine we lasted as long as we did. When I think of it now, I wonder if I am remembering it wrong. Perhaps it was no more than a week, each day so full of you it stretched in my memory to the length of two days, three. The story I told Paul in the taxi amounting to little more than fabrications and approximations, after all, a story stitched together like one of my mother's samplers, bits of this and that sewed together to form a whole, a sum that might appear—the thinking goes—more pleasing than its parts. Alex had asked me to take you for a few weeks while she recovered, I said. She was in no condition. A sanatorium was in the cards, somewhere where she could rest. The healing effects of a little peace and quiet not to be underestimated. The stress of the new baby, I said, too much, and poor Bertrand already struggling at work and the twins—God, the *twins*.

Not that I believe Paul bought it for an instant. He may have proven many things over the course of our years together—vain and careless, self-absorbed—but he was never a fool. I believe he simply needed time to think, that because of that he allowed it to go on longer than I might have anticipated. Divorce in those days was still frowned upon, understand. Certainly it was nothing to be entered into lightly, not to mention the disappointment to Bitsy and Jed. He would have thought very hard about that. The boys, meanwhile, seemed alternately amused and bored by you, your china-doll face, the unpredictable timing of your screams. We are having a new experience, I told them. We are opening our eyes.

When Paul came into the bedroom those weeks or days later, whichever it was, he had to tell me he was leaving twice before I heard. I was holding you in my arms when he said it. I would do as I pleased, it seemed clear, and he had no intention of getting in the way. Neither did he care to fight. Things had been headed this way for years now, hadn't they? Now was as good a time as any to cut our losses. He actually used those words: *cut our losses*. Frankly, we both deserved better, he said, his voice warming the way a politician's does when he's ready for the applause. Didn't I think we deserved better?

"All these years we were living like this . . ." he said, running his hand through his mane. "Stupid to have let it gone on so long, in the end. Stupid and dumb." He stood in the doorway with one hand against the frame. "Though we had our moments, didn't we? There are the boys, for God's sake. We did well there." He gave me a tentative smile, his face made suddenly youthful. For a moment he looked like the man I had fallen in love with, the face that had appeared in the darkness all those years ago, radiant with concern. "We had a good run, didn't we?"

I held you tighter. "I think we understand each other," I said—oh, I was capable of such cruelty!

But he only shook his head. "That's just it," he said slowly. "I don't think I ever understood the first thing about you."

I smiled then; your hand had uncurled itself from a fist and it lay against my chest like a flower.

"What?"

I slipped my pinky finger into your hand and you gripped it. From the beginning, there was such a strength to you it took my breath away. "The heart wants what it wants."

He looked at me, his handsome face surprised: Who knows what the lion sees? "Yes," he said slowly. "I suppose it does."

My lawyer said in all his years of practice he'd never seen such a civil divorce, Paul signing the apartment over to me without a word, taking only his clothes and his books when he moved out that next week, no furniture save the desk in his study and his favorite chair from the living room. It's a terrible thing to say, but in many ways the whole thing came as an enormous relief. Paul had been right to say what he did. Stupid to have let it go on so long, stupid and dumb. We were kinder to each other in the aftermath of our marriage than we had been since those early days. There was space now for kindness, a new and welcome freedom, as though each of us had been sitting all those years in our own cramped little room, desperate to simply stretch our legs. When we moved to Brooklyn that winter— you needed room to run, you and your brothers, I decided; you needed *air*—it was Paul who called the moving company himself and arranged for everything to be packed up. He came out to our place on Cranberry Street and picked up your brothers every Friday for the weekend, and when you got older, it was he who asked if he could take you along. Would I mind, he asked. You were for all intents and purposes his daughter too.

As for Bertrand and your mother—I'm sorry to say I know very little of what happened after they left the restaurant that night. My lawyer said it was best I not speak with them during the adoption process. Mr. Lowell, he said, a bit of a loose cannon. Divorce proceedings began immediately after they arrived back in L.A., he told me, though custody of the twins remained under debate for some time. It must have been a terrible few months for them. Your sisters, Violet. You'll want to be in touch with them now.

You should know your mother told her lawyer he was to place you in my custody before he got a dime. This he reported to me himself. She refused to so much as speak until the adoption papers had been signed, he said. Not one word. She wrote down everything she needed to say on a notepad and held it up at the divorce meetings.

GET THOSE PAPERS, she wrote. OR I SWEAR.

\\|/

I began writing her again immediately—these letters I actually folded into envelopes and addressed, smoothing the stamp against the front with my thumb. I had them written into the official papers, stating that I would send *no less than twelve reports annually on the progress of the aforementioned child, Violet Lowell Turner*. And I did. I took down your first steps, the first cruel white corners of your baby teeth. I did my best to describe your repertoire of smiles. I copied down the words you said so deliberately, your serious mouth shaping every vowel. *Mama*, you said one morning on the park bench. *Mama*, and I tipped forward into love. And then, later, came the moments I found harder to describe. The ones when you started walking ahead of me on the sidewalk. The time you ducked, irritated, as I went to pin back a stray piece of hair your first day of junior high here in Marblehead. The day I started my work with the hospice and you asked, smirking, if I was going for Humanitarian of the Year Award. *Mom's saving the world*, you told Lucas over the phone. *One sick old fart at a time.* But I told her about those too. *She's asserting her individuality*, I wrote, because that was what the books said it was. I slipped in a photograph I'd managed to snap of you walking across the parking lot that first morning of high school, dark hair shorn to something daring—your strict instructions, as I understood them, for me to remain hidden from view.

Independence, I wrote. *Exhibit A.*

Chapter 2

WHO knows what might have happened if I hadn't picked up the phone the other day? I might have kept quiet the rest of my life. I always considered what happened *our* secret, understand: hers and mine, Paul and Bertrand be damned. Ours a schoolgirl pact, signed and dotted with blood. Of course I realize now how selfish that was. Nothing about this has been fair to you in the least.

But I did—pick up the phone, I mean. And now, today, even that is broken, that last tacit promise we made on the floor of that restaurant whose name I can no longer remember—or I refuse to remember, I suppose, on the grounds that it may incriminate me. Or else it simply makes me too sad. There are more of those moments in my days now than I care to admit.

Your mother was the great love of my life. I suppose that makes me one of the lucky ones.

"Well," I say. I let the spoon clatter against the sugar bowl to make a little noise. "Here I am." This is what I've become with all of you gone, the kind of woman who speaks into her empty rooms just to hear the sound of a human voice. Strange, because I have always thought of myself as someone who enjoys a certain kind of solitude—seeks it out, even. But my days have taken on a new silence now, one I'm startled to find I mind from time to time. That's something I've only recently come to realize children do, lend us the sense for a few passing years that we are never really alone. The awakening, when it comes, cruel.

But I don't mean to make it sound too dismal. I read to my patients four days a week now, and the hospice started me on a salary just before Thanksgiving—did I tell you? A small check every month, nothing to live off, but still. I like to think it means I've come to be valuable to them over the years, though I'm aware I have the easiest job of all: no changing bedpans or bandages, no telling the relatives the time has come to let go. All I have to do is sit in a comfortable chair and keep my voice even, my consonants clear. They say the sound of the human voice is comforting, that it eases the pain. There have been studies; I've read them in some of the journals I flip through from time to time at the library, though I don't need to read anything when the proof's right there under my nose. I've got one right now, a Mrs. Fortham, who's hung on a full three months longer than anyone predicted. Refuses to hear anything but Dickens, Mrs. Fortham. Cheers the heart, Mrs. Fortham says, and I pick up *David Copperfield* and begin.

But: the call. I was here in the kitchen yesterday, making tea, when the phone rang.

"Is Rebecca there, please?" It was a woman, her voice deep. "Rebecca Madden?"

"This is she." I stood a little straighter. The sound of that name strange, unfamiliar. It was like someone ringing a bell.

"Rebecca, it's Betsy." There was the clatter of something dropping. "Darn it. It's Betsy Bromwell. Bromwell-Atherton."

What could I do but see her as she'd been? That round, pleasant face, the shy smile.

"Betsy," I said. A woodpecker started up in the yard: *rat-a-TAT-rat-a-TAT-rat-a-rat-a-rat-a-TAT*. "Isn't this a surprise."

"I'm sorry to catch you like this. I've often thought . . ." She paused. "We've all wondered how you were. I used to get little bits and pieces, you know . . . Well. I finally dug up this new number for you after I tracked down your husband, who told me you two had—I was sorry to hear about that, by the way. Divorce is no picnic." She laughed a little. "Believe me, I know. I'm on my third, if you can believe it."

"Goodness." *Rat-a-tat-a-TAT!* "Well—congratulations, I guess."

"I just called to say we're sending flowers and I thought maybe—that is—" She stopped. "Oh, dear. I don't know why I assumed you'd heard the news—"

"What?" My head emptied itself in a rush. "What news?"

"I'm so sorry." Betsy let out a little sigh, and it made a rustling noise across the receiver. "It's Alex," she said. "She's"—there was a small hesitation, no bigger than a swallow—"well, I'm afraid she's passed."

Cancer, of course. By my age everyone knows someone, if not endless parades of someones. Lungs, ovaries, kidneys, stomachs, tongues—nothing's safe these days. People wake up one day and their bodies have turned on themselves; their flesh revolts. Primes itself, attacks. Most of the patients I see are dying from one kind or another, though we get the occasional liver case. A heart disease or two. But most—most are cancers just like hers: a tumor that curled itself around the bladder like a snake, a knot of cells bloomed in the lungs and gone unnoticed until it was too late. The way Betsy tells it, your mother knew long before they told her. She wrote out specific instructions forbidding a funeral and left a will that provided for all the arrangements. She planned accordingly, in other words. Battened down the hatches. And then she took matters into her own hands.

She was nothing if not selfish. I don't say that to be cruel.

I learned from Betsy that your mother had been living in a little town up the coast from L.A. for years when she died, your sisters remaining in Bertrand's custody until the age of eighteen and then released to college, free to do as they pleased. It seemed she lived a mostly solitary life, though the neighbor who found her remarked that she had often seen her walking along the beach, that she appeared, the neighbor said, to have gone into the water nearly every day. She left behind a garden, which I found surprising, and a little dog, which I did not. Marlene was the dog's name. I laughed when I heard that.

It was hours before the neighbor discovered the car in the garage, the noise of the engine just audible from the sidewalk. The fumes when she lifted the door, the neighbor reported, blinding.

Except even that's not it, exactly. The truth—I've sworn to write it here. Your mother said something else to me that night in the restaurant, three words I pushed down under the murk. A fool, I admit it now. Both of us fools in the end. Fools living out our separate lives on opposite sides of the country. The shame of it now a thing too great to imagine. There is, I'm afraid, too much to apologize for. To think what might have been is to lose myself entirely. *Je ne regrette rien*, your mother said. Piaf, though I didn't know it at the time.

Picture it one more time: Bertrand standing over us, Paul trying to restore some semblance of order. It smells, on the carpet, of bread and fish, the faint yeasty odor of your small body. She crouches there down on the floor with you squalling in her arms, her expression in that moment beatific, some part of her I have known all too well over the years suddenly vanished or stamped out, thrown to the curb. I will lose her, I know. I already have.

And then she smiles. Your mother: There is nothing like her in the world.

"What if we made one goddamn choice for ourselves," she says.

"Rebecca," she says. "Come with me."

Listen: *I* was the coward. I regret everything.

Chapter 3

October 2, 1981

Dear Alex,

She really is developing the most stubborn little mind. Apparently she's at that age. The books say this is it for girls: "Seven is learning heaven," if Dr. Z is to be believed, which I'm not entirely convinced he is. They're all full of it, these doctors. You were right about that. But if I tell her there's something she absolutely can't do, she goes ahead and makes sure she does it. If I tell her she can't walk any farther than the third tree from the stoop, she barrels toward the fifth. If I tell her not to eat something in the cupboard, off she goes with the stool the second I leave the room, dragging it across the floor. I can hear her on the prowl—*thump, thump, thumpity-thump*. I'm embarrassed to admit I tried something the other day I'd heard one of the other mothers talking about at school. I let her eat a whole box of Mallomars just to prove the point that, yes, indeed, there *can* be too much of a good thing. Of course she was up all night, and so was I. It didn't teach her a thing. What do you think I heard the next day after lunch? *Thump, thump, thumpity-thump.*

Then there's this, the latest disaster. You'll never believe it. Paul took all three of them into the city for the weekend, and early Saturday morning the bell rings, loud and clear. I was in the kitchen doing the dishes, and when I looked down from the window, there she was. *Violet?* She nodded her head—she's always so serious, such a focused little girl. And so lovely— God, she's just the loveliest thing. Eyes like water, green as any- thing. She waited for the buzzer with her hand against the door, looking like she was about seventy instead of seven. I stood there a moment, still searching for Paul and the boys out the window, not understanding, and then I ran down the stairs. When I opened the door, she trotted right through and went up the stairs into the apartment and sat down on the couch. *I've had a day,* she said wearily. She's an old soul. It'd kill you, some of the things she says.

She was so tired, poor thing, but she insisted on taking off her own shoes. *Sweetheart?* She cut me off. *I'm very tired from my walk,* she said. *It was a very long walk. The buildings got bigger,* she said, *and then they went away. The part on the bridge was nice but there were too many people.* She wanted to know what all those people were doing up so early. Why were they taking pictures of the bridge? Why did they keep stopping to take pictures? And then she fell asleep, right smack in the middle of a sentence. She was every bit as determined to finish her story as she had been to make that trip, though, stubborn as anything. Every time her eyes closed, she shook herself and started up again. I can't tell you how furious I was. Too furious to move, honestly. I just sat there listening to her tell me what she'd seen and where she'd been, and when she finally let me tuck her into bed, she rolled over on her side. Her hair was tangled from the wind, her cheeks still red, and she stuck her finger out at me like she was making a point:

I was just trying to find you, she said.

R.

Acknowledgments

For reading, editing, advising, and encouraging, thank you to Ethan Canin, Lan Samantha Chang, Leslie Jamison, Maggie Shipstead, and Vinnie Wilhelm. Thanks especially to Kate Walbert, whose generosity ought to be bronzed.

For the gift of time and freedom, thank you to the Iowa Writers' Workshop, the Iowa Arts Foundation, the Yaddo Corporation, and the Vermont Studio Center. Thank you to Connie Brothers, whose phone call changed everything.

For cheering me on along the way, thanks to Linda Swanson-Davies and Christina Thompson, editors who go above and beyond.

For many, many years of patience and good faith, thank you to my family. Without my mother and the house on El Molino, there would be no story.

For tireless revising and championing, thanks to my brilliant editor, Sarah Bowlin. Thanks also to Joanna Levine, Rebecca Seltzer, and everyone else at Henry Holt who helped bring these pages to life.

For telling me this was a book from the beginning—and then making sure it became one—I am forever indebted to my agent, the inimitable Claudia Ballard. Also at WME, thanks to Laura Bonner, Ian Dalrymple, and Eric Simonoff.

For all this and everything else, thank you to Dan: You made me one of the lucky ones.

About the Author

ARIA BETH SLOSS is a graduate of Yale University and the Iowa Writers' Workshop. She is a recipient of fellowships from the Iowa Arts Foundation, the Yaddo Corporation, and the Vermont Studio Center, and her writing has appeared in *Glimmer Train*, the *Harvard Review*, and online at *The Paris Review* and *FiveChapters*. She lives in New York City.